The **aware**

THE **aware**

Ian Dallaway read hundreds of mysteries before deciding it would be even more interesting to bring his own characters to life set in surroundings he knows well. He moved from an established senior buying role to take up pen and laptop, throwing away the economics books to complete an MA in creative writing at Christchurch Canterbury. He has often visited all the places described and lives in Somerset.

Also by Ian Dallaway:

Artistic Endeavors
The second world of Alex Ash

London Calling (All jazzed up)
The third world of Alex Ash

For more information about Ian and his books, visit www.iandallaway.com where you can also email him.

The **aware**

The first world of Alex Ash

By

Ian Dallaway

THE **aware**

The first World of Alex Ash

First published 2021 Moonlightcrystal Ltd

www.moonlightcrystal.com

ISBN978-1-8384506-5-6

copyright © Ian Dallaway 2021

The right of Ian Dallaway to be identified as the author of this work has been asserted by him in accordance with the Copyright, Designs and Patents Act 1988.

This book is a work of fiction. Names, characters, organisations, places events and incidents are either products of the author's imagination or are used fictitiously. Any resemblance to actual persons, living or dead, is purely coincidental.

For Briony

CHAPTER ONE

They were sitting at a table outside the Resonance café in Bath, in a street that ran near the Roman Baths. A spring day and the sun was out, shaded by a red umbrella spanning their table.

'You alright?' Mike asked. 'You seem distant this morning.'

Alex shook himself. He hadn't realised that he was slipping, and that wasn't good.

'Sorry, miles away.'

'Anything special?'

He hesitated. 'Look, I know this is out of the blue, but I connected just for a moment to another life.'

Mike stared for a moment and then burst out laughing. 'Hey, mate, it was just a concentration slip. You don't need to make stuff up. I do it all the time, most people do, they just slip away and think about something else.'

'Mike, has no one talked to you about your other self?'

'What do you mean, other self? You're getting spooky now.' He made a play of looking over at Alex's coffee and then up to stare into his eyes.

Alex sighed, he'd got it wrong, and he'd been sure that Mike would understand.

'Come on, Alex, you've got to explain. What did you mean?'

Alex took a deep breath. 'When you feel disconnected from this world, did you ever think that you might connect to somewhere, or someone else? That you're more than one person. That you're present in another world. That there's more than one you?'

'You're kidding me. Aren't you? Or have you lost it? Has your writing been getting to you lately? Is a relationship getting you down? I don't know, it must be something.'

'Mike, listen to me because this affects you, it's just that no one has ever told you, and they should have done. It divides the people you see around you into two groups, those that have been here before, and those that haven't, virgins if you like. I'm sure you're not a virgin, in this sense, but you're an **unaware**.'

'Yea, right? So, you're saying you've been on the earth before, and others have too. Yes?'

'That's right, it's just that you don't know it, but you exist on other worlds as well.'

Mike sat back, his jaw tight. He kept looking at Alex as though he'd never seen him before, and then he shook his head. 'You've flipped, mate. I don't know what to say. So, prove it to me, OK, prove it, or I'm off.'

'I know I can, but…'

'No, no excuses, you just prove it to me here and now.'

Alex looked around, then nodded. 'You see that girl coming down the street?'

Mike looked up and saw an attractive, long-haired, long-legged blond walking towards them, he'd fancy her alright.

'So?'

'I'm sure she's an **aware**.'

'So?'

'So, I can use that, even though we've never met.'

'Go on then.'

Mike looked at the girl and let his mind float. This really should take more time than he had. If he wasn't careful, she'd walk past before he made a connection. He reached out to her. She walked on.

Mike laughed. 'Some trick, that was,' he guffawed as he watched her go. Then stopped as the girl turned around and made for their table.

'Hi there, which of you guys was calling me?'

'That was me,' answered Alex. 'I'm Alex, and this is my friend, Mike. Care to join us?'

'I don't think so, not now anyway.' She frowned at Mike, looked hard at Alex, and raising an eyebrow, gave him a questioning look. 'Here, take my stuff, and maybe we can hook up later.' She took out one of the latest golden flip phones, and Alex did the same. They put them together for a moment, and then, with a smile and a wink, she walked off.

'So, what do you reckon?' Alex asked.

'That was just a fluke,' Mike said, but not with great conviction. 'She just fancied you. Though why I don't know. I bet you can't do it again.'

Alex shrugged. 'I could, but let me explain because someone has to. Your parents could have done that, maybe.'

'Ah, but I'm an orphan, didn't you know? I never knew my parents. They died in a car crash a few months after I was born.'

'Ah, so they **repositioned**.'

'Eh?'

'You don't die, no one dies, you **reposition**. You then live mainly on another world, or at a different frequency.'

'So, you're saying my parents are still alive?'

'Not alive as in they inhabit a human body on this planet, but they're around somewhere. Not that you're likely to meet them anywhere. But it explains why no one told you, doesn't it?'

'Maybe. I don't know. So, what happens now? Like your **phone**, by the way. She had one just like it.'

'Yes, it's odd.'

'Why?'

'Because only **adepts** have them.'

'Hey, stop it. **adepts**, what are they? Anyway, those phones came out this year, so anyone can buy one. Expensive, though.'

'The **phone** isn't what it seems. The design might look like something you've seen before, but it's not the same. You can only tell by what it can do, and one thing it does is transfer information. It's what we did when we put them close together.'

'Yes, but phones Bluetooth, don't they? That's nothing new.'

'It's more than that.'

'Well, so you say, but I reckon you're making it up as you go along. What did she send you?'

Alex checked his **phone** and then showed Mike. It showed four pictures; the girl they'd just seen, a man of about forty dressed in a tracksuit, an older woman sitting at a table, and a young boy. Mike shrugged. 'So?'

'They're her other lives. The name under the picture of her as we saw her is Jayne, Jayne Sutherland.'

'They're all human though, aren't they, what's so special? They're probably just her family. Odd to share that though.'

Alex sighed. This was going to take a long, long time. 'Yes, they're all her human forms. They're the lives she's lived on and around this planet. I can go deeper, but I wouldn't be able to do that until I know her better.'

'Why not?'

'Convention. It's just the way it is. I now know that she's an **adept**, because of the **phone**, and…'

'You didn't say what an **adept** was. A magician or something?'

'It's just how good you are at switching between lives and worlds. There's no bit of paper or an exam you have to do, it's just that when others think you've reached that level one of them gives you a **phone**.'

'Do they talk about you, then?'

'Not really. How do I put it, when you meet someone your subconscious puts them into a group, just like when you meet, say a fellow artist and see their work, then you almost immediately see how experienced they are, and what they can do, yes?'

'And?'

'Well, then the person is nominated as **adept**, and if others agree, then that's what you are, and someone gives you a **phone**.'

'Yes, but that makes little sense. Who gives them a phone? Where do they get it from? Or do you have a special phone shop on another world?'

'Mike, I don't know where they come from. A friend who was in a group I joined gave me mine. Sorry, I really don't know where he got it from.'

'They just give you a top of the range phone for free. I think I might join.'

'It's not free, of course, I mean you have to pay for it.'

'How much then?'

'Well, you know…'

'Let me guess, you pay over the odds for it, don't you? Alex, I'm going to leave you now, and I'm going back to my hotel and have a lie-down. Frankly, I don't believe a word you've said, although you pulled that girl alright, but then you always had a way with girls. It's your naïve, little boy manner. No offence, I could do with a bit of that. Maybe when I've had a think, I'll find you and you can teach me that?'

Alex nodded slowly. Maybe this was all he could expect. 'I look forward to it, Mike, see you soon.'

Mike stood, nodded a goodbye, and walked off, but Alex stayed seated and watched him make his way down the street, maybe going back to the Abbey Hotel where he was staying. A one, or maybe two weeks stay, that he'd let Alex know about only when he arrived from his Isle of Wight home. No one looked at him as he passed by, nobody felt the tug of an **aware** passing but, Alex thought, he could change that.

CHAPTER TWO

Jayne Sutherland walked home to her flat above a café in a Bath backstreet. She let herself in through a green door next to the café's entrance while smelling the wonderful aromas of coffee mixed with freshly baked pastries. It was so tempting. Determined to carry on with her diet, she hurried through her door, up the stairs, and into her front room. Front room sounded grand; there was only one room, plus a bedroom, bathroom, toilet, and a kitchen. Enough for one.

She was still in a whirl. It wasn't every day that an **adept** made contact, and she was wondering what it was all about. There must be a reason, surely? He would not contact her just to say 'hi' and then wander off. Maybe he just wanted a date? Well, there were plenty of those going, and he looked nothing special. His friend was odd. She hadn't picked up anything from him at all, and yet he was with an **adept**. Not just an **adept**, but a **dramatist**. She'd seen him signing books in the big Waterstone's. Oh well, it took all sorts, as you soon found out. She went into her kitchen to make tea and came out with a glass of red wine. She looked at it as though it wasn't hers, shrugged, and took a slug. Nice. Rounded, full-bodied, slightly sweet. Wonderful stuff.

She pulled out her **phone** and looked at the profile that he had transferred to her. It showed a plethora of information. Not like her own neat four squares. But then he'd guess there were more behind there. He had just dumped the lot as though he didn't care who knew what he was or where he'd been. On this planet, it was like giving your Facebook history to a stranger, with all the personal stuff filled in. Who did that? Maybe there was a method to this madness. Maybe he thought she'd just shrug and not look at all his shit. Well, he was wrong there. Walking over to the windowsill which overlooked the busy street below she picked up her **phone**. She had thought she had finished with the world of the **aware** and George Marlin, with all it had entailed. But, of course, she still had the **phone**. She tapped out a number and waited, and then and she told him about Alex.

'Well, you've hooked yourself an interesting fish,' he said. 'How did you manage that?'

'That's the odd part,' she answered, taking another sip of wine. 'He was just sitting outside a café. I was passing, he hit on me. Does it mean anything?'

'Anyone with him?'

'Yes, he had another man with him. Nothing going on there. An **unaware** I think, although I'd need more time to be sure.'

'Might have just been showing off, might have just been bored…'

'Or might have fancied me. Thank you. You don't think there's anything else to it though, do you? I mean, it's odd, isn't it?'

'Not that odd. Did he suggest you meet?'

'He asked me to join them. I gave him my stuff and said we might hook up later.'

'And has he made contact?'

'Hey, give him time, it was only…'

'OK, OK, give me a break. I only asked. Are you going to? He clearly intrigues you.'

'Yes, I think I will. I'll suggest tomorrow and see how keen he is.'

'That's sorted, then. Keep me in the loop, and you can always bring him along.' And he had gone.

She chucked the phone down on one of the snuggle chairs that surrounded an old wooden table and threw herself onto another. Men. What was it with them that threw a spanner into a girl's world? But then, she thought, it must be the same for them. With a start she realised the time and that she hadn't eaten. With only an hour for lunch, she'd left it too late now. Scurrying back down the stairs, she raced into the café, grabbed a couple of croissants and coffee from Jellie, the owner, and raced out. She'd see her later. Now, though, it was back to the shoe shop, and an afternoon filled with irritating customers. And Vicki.

Vicki started at her as soon as she walked through the door. She looked at her watch, looked at Jayne, looked at the coffee and the bag of pastries. She didn't say a word. There was no need, but if Jayne took one minute more than her allotted one hour, there would be trouble. Jayne scooted through the shop and out into the dreary staff area. She bolted down the croissants, quaffed back the coffee, threw the remnants into a bin, smoothed her dress, and walked back into the shop. Just as Vicki was about to walk in. She was exactly on time. She smiled at Vicki and got a scowl in return. Vicki didn't like being beaten, so she'd be checking everything now. But was there anything she could do about it? Maybe. Jayne smiled to herself. It would have to be later, maybe after she had met the man from the café. Yes, that was the way. In two days, the area manager would call in on her rounds, and things might happen then. Jayne smiled some more, just as a customer walked towards her.

'Excuse me, Miss.'

CHAPTER THREE

Alex texted Jayne. He'd splashed out and was able to book the Olive Tree for that evening, reassuring her he'd be paying. She said she would meet him there at eight, but it would have to be tomorrow; a quick call to the restaurant, and he was lucky they could do just that. He just hoped this wasn't a terrible decision. Meeting someone you thought was **adept** was always tricky, because you never knew what they could do. But then you had to take that risk, you just had to.

Their conversation went more like this:

Olive Tree at eight OK?
Olive Tree great: Tomozz?
Done that. My treat.
Love it. See you J x.

CHAPTER FOUR

With Jayne not around until the following evening, Alex rang Mike, and they soon settled down to an evening in the pub. Mike had decided to humour Alex because there might be a laugh in it. After all, Alex had always talked bollocks. As for the **phone** scam, they must have seen him coming. But then, he'd always been naïve.

'Everyone has a **lifeplan**, not just the **aware**, everyone,' Alex was saying.

'Me then?'

'Even you, Mike. From the moment you're conceived, there's no waiting until you're born.'

'So, what does it look like?'

'I'm coming to that. Take a tree, a deciduous tree, look out of the window over there, one of those. See how the branches splay out all over the place, but some reach up to the sky. Now take another tree and invert it, so that its roots are coming down from the sky and place it on top of the first tree. Most of its branches will splay out too, but some of them will touch the branches reaching up from the first tree. Your **lifeplan** should follow a route from the roots of one tree, up the trunk, and into the branches. If you're lucky, it will follow a course that's a **bestlife**, up into the upside-down tree, and along a branch that will guide it to the trunk and the upside-down roots. Your life provides you with **decisionpoints**, times when you have to make a **lifechoice**. It may be a simple one, a random one, but with major effects on your life, such as who you marry, or who you have an affair with. If you have an affair, even. What job you get, whether you decide to stick with that job or grab at something that seems better. Choices, always choices.'

'And this is all worked out in advance, is it? For everybody?'

'That's right. Plotted out.'

'Can I change that **lifeplan**?'

'Of course, but, it's more likely you will just be following another branch. It's still part of the **lifeplan**.'

'So, I can't change things? If I suddenly decide to be something different, you're saying that I can't unless it's part of the plan?'

'Yes. That can be good or bad, depending on the original plan.'

'Sounds rubbish to me, like the caste system. I'm born into a particular caste, and that's it, that's my lot, I can't change it. I suppose I'm in the lowest caste?'

'There's no lower or upper, just how much experience you've had overall. It can be in any type of life.'

'Can anybody else change it?'

'Ah, now there you have it.'

'Is that a yes?'

'The more experienced can nudge the lives of others, of any level of experience.'

'For good or...?'

'For the good of the person you're nudging, but that might be to the detriment of someone else. What one person thinks of as good, another might think bad. You can't help that.'

'Sounds a bit rubbish to me. You're saying that my life isn't my own, aren't you?'

'No, I'm saying that you have a plan that can be changed because others have a say as well.'

'So how do I change my life?'

'What would you like to change?'

'Serious? I can just change my life?'

'Not just change it, you have to put some effort in. That's often the problem, people don't like putting the effort into it, or don't feel they can, sometimes they're just overwhelmed by circumstance. It's a plan, it's not set in stone. It's hope, it's a chance, it's what could be.'

'Hey, but what about the bad guys? What goes on there then?'

'Choices, circumstance, and remember, those choices aren't just yours, they're everybody's. Not only that but there are lots of individuals off-planet that can have an influence as well, but most can't be bothered, or are **unaware**.'

'Are you saying that those who aren't **aware**, I mean aware of all this, have less of a chance? That I have less of a chance?'

'Bluntly, yes. But remember, it's you who are responsible for both your successes and your mistakes. Well, mostly anyway. Are you ready for that?'

'Shit. Are you saying if I knew nothing about this then I could just let life happen?'

'Absolutely. You could just let it sweep you along, ignorant of so much that's going on. Until the moment you move on.'

'What did you call it**, reposition**? See, I remembered.'

'That's it. Until then. At that moment you get to look back at what you have or haven't done. It's something that will stay with you forever and ever. Part of your history. Part of what I passed on to Jayne, and she passed to me. Part of something that others will know you by. For always.'

'Shit.'

'It's up to you, no one's going to force you.'

'I'm not up to this.'

'No probs. Another?' He picked up the empty glasses and went up to the bar for a refill. It would be good to have Mike along, but if it wasn't to be then, well, so what? Frankly, it wouldn't make much difference, but he'd always wonder. A big what if? He returned slowly to their table.

'I've been thinking, Alex.'

'Drink up. Go on.'

'If you can influence other **aware** and even **adepts**, then what can you do with the **unaware**, like me?'

He wanted to say have fun, but he checked himself. 'Oh, we just ignore them. After all, they're not a danger, are they?'

'Hey, don't ask me. I don't know. So, you're saying we're alright then, is that it?'

'You'll still have a **lifeplan**, you just don't know about it, and will only think of your life as just that, your life, for better or worse.'

'I don't know. I'm not sure it makes sense to me.'

'Sleep on it, then. Come back if you're ready. There's no pressure.'

'You know, I think I'll do that.' He sunk his pint, got unsteadily to his feet, and as Alex watched him, he waved and weaved his way to the door. People moved to let him pass, and one or two gave a helping hand.

Alex walked out shortly afterwards, leaving a long enough gap between them so that he could keep an eye on him without being seen if Mike turned around. Not that that was likely. Mike had said he was staying at the Abbey Hotel, so not far away, in a quiet city with plenty of tourists still around. In Bath, you were more likely to find someone helping you than mugging you, but it was best to be safe. It took Mike twenty staggering minutes to pass through the centre, the abbey, and round to the hotel. Alex watched as he made it through the hotel doors without incident.

For Alex, something else was afoot. He kept feeling the pull of a summons, and not just one summons, but several. What the heck was going on? He'd never been this much in demand. He could just ignore them, but they would either get more insistent, or they might get annoyed, or they might just go away. It was best not to tempt them, though, so he walked on. He needed to find a quiet place, somewhere he couldn't be distracted. He walked down Manvers Street, around the station, over the Halfpenny Bridge, and onto the path beside the River Avon. There were plenty of seats along this stretch, and he could watch the river rush over the Pulteney Weir in peace. It was peaceful, and the rush of water cut out extraneous noise from the city. He found a bench and set about clearing his mind, which wasn't so easy after a few pints. Questions kept dropping into his head, questions like:

So, what made you pick her then?

You know who she is, don't you?

What do you really know about her?

She won't let you go, not now, not when you've asked her.

Better think what you're going to say, better be careful.

Careful! You're going to have to be more than that.

Do you really not know?

He wondered if it was something to do with the beer, but no, it must be the voices of others. There was no way of knowing if what they said was true, or they were just having a bit of fun. Maybe he ought to be careful when he met up with Jayne again. Maybe he'd been rash about booking the Olive Tree. Oh well, too late now.

CHAPTER FIVE

Alex sat next to a black cat, or rather the cat allowed him to sit beside her, feigning ignorance of his presence. There was bound to be something else she wanted to do shortly, like lick her bum, but for the moment, she let him be. She wasn't even his cat, but belonged to a neighbour. When he bought the house, there was a cat flap in the back door, which the cat was used to using. Either the previous owner had programmed its chip recognition for the neighbour's cat, or it had done it by itself. He thought the latter, anything for another meal.

Alex lived in a house that was too large for him, mainly because his fiancée had walked out six months ago and left him to sort it and their marriage plans out. He wasn't sure why she'd left, and it obviously wasn't because of the fireman who'd insisted on carrying her out when they had a chip-pan fire. Even though he'd seen them together since. That was just too shallow. She wouldn't, would she?

That was the thing about being **aware**. It could happen to anyone. A lawyer, a tramp, well, anyone. It was no respecter of class or education. One moment you weren't, the next you were, whether you were five, fifty-five, or a hundred and five. It simply didn't matter. Nor did your colour or your creed. Ideally, your parents, or at least one of them, or a kindly aunt or uncle, let you know at an early age, and gave you a bit of guidance, but often it seemed to just happen. Alex didn't know what that was like but could imagine. Frightening. Like being told to fly a plane without an instruction book. Luckily a friend had guided him, and it had been a gentle adventure rather than a panic-stricken plunge. It had cost, of course, but that was only to be expected.

Some people charged a shed load of money for **awareness**, although they didn't always call it that. They dressed it up as some religious or magical experience. But they didn't last long. They got **blankwalled**. Not literally. It just happened that several **aware**, usually **adepts**, grouped together and diverted the life of the annoying sod into a place they really didn't want to go. Milton Keynes, for example. Not, thought Alex, that he had anything against Milton Keynes, apart from the fact that he had spent an afternoon trying to find out which roundabout he had to come off at, and when he did, all the buildings looked the same. Of course, there was also the annual subscription. The money you gave to your local group voluntarily to help with expenses. But he hadn't joined a group since he moved to Bath. Maybe he should?

All this was just a distraction from work. He reached for his laptop, which annoyed the cat, who, after an indignant meow, stalked off. Then he took his **phone** out of his pocket and looked for Jayne on social media. It was interesting that she'd only revealed four lives. He'd been quite open with her and shared all the information he had. Maybe because he was hoping to impress her, but actually because he could never be bothered to find out how the **phone** worked so he could change the settings. He studied each picture closely. Maybe these were who she was at this moment, maybe she was **multipersoning**. Now that took skill, let alone time and patience. It was certainly possible, though, or so he'd been told. The trouble was you had to keep each person separate, every aspect of them, and especially any contacts they had. Mix an element up and all sorts of hell awaited, they'd told him. Imagine, no, no need to imagine. He shuddered.

And so to Jayne. It was easy to track her down, and he clicked on a picture of her. She was from a family in Dorset, was twenty-four and worked at a well-known shoe shop in the city. All gleaned from three sites. He'd experienced nothing like this before, contacting an **aware** girl and her responding. Well, the only thing he could do was to meet her. Or would he be walking into some sort of trap? He shook his head and gritted his teeth as the cat jumped up onto his lap, using its claws to steady itself after the jump. It looked up at him, hoping for affection, or maybe just smirking, knowing full well what it had just done. He gave it a few strokes and then carefully placed it on the floor. Work to be done. An author had deadlines, and none of them his.

Once he was applauded for dropping hints into his books about **awareness**, but as he pointed out to those who cared, a hint did nothing, even if he'd intended it. He was now writing for the seven to eleven age group as well, although his agent said even these were read more widely. Maybe his readership had picked up on something, who knew, but it was unintentional. At first. When they pointed it out to him, he refuted the claims, and then, after reflection, done consciously what he had previously included unconsciously. There were no **phone**s in his stories, nothing that obvious, but some of his characters had an uncanny knack of getting others to do what they wanted.

He sat at his desk and looked out of the window. His was a period terraced house on Poet's Corner, which was on Bear Flat to the south of the city. Called Poet's Corner because the roads here were named, well, after poets. There was Shakespeare, Chaucer, Kipling, Milton, Longfellow, and so on. His house was well placed so that he could see out into the distance and a grassy protrusion, surrounded by the closely gathered houses of Roundhill. As evening drew in, intrepid balloonists from Bristol would drift across the sky under multicoloured canopies with flames shooting up to come raining down somewhere near Bath racecourse. But it was too late for that now, and all he had to look at were the twinkling lights of distant occupation. He sighed, opened up his laptop, and typed.

CHAPTER SIX

Jayne, (no, he couldn't include her name… no? why not?), *sat under the leafy apple tree in the garden. She was drifting off into a world of her imagination while keeping half an ear out for her mother's call so that she could ignore it yet know that she was wanted. She enjoyed being wanted, a cosy feeling that warmed. Out here in the country, she had few, if any, friends. They'd left them behind when her father had lost his job and they had moved house when he managed to get a new one. Away from the expensive suburbs to this hamlet, with its winding roads, its few shops, and non-existent transport links. All this meant that Father was away a lot. He drove out early in the morning, often for several days, and when he returned, he grumpily shut himself away.*

Her mother was unhappy at first, but then perked up as she made friends. Especially with Jake Parsons, who often came to help with this and that. It was amazing how many little jobs needed doing, but that must be because it was such an old house. These days Mother positively skipped around the house and down to the shops to see her new friends while checking with Jayne when she would be back at school.

School. Instead of the hordes she'd known at their other house, there were so few potential friends here. They'd all known one another forever. She was the "Incomer", the one left out of their games, who saw them gathered together in little groups muttering, with glances over their shoulders at her. If only there was a way to break into their circle. She had picked one of them at random, or maybe because she wore the most colourful clothes. Davina Parsons, who could be quite nice on her own and had even accepted an invitation to come to tea. But she didn't turn up, much to Mother's annoyance. Davina had denied all knowledge of it when challenged, but there had been an odd smirk on her face. Jayne focused on her, her golden hair tied into a ponytail, her bright blue dress, which probably was against all the school rules. But then her daddy was a school governor. Her pristine knobbly knees were not scraped like Jayne's (there were lots of trees to climb), and her highly polished shoes. Now here was someone she would like to bring down a peg or two. If there was a leader, then Davina was it. She liked to have everything her way, and that, it seemed, meant the absence of Jayne.

She absently wondered what Davina would be like if her father wasn't a governor. She didn't have as much money as Davina for clothes and couldn't invite friends around for tea whenever she wanted. A hint to Davina's success lay there. But there was nothing she could do about it, so she might as well just get on with life, which, she thought with a sigh, meant catching up with her schoolwork and not daydreaming. She levered herself out of the wooden steamer chair, a decaying reminder of their previous home, and made her way into the house.

The next morning, she did her paper round as usual. It gave her a small income, which her parents let her keep instead of providing her with pocket money. Back to the house for a bacon sarnie, which her mother cooked for her, a quick check that she'd put the right books in her bag, and away. The walk to school wasn't arduous, just boring, because no one wanted to walk with her. They already had their pairs and were quite happy with that. She'd tried to tag on to one or two, but they just ignored her. It was with a heavy heart that she watched Sheila and Ellie walking on the other side of the road, chatting away. If only. Then they turned around, saw her, and beckoned her over. She was so surprised that she just stopped and stared for a moment, but Ellie gestured again, so she walked over. Cautiously.

'Jayne, come on. We don't want to be late. Have you done the homework?'

It was as if they always did this, as though they thought of her as their friend. There must be a catch.

'What are you going to do now?' Sheila asked.

Jayne looked at her, puzzled. Here it comes, she thought. 'What do you mean?' she asked cautiously.

'Well, now that your mother is leaving.'

'Is she?' What to believe, was this just a windup as she expected, or was there really something to this?

'I heard my mum on the phone to Daphne's mum, and she said that your mother was going off with Jake, you know, the handyman.'

They were both looking at her intently now, maybe seeing how she'd react, maybe just looking for tears. Well, she was going to disappoint them.

'Maybe. I don't think she's made her mind up. But then, if she goes, I'll have a lot more time to do as I want, won't I?'

Sorted. Adversity changed to triumph, especially since she knew that Ellie's mum kept her in until she was satisfied with her homework, which didn't happen often.

'But, but what does your dad have to say about it?' Sheila asked, looking at Ellie as she spoke.

'I don't know, he's never around much. I expect he'll be glad he doesn't have to be home at a certain time for her. Yes, I expect that will be it.'

They arrived at the school gates, and just as suddenly as they had adopted her, Ellie and Sheila scooted off. She saw them talking intensely to others in her class, looking over their shoulders at her as they did so. So that's what it was all about. Jake's frequent visits, her mum's absences. One thing was true, she wouldn't miss her, and wasn't that an awful thing to think.

Alex stopped typing and looked out at the twinkling lights in the distance. It was too sad. Or maybe it wasn't, maybe it was a tale of hope, of courage in adversity. He hadn't decided yet. The story would flow in its own time, words coming out of the ether and onto the page. It always amazed him how that happened. Something from nothing. Where did it all come from?

He closed the laptop, found himself a beer, and settled down to watch the TV.

CHAPTER SEVEN

Jayne was already waiting for him at the entrance to the restaurant, even though he was early. She'd dressed all in red, except for the black coat that rested on her shoulders, showing off her long blond hair. He kissed her lightly on a cheek, taking in her perfume, waved her down the steep steps, and quickly followed. Maybe he was a little underdressed for her in a camel coat, blue striped shirt and light linen jacket but with jeans and trainers, but it wasn't a look he wanted to change. Their coats were taken, and they were escorted to a table for two in the seemingly full restaurant. He waited for her to sit before he did, and then she leaned towards him.

'It's so long since I've been here. Thank you.' She reached across and squeezed his hand. So far, so good. 'So, tell me all about yourself,' she went on, 'and why you picked me out.'

Shit, what a question, and one he wasn't stupid enough to answer honestly, otherwise the evening would come to an abrupt halt.

'Two things,' he said, thinking rapidly. 'First, you looked so attractive as you walked down the road, and then…'

'Yes?'

'Then there was an air of mystery about you, something I couldn't fathom. It intrigued me.'

She sat back, looking at him closely. Had he blown it?

'How lovely,' she said, 'and exactly what I'd expect a **dramatist** to come up with. It's interesting, flattering.'

He looked at her.

'Don't look so shocked,' she said. 'I knew from the moment I saw you. From the moment you called me, and I also know you were just playing about to impress your friend. You see, I can tell.'

'You're an **adept**, aren't you?'

She laughed, and it was delightful. She reached forward again to place her elegant hand with neatly painted red nails on his arm. 'And?'

'And?'

'Oh, come on, open up to me,' she said in a teasing voice.

'You don't open up much in your...'

She interrupted him. 'Of course not. Why would I? You, on the other hand, show everything and expect me to believe it. It's like hiding a leaf in a forest, no one's going to wade through it all trying to find the real you. Brilliant. You impress me. As I suppose you expected to, me a mere **adept**, and you the **dramatist**.'

He shrugged. She was giving him more credit than he'd ever thought of. He dumped everything because it was easier than sorting out a few points he wanted to make. If it impressed though her, so be it. Then he had a thought.

'But you're not just an **adept**, are you?'

'Of course not, as you very well know. After all, we've got history, haven't we? So much history, and so, disruptive.' She laughed. She had a glass of champagne in her hand, which he didn't remember ordering, and she looked over the rim and toasted him.

'But that's just history,' he said, playing for time.

'True. We must move on, you're right, and I look forward to finding out where you plan for us to be next. I'm thinking of a sunny beach somewhere hot, not too hot, with a bar not far away, and a lovely gentle sea. How about it?'

'Well, I'm writing at the moment.' It sounded lame, but what else could he say.

'Of course, you are. At least I hope you are. I suppose the story cannot stop, can it?'

'Maybe later, when we know one another better. If you'd like that?'

She laughed again. Such a light laugh. 'Oh, I'm sure we'll do that. Aren't you?'

He was becoming irritated with this game, the rules of which he didn't know. Hell, he didn't know where he was at all in it, and yet she thought he was its master. He needed to get out of this and seek advice. But who could he ask?

Food arrived, food that he didn't remember ordering. Then they were on to the dessert. How had that happened? He remembered that he'd enjoyed the courses so far, very much, but he could not recall a single element of them. Time seemed to swirl around them, distorting life, and yet here they were, as real as real could be.

'What about you?' he asked. 'What do you do with your day?'

'As if you need to ask. But I suppose we should go through the motions, reinforce the narrative. But then, no, why would we do that, you and I, there is no need. Coffee? A liqueur?'

And indeed, they had reached that stage of the meal, and he still hadn't the faintest idea who she was, nor what she did. But warnings rang around him. He could hear them now, as he had before. "Do not trust her." "Leave her be." "Keep her out of your story." They all had the same tenor, but were they just in his head, just his imagination, or something more?

'Your place or mine?' she asked. 'My bed's really soft.' Her head tilted on one side, a beguiling smile that matched the eyes, the oh such blue eyes that swept into his. He gave himself a mental shake.

'Another day, if you don't mind, Jayne. I have so much on that I can't relax. I would love to another day. I hope you don't mind.' And he was at the desk, tapping his code in to pay as they gathered their coats for them. 'It's been a lovely evening, as I knew it would be.'

'Ah, you're running away from me. Well, if you're sure, but I might not be available the next time you come calling.'

'But that depends on the story, doesn't it?' he answered, although he wasn't sure why. With that she cupped his face in her hands, kissed him fully on the lips and was off, walking briskly, heels tapping away, red coat flying, to disappear around a corner. He drew a deep breath. He felt that he had escaped something, but he had absolutely no idea what.

Strolling back, taking time to savour the city and its floodlit features. His head swam with thoughts of the evening and Jayne. Why so mysterious? It had been as though she was playing a part, a part he responded to in kind. Did she know something about him? She must do something fantastic by the sound of it, something he should know. There must be someone who could help him, but he had kept away from the **aware** world, away from the cliques they gathered in. They had tried to get him to join them when he'd moved to Bath, but he had turned them down. Was that a mistake? Maybe he should have joined in because they'd know about Jayne, what she was, what she did.

They met in the home of one of their members, in the Royal Crescent, probably because it gave them a prestigious address. If you were into that sort of thing. When they'd talked to him about joining, they'd emphasised the rules, the regulations, the bureaucracy that they'd brought to the art. At the time he'd thought them nothing more than jobsworths, bent on creating jobs for themselves, funded by the likes of him. He wasn't sure that his opinion had changed, but now he needed them.

He walked around the abbey to the taxi rank and took one home. It made life easy. There he poured himself a brandy and sat at his laptop, once again looking out over the twinkling lights denoting so much human habitation.

CHAPTER EIGHT

Jayne awoke with a headache. She had drunk too much. She groaned as she sat up; the room coming into and going out of focus. She had to face the shop, and the customers, and Vicki. She ran to the bathroom and threw up.

What the hell had she been doing baiting a **dramatist**? Why hadn't she just talked to him like a normal person? It was as though another personality had taken her over. Truth be told, she was scared, overawed, and worried. He had found her; he had called out to her, and she had accepted his call. She had thought herself finished with all that. The Marlin group, the Bath **aware**. They had pulled her in deep, but, despite their entreaties to stay, she had broken away. Now this man was dragging her back in, and there was no way of avoiding it. Now she would have to face the consequences, although she hoped they would use Lizzie rather than her. Lizzie, who had trained her, mentored her and blanked her when Jayne said that she was leaving. Well, maybe this would settle any debt they felt she owed them.

She washed, then changed her mind and showered, slowly going through the motions until she left the flat late, grabbing her usual cappuccino and croissant from the café. The café was only a few minutes away from the shop where she worked, but it would be a stretch to make it on time. But she wasn't too late, because Vicki wasn't at her usual position by the front entrance. She slowed, breathing deeply, nodded to Amy who was by the back area and composed herself as she wolfed her breakfast. Her starting time was three minutes away. What a way to live. Clock watching, waiting for it to be over, lunchtime, home time, any time but work time. Then Vicki walked through the door, and she and Amy gasped, for Vicki looked a wreck. She ignored them and strode through to the back area, where they heard the toilet door slam shut. What on earth had happened? Had Vicki, perfect fucking Vicki, actually got a hangover?

Alex made his way from a dream he'd never remember to consciousness and then to the kitchen, blearily dropping a sachet into his fancy coffee machine and pressing the cappuccino button. A grind, a whir, a gurgle, and hiss, and he took the mug of cappuccino over to his laptop. Naked, he sat and yawned. It was like this most mornings. But now Jayne was occupying the story. She was on his laptop, waiting for him to open the lid, haunting him, teasing him. Maybe he should just change her name and have done with her. But no, his stories didn't work like that. Once a name had come to him, it stayed. He'd never changed a name. Ever. A ritual maybe, but, oh hell, he needed to write.

It was some time after Elli and Sheila broke the news of her mother's infidelity, and the end of term was approaching. It had hardly been the best term for Jayne. Her mother had gone. Had just packed and left one day without even saying goodbye, and her father had become even more absent and uncommunicative the few times he was around. Social services had visited, alerted by the school, but had taken no action that Jayne knew of. So, life went on pretty much as it had done when she had both her parents around. Except now life just seemed emptier, and if it hadn't been for Amilie West, it would have stayed that way.

Amilie appeared at Jayne's house one day. Jayne knew she existed, but they hadn't spoken before, so it was a surprise and a little awkward to start with. She had walked around the house to find Jayne sitting under the tree, book in hand, although Jayne looked as though she was daydreaming more than reading. She stood for a moment before Jayne looked up.

'Hi, it's Amilie, isn't it?'

'Yes, that's me. Sorry, I didn't mean to interrupt.'

'That's alright. Is there something you want?'

'There's something I want to talk about, yes, but it's awkward.'

This sounded more interesting than her bruising encounter with Ellie and Sheila, but Jayne was wary.

She had no friends now, not one, and had become used to that, so anyone thinking that they could just walk into her life was a threat to be repelled. Amilie seemed nice enough, though.

'You're in the year above me, aren't you?' she asked.

'Yes, but in some ways that helps with what I've got to say. I want to tell you something. Not something bad, but something that might be of use to you.'

'Go on then. Oh, would you like some squash or something?'

After Jayne had fetched a jug of squash, they settled down together cross-legged on the grass, and Amilie began.

'A few years ago, my parents told me something. This will sound weird, but I promise it's true, and it's something you can test out for yourself. They told me I had an aptitude.' She paused and looked up at the sky, and then at Jayne. 'They said I could communicate with people just by thinking. Not only that but when I did it, I could change their mind about things.'

It took quite an effort for Jayne not to smirk. Why? Why did she get the weird one? All this time with no friends and then this. She put her arms around her knees and rocked gently, nodding, which seemed to encourage Amilie.

'My parents told me that this was quite common and that those who could do it are the **aware**, *and those that don't know they can do it are the* **unaware**.

I have to admit, I laughed. But they kept going, and they showed me what to do, and you know, they were right.'

'But,' Jayne said, 'I'm don't get what that means. Surely you can just talk to people. You don't have to have a sort of secret way of getting your point across.'

'Oh, there's more to it than that, and especially for you. My mother saw you in the High Street last week, and she couldn't stop talking about it. She said that you have some sort of special… now she didn't say power. What did she say? I know you emanated something special and that we needed to talk about it because it was going to waste. That's why I came. She'd like to meet you.' She looked cautiously at Jayne from under the fringe of black hair that curtained her face. Jayne looked at her. Looked at her properly for the first time. Amilie was taller than her, with straight black hair, cut to shoulder length, then a plain dark blue dress that reached to her knees when she was standing, and sensible black shoes and socks. If she remembered right, then she was quite bright. Brighter than Jayne anyway, who was always near the bottom of her class for just about everything except English.

'I'm not sure, Amilie, I mean it sounds weird to me.'

'Look, it won't hurt, will it, and Mummy's really nice. She said she'd make food for us both if you came over, and she's a fantastic cook. When she's got time that is because she's a doctor as well.'

That was it, thought Jayne. Amilie was the daughter of Doctor West, which meant that she didn't have a daddy. He'd died, but she knew only that. It made her like Amilie more. How strange life was that she felt drawn to someone because of the bad things that happened. She smiled up at Amilie.

'That would be lovely Amilie, you can tell your mum that I would love to come. I'm looking forward to it already. When was she thinking?'

'How about tomorrow? I know it's her day off, so she'll have time to make food. It doesn't happen often to be honest because she works so hard.'

'That sounds great. After school?'

'Yes, I think so, but I'll check with her first, and then I'll see you tomorrow. Is that alright?'

'It sounds divine.'

She noticed Amilie was hesitating, looking down at her feet, and then into the distance.

'What's wrong?' she asked.

Amilie just shook her head before saying. 'Mummy was right, I can feel you. You have something there, something powerful, Jayne, and I think Mummy's going to be helpful. I don't want to worry you, though. It's really useful, you see, not something to be afraid of, and Mummy's fantastic at it. Honest.'

Jayne changed the conversation to school, to the village, to anything but the reason for Amilie's visit, and they found that their conversation became easier, that they thought the same about many things. It was nice to find someone like this, Jayne thought. If only there wasn't the weirdness. After a while, Amilie left, and Jayne sat alone with her thoughts. Could she have something special about her? She'd always felt different, but this was something else, and it was a doctor who had recognised it, so there must be something there. But what?

Alex stopped typing, checked his word count, and looked down at his empty mug. Time for another, and to sort out what he was going to do for the day, apart from thinking about Jayne. She really was a disturbing person, and the way they had sparred last night was just weird. He checked the time. Too early to wander into the city and seek help from the group. He was sure they weren't early risers. So he would walk over to George's around twelve. Hopefully, he could catch someone who wanted lunch and would swap information for it. With that, he went to shower, shave, and dress for the occasion.

At five minutes to twelve, he walked into the Royal Crescent and along the imposing frontage and the equally inspiring view across the countryside it enjoyed. The Georgian building dated back to the 1700s, but now many of the terraced buildings were split into smaller lets. George Marlin probably owned a lot of things, but his house here had to be his pride and joy, as he often told people. Although he hosted the group, he wasn't, he told people, an **aware**, but because he said that people seemed to assume that he was a powerful **aware** who could hide his power. Or maybe he was too rooted in the material to achieve full **awareness**, they said. But who knew? As Alex walked past each of the terraced houses, he looked in. Often it was too dark to see much, but sometimes he glimpsed beautiful pictures on their walls or carved furniture. Not always, though. There were several that showed more basic tastes. He walked on past the Royal Crescent Hotel, with its uniformed greeter standing ready, to a house further on. It had an imposing black door, and net curtains screened the windows. As he approached the door, he could hear an indistinct murmur of conversation and hoped he was doing the right thing. He wasn't one for clubs and societies. His finger hesitated over the bell push, but before he could press it, the door opened.

'Ah, Mr Ash, so pleased you could make it.'

That was the trouble with **adepts**. They could feel your approach. He'd never become used to it, even though he could feel others. It was eerie. He was ushered into a finely decorated hall with exquisite oil paintings, mainly of horses, on the walls, and then into the front room. There were too many people there, men and women in almost equal proportions, and they all turned to stare at him. He wondered whether to just turn around and go when a glass of champagne was pressed into his hand, and a man approached him.

'Alex, we're so pleased that you've come to our little group at last. We were despairing. We need to stand together, you know, ready for whatever life throws at us. Better together, that's my motto. Now I won't introduce you to everyone. It would take too long, and anyway you can just touch and go as they say, and you'll have a complete record, won't you? One thing though, we're all agog about you and Jayne. I hope you can tell us something about the two of you. Quite a surprise, I can tell you, we've been abuzz with it.'

Alex swallowed some champagne and had to check himself from gagging on the bubbles, which gave him time to think. He was being addressed by George Marlin himself, which was an honour. But what could he say about Jayne? Maybe if he could just speak to one or two **adepts**, then he might find out more about her, rather than display his ignorance for all to see.

'Come over here,' George placed a guiding hand on the small of his back, nudging him forward to a small group that had placed itself a little away from the others. There were three women and two men, none of whom he recognised. They all raised their slim gold **phone**s, and he touched his against each one. Their presence overwhelmed him. Oddly, they seemed to have the same reaction to him.

'Mr Ash, Alex,' one woman spoke up, looking up at him as though in awe. 'The **dramatist**. What an honour. George has told us all about you. We're so pleased to see you. Maybe you'd like to come more often, we'd be so happy to welcome you.'

He stood stock-still, wondering what to say for a moment, but they quickly filled the space as they all rushed to welcome him. Others clustered around, and they were all talking, so he could just stand there and listen as they pressed more champagne upon him. It was heady and dizzying. Canapes were offered, and he struggled to hold his glass, eat, and nod, let alone take part.

It all came to a sudden end. He noticed that the room was cooler and, looking around, saw that the group he was with was the only one left. He'd been right with his timing, for lunch had called them. He felt a touch on his arm and found the first woman who had spoken to him looking earnestly up.

'Alex, we wondered if you would do the honour of lunching with us. George has set out a small table, just for us. It would be so lovely if you could, but of course, we know what important things you have to do, and we don't want to impose.'

'But of course,' he answered. 'I'd love to, and to be honest, I was looking for some information myself and wondered if you might assist me.' Well, that stopped the conversation. Marlin was suddenly still, and there was an awkward pause.

'We would love to assist you in any way that we can, wouldn't we?' He turned to the others, who nodded. 'Now this way, and we can tuck in and talk.'

George led the way to the back of the house, where a dining room decorated in the original Georgian style led through open doors to a large expanse of garden. In the centre of the room was a vast expanse of a table laid out with cold meats and salads. The group ploughed in with all other things forgotten. Alex felt a hand on his shoulder.

'You know, it might be better if you talked to Lizzie there.' George pointed to a woman Alex hadn't noticed before. She was about the same height as him, with long dark hair and smartly dressed in a black suit. She was watching them and raised her glass in acknowledgement. 'It doesn't pay to involve some of the others. They do not know how to treat personal information, so whatever you say will be around the city by nightfall. Don't worry, I'll keep them out of your hair.'

As the others drifted out into the garden, all thought of his request for information forgotten, just he and Lizzie remained.

'Well,' she said, 'this is a surprise. The **dramatist** wanting more information on our Jayne. How interesting.'

He looked at her and realised that he was staring into her dark brown eyes. He stopped immediately. Maybe she had been staring into his.

'Yes, that's right. You must have read me.'

'Of course, but you're lucky. I blocked the others, even though it's given me a headache. They've forgotten all about it now, but you really are going to have to be more careful. I suppose, being a bit of a recluse, you're not used to dealing with the **aware** en masse. Not to worry, we can soon sort that.'

'I'm a bit at sea altogether, really, Lizzie. I mean, I don't even understand why I'm an **aware**, let alone the **dramatist** thing, I'm just an author. A friend made me **aware** years ago, and, frankly, I'd be grateful for any help you can give me.' It was the first time he'd ever asked for help from anyone, and it felt empowering. How odd.

'That's exactly what I'm here to do. George spotted that straight away, he's good at that. Even if he isn't a developed **aware**, he's a good organiser. Now, how about we disappear and find some lunch somewhere quiet? He won't mind, in fact, I think he'll be rather pleased.'

They left without seeing George, and with Alex making a mental note to apologise to him, set off into the city.

At Lizzie's suggestion, they walked to the far end of the Crescent, turning right beside Marlborough Buildings. More Georgian architecture, and a view of the messy backs of the Crescent when he glanced around. At the top of the road, where it met Weston Road, she steered them towards the Marlborough Arms. He'd been here a long time ago, and the food had been good then, but today that was secondary. Walking out into a garden packed with tables, Lizzie made for the quietest one.

When they had finished eating and had coffee in front of them, she began.

'I'm getting the feeling you don't know as much as people think you do. In this life, anyway. Do you think I'm right?'

'Absolutely. I'm sure everyone else knows more about me than I do, and as for Jayne…'

'Yes, we'll come to her in a minute, but let's talk about you first. I think we ought to start there. No, I'm wrong. It's best if we talk about me first, then you'll know where we stand. The trouble with you is that you're too trusting. Or you just don't care what people think about you. Or you can't be bothered.'

'Probably the last one. Sorry.'

'Don't be sorry, it's just that you're getting involved in things that are going to cause you problems. But you're going to have to get involved, whether you like it or not.'

'Really?'

'Yes, really. My goodness, you are in the backwoods, aren't you? I think we're going to have to have lots of meetings to sort you out, don't you? Maybe many a long night too. Just to make sure.'

He looked up then, and saw the twinkle in her eye, and felt the press of her foot against his ankle. Not again, he thought, but then, with a smile, gave in.

'Your place or mine,' she said with a grin as he looked into her brown eyes.

CHAPTER NINE

The next morning they sat together in a small café in the backstreets of the city, a hand on each other's thigh, sipping coffee and munching pastries. It had been a long night.

'You're good,' he said, not for the first time.

'So, are you, but then we've had thousands of years to practice, and at heart, it's a fairly simple process.'

'Yes, but it gets mixed up with romance, and then there's a story.'

She looked up sharply. 'You're not talking...'

'No, I'm not.' He looked at her, concerned. 'Are...?'

'Of course not, I just wanted to be clear.'

'Anyway, it's not always a simple process, but you're right, the mechanics are.'

'Unless you fall off the bed. Sorry, sorry, I wasn't going to mention that.'

'Or...'

'Don't you dare...'

'Alright. But you are incredibly, err, flexible. It's a lovely day, isn't it?'

'Yes, and now we need to continue with your education, don't we? You know, for someone who has been around for so long you're surprisingly, err, fresh.'

'I'll take that as a compliment.'

'I didn't say it was… we need to think about Jayne, and her past, the sort of tricks she gets up to, and what she might have in mind now. The difficult thing is that she might not know, might not even know she's doing it.'

'Seriously?'

'Everything I say is serious.' She saw him look at her. 'To do with Jayne, that is.'

'There are so many names for **aware** things, aren't there?'

'It happens in any job. A plumber has Yorkshire fittings and compression joints and…'

'How do you know about plumbers' joints?'

'I am one. I run **multilives**. If you need a plumber, make sure you let me know.'

'You need the work?'

'No. So I can make sure I don't turn up. Do you want that last croissant?'

'What should I do if I see Jayne?' He pushed the plate with the croissant towards her.

'Act naturally, ask her out again, but don't let her come too close, and do nothing without checking with me first.'

'Even…'

'Now you're getting kinky. But ideally, yes. Though you can give me a blow by blow account afterwards.'

He looked at her closely, but she wasn't smiling, although she was stroking his thigh very pleasantly. He'd never understand women, certainly not in a few thousand years, anyway.

'So, the plan is we continue as we would normally do, and I wait to see if Jayne gets in touch. Right?'

'You could always get in touch with her, there's no harm, she might expect it especially if you had a fantastic time with her.' She was looking at him again.

'Right, I'll think about that.'

'Yes. Now how about we practise the bed bit again? My place.'

Sometime later, he staggered from Lizzie's spacious terraced house on the Circus, with the random thought that everything looked white there, white and grey. Now he noticed that all the woodwork of the houses in the Circus were painted white too. Bizarre. It had been a lovely house, but how had she kept it so clean? He shook his head and sauntered down the hill. Stoked up with her coffee, which she was perpetually brewing. He was buzzing and lightheaded. Not the best way to write, so he ought to think of something else to do. He toyed with buying a pair of shoes, just to see Jayne again, but ruled that out too. It was too close to his time with Lizzie. Mike, then? Well, the pub anyway. Sorted, he walked on, a smile on his face. He might not have smiled quite so much if he'd given a lot more thought to all that had happened since Jayne had come into his life. But sometimes you just have to enjoy the moment.

At the same time as Alex was walking away from the Circus on a mission to find a pub, preferably with Mike in it, Jayne was in trouble.

'I'm not having it,' Vicki shouted, ignoring the customers who were hanging around enjoying the show. 'You've gone too far now. I specifically told you to bring me the size sevens. These are eights.'

'Actually,' the petite woman in a green coat, a scarf tied around her head piped up, 'you asked her to bring the eights. I thought it odd at the time.'

Vicki turned every shade from red to purple before thoroughly losing it. 'How dare you contradict me. I'm the manager.'

'And I think I'm the customer, dear. So, I think you'll find I'm right.'

She noticed Vicki was glaring at her, so she picked up the unwanted box and hustled back to get the right ones. It hadn't been Vicki's day. Everything she'd touched had gone wrong. And now this. She found the box she needed, stowed away the other, and walked back into the shop. The customer was still sitting there, Vicki was still standing there, but overlooking both of them was Mrs Thompson, the area manager. Jayne slowed her pace until she was close by.

'I come in here quite often,' the customer was saying, 'and usually, that nice girl serves me,' she smiled up at Jayne, 'but today, well, it hasn't been a pleasant experience at all, and she,' she looked daggers at Vicki, 'tried to blame it all on her.' She smiled beatifically at Jayne.

Mrs Thompson looked at the three of them. 'Miss, err,' she checked out Jayne's badge, 'Miss Sutherland, please look after our valued customer.' Then she turned to Vicki. 'I think we'd better talk. This way.' She strode off, with Vicki trying to keep up behind her.

'There,' said the customer, 'I think she's sorted now, don't you?'

Jayne went cold, remembering that she had seen this woman at one of George Marlin's soirees. She had 'sorted' Vicki, who was totally an **unaware**. It was like being in a club where the members looked after one another, and it was disconcerting.

'Yes,' she said, looking over to where Vicki had left. 'I think you have. Thank you.'

'Oh, no trouble, I sensed she was a wrong 'un as soon as I saw her. You shouldn't have any more trouble now. How about we try those eights? Or maybe the sevens?' She smiled innocently up at Jayne.

An hour later and Vicki said that she had decided to work at another branch, although in what capacity she didn't make clear, and the area manager had made Jayne the new store manager. How had that happened? She was in a whirl; a promotion, Vicki out of her life, and a pay rise that meant she could save some money. It was incredible. As she thought about contacting the agency to find a replacement for herself, she thought about the lady in green. She's said she often came into the shop, but she couldn't recall ever seeing her. She shrugged. These things happened. Then she thought about Alex. It would be nice to see him again and tell him what had happened. They could laugh about it, and then… She could only hope.

CHAPTER TEN

Mike wasn't in Alex's usual haunt, the Old Green Tree, in Green Street, so Alex thought about another favourite, the Raven on Queen Street, and made his way there. Still no Mike, but he needed fuel, so a pie and a pint were just the things. As he settled down to eat, and sup away at a pint of Raven's Gold, he heard a voice he recognised. George Marlin had arrived with a friend. Alex concentrated on his pie but couldn't help overhearing them as they took their seats.

'Pleasant time we had, George. Quite a gathering. Pity, it's so long 'til the next one. Good, you invited that author chap along, though he had little enough to say for himself.'

'Introverted lot, authors, need to get out more. For a **dramatist**, he appears remarkably coy about his knowledge, but maybe that's a good thing. I set Lizzie on him; she'll sort him out.'

'You're good at that, George, a superb organiser, everyone says, and Lizzie has her ways, if you know what I mean. I feel that we're going to need them in the coming days.'

'There's something brewing, Arthur, but I don't know what. Any ideas?'

'Oh, keep me out of it, George, I had enough trouble the last time.'

'Yes, we lost a couple then, didn't we? Couldn't help that though, they ignored my advice.'

'What advice was that, George?'

'Why, not to see one another, of course. Patty and Jerry, now they were having it off, and Jerry's wife got uppity. Not surprising, really. He was seeing more of Patty than her. No sense of diplomacy, Jerry, always diving in without testing the depth of the water.'

'His wife's an **adept**, isn't she?'

'Oh, more than that, but she won't talk about it. Doesn't talk much at all these days, not since Jerry. It all got out of hand.'

'The river, wasn't it?'

'Yes, swept away, but no one knew why they were there or how it happened. All very strange, and his wife wasn't saying.'

'Anyway, this author, this **dramatist**, do you think he's a danger?'

There was a long pause. 'Lizzie will sort him. Don't worry on that score. Good sort, Lizzie.'

He heard them place their order and focused on his food, feeling trapped. There was no way he could leave at the moment. What did George mean, saying that Lizzie would sort him? He had no wish to be sorted. Unless? No, he hadn't meant that, surely.

'The trouble with **dramatist's** is that you never know what they're working on until it happens.' George was speaking again.

'Difficult one, I haven't had dealings with one before.'

'Tricky characters. You think everything's sorted just so, and it all gets rewritten. Best to keep on their good side, I'm told.'

'Who've you been talking to?'

'Oh, Lizzie's got past knowledge. Been around for a while, has Lizzie, knows what's what and what she needs to do. Not a sentimental type, either. Pity I haven't had more to do with her myself, but she's never been interested.'

'I heard she steers clear of married men.'

'Pah, that doesn't stop some of them, I mean…'

'I know, I know, but still.'

'Enough said, Arthur, now, about the tennis. We need fresh blood in the club, we're being slaughtered at the moment, and it's because it's the same old hands turning up.'

Alex tuned out, but his brain kept turning over what they'd been saying. What did they mean by "Lizzie's got past knowledge", and "Lizzie knows what's what, and what she needs to do," let alone, "not a sentimental type?" It just went to show how little he knew about her. He grinned to himself. But maybe more than George. In some respects, anyway. He was still mulling all this over when he heard George call for the bill. He glanced at his watch, they'd raced through their food, he was only just finishing his.

'Sorry I've got to rush, George, on me next time, eh?'

That explained it. George usually looked far too relaxed to hurry his food. Not that he'd expected George to eat in a pub, but then, what did he know?

He had dessert and a coffee to give them plenty of time and then walked out into a day that had changed from sun to rain. Cursing, he ran down the street, their conversation forgotten. As he ran, a place of shelter occurred to him, a certain shoe shop. Surely, he'd find a friendly welcome.

CHAPTER ELEVEN

George Marlin was never one to leave things be or to take no for an answer. It had started to rain. The chat with Arthur had got him thinking, and because of that, and the fact that he was getting wet, his feet led him to Lizzie's door. He rang her bell and waited, rang and waited. Oh well, another time. He stepped back and looked up at her rooms, sure that there was movement there. He thought of ringing again, but the rain was becoming heavier, so he stomped off. There were easier pickings to be had than Lizzie Westbrook. It took him just a few minutes to arrive on another doorstep. The door opened quickly, and she ushered him in, arms raised ready to take his wet coat.

Alex ran through the city and he was getting soaked. When it rained in Bath, it rained heavy saturating raindrops from leaden clouds that often came up the Bristol Channel and the Avon Valley from the Atlantic. He saw the shoe shop and hesitated. Then, heart in hand, he walked in.

Jayne wasn't to be seen, and he was about to walk out again when another woman stepped over to him.

'Can I help you, sir?'

What to say? 'I was in here before and saw another…'

'There's only three of us, and one has moved on, so you must have seen Jayne. She's just popped out because it's quiet and she hadn't had her lunch, but give her thirty minutes and she'll be back, or I'm sure I can help.'

He thanked her and plunged back out into the wet. He saw the library before him, ran over to it, and stood on the escalator that went up to the library and a café. He wasn't sure why he was here, apart from the absence of rain.

Jayne was sitting in the café. It wasn't the weather to go far, so she had just dashed across the road to the Waitrose café above the store and next to the library entrance. She was mulling over whether to call Alex, not sure of his reaction. It would be nice to tell someone what had happened and how Vicki had moved away. She could see the shop entrance from here, so if it got busy, unlikely in this weather, she could run back to help. She saw a familiar figure walk out and then run across the street. Alex. He was probably going to the library, but she watched the door in case. Then he walked through, shaking himself like a dog. She watched as he queued for a coffee and called to him as he turned to look for a table. She loved the way his face lit up as he saw her and hurried over.

'Hi there, I looked in the shop for you.'

'I saw you. You're looking wet.'

'No surprise there. How are you?'

She shrugged. 'I've had an interesting time.'

'Go on.'

'Things happened at work. Remember Vicki? My manager? Well, she had a go at a customer, just as the area manager walked in, and as a result, Vicki had to walk. She doesn't work there anymore and guess who's the new manager?'

'It must be you then.'

'Yes, it's wonderful, as though a great weight's been lifted off me, and Amy, too. She works for me now, and she's great. I reckon our sales are going to be well up now. Vicki was useless. All she did was boss us around. I can recruit a replacement for myself now.'

'That's fantastic, well done you. Would you like to celebrate this evening?' He said it without thinking, swept along in the moment, no thought of the future.

'I'd love to. Where shall we go?'

He had to give it some thought. 'I know. I'll see if I can get a table at Lucknam Park. Would you like that?'

'Oh. Alex, I'd love that. Would you really?'

He reached for his ordinary phone and tapped away. He looked at Jayne. 'Seven-thirty alright?' She nodded, and he tapped some more, ending with a flourish. 'There you are, tonight at seven-thirty. Is it alright if I pick you up at seven, I'll order a taxi so we can both drink?'

'It sounds divine. What a day.' She stood up and reaching across, kissed him on the lips, softly and he felt meaningfully. He wondered if he was up to that tonight. Life was suddenly getting hectic, and, he thought in a moment of panic, the writing was suffering. Jayne saved him.

'I have to get back now. I don't have to worry about Vicki, but I need to set an example. Is that alright? I'll see you at seven. Here, I've written my address down.' She handed him a small piece of paper. 'It's next to the door for the café.'

He glanced at it, but somehow already knew where it would be. How did that happen? He smiled, helped her on with her coat, and followed her down the escalator. A few minutes later he was walking away from the shoe shop and thinking about the writing. He saw a taxi with its light on and flagged it down. Minutes later, he was home and making a coffee, which he took into the front room. Jayne had changed. There was none of that sparring they had gone through on their first evening out. He picked up his laptop and opened it up, and sat down cross-legged on the floor with it in front of him. Then he began to type.

Amilie and Jayne walked to Amilie's house together, holding hands, chatting about their day. It seemed so natural, and yet there was a feeling of dread in Jayne's mind. What was it that Amilie's mum wanted to tell her? Would it change things between her and Amilie? She so hoped it didn't because it looked as though Amilie would be the first genuine friend she'd ever had and it would be heartbreaking to end it.

They were at Amilie's house so quickly. She hadn't realised where it was and what it was like. Amilie's mother had inherited some money after her husband had died, and with that and his life insurance, she had bought a detached house. It wasn't big, it was just lovely. She stood at the gate and looked at it for a moment, wondering what it was like to live in a place like this.

'Jayne, come on, Mummy's here.'

They walked in through the front door that had coloured glass panes in a pattern that the light shone through when she closed it. Amilie led her down a long hall and into a kitchen that stretched the full width of the house. It was huge.

'Hello, Jayne.' Jayne stopped right there, her mouth open. She felt something, but she didn't know what. It was as though Amilie's mother had reached out to her and given her a great hug. But she was there, one hand on a mixing bowl, the other stirring. Smiling.

'Ah, see, I told Amilie you were special. I can see that you can feel it too. How wonderful. After our meal, we can talk, but now you and Amilie can lay the table, and then play in the garden. That's if you don't have any homework you ought to do first.'

The way she said this meant that they could play, anyway. Jayne smiled.

'Thank you, Doctor...'

'Oh, don't bother with that here. Here I'm plain Anne. No titles in this house.'

They ran off together into the garden, with a summer house at the bottom where Amilie gestured to Jayne to sit in one of two womb chairs that swung from metal frames.

'See, I told you, Mummy's always right. She says I'm a late developer though, and I'll be like you one day, but for now, you're the special one. I don't mind, not much anyway, as long as it happens to me, and preferably soon.'

'I'm sure it will, Amilie. Then we'll both be special, not that I know what that means yet.'

They talked of school, of their families, what was left of them, and what they hoped to do after school. While Amilie wanted university, Jayne realised she had no aspirations at all. She wasn't bright enough for uni, and not that keen on education.

'I'll probably end up working in a shop or something. Boring, I know, but…' She shrugged her shoulders and looked down. She would lose Amilie. Not now, but as Amilie realised the gap between them. It was the first prophetic thought she would have; it was just that her reasoning was wrong.

'Don't be down. Lots of things happen, and remember, you'll be special, whatever that means. We'll find out soon, won't we?'

But it was not to be. Anne did not allow Amilie to hear what she said to Jayne. She told Jayne that she must never tell Amilie what happened between them. Not ever. It hurt Jayne so much she nearly cried. Nearly.

Alex sat back and looked out of the window. It was still raining. He rang the taxi firm and arranged their transport for the evening, and went to check on his jacket. He had a habit of getting stains on the sleeve, but all was well. He turned back to his laptop just in time to see the unexpected figure of George Marlin walking up the path. George saw him and waved. Alex jumped up to open the door, and with a brief handshake, George came into the house.

'Ash,' he started, having waved aside the offer of a drink, 'we have to talk.' He looked across at Alex's laptop as he spoke, as though it held some ancient magic. 'I need your help.'

Alex casually walked over to his desk and closed the laptop lid. He wasn't sure why, but instinctively he felt it was important that George didn't see what he had written.

'Of course, George. What do you need?'

'As a **dramatist**, you'll know the power you hold, and I would like to call on you, in that capacity.'

'Right, I'm not sure I have that much sway, but ask ahead.'

'I've been a bit of a fool, you see…' he faltered.

'In what way, George?'

'It's delicate, I hardly know where to start.'

In Alex's experience, this was usually the prelude to a long discourse, so he looked at his watch.

'I'm happy to listen, George, but I have a taxi arriving at quarter to seven.'

George checked his watch and nodded.

'Right, right, it's like this. I've been talking to a friend of mine, a close friend of mine, and she believes you're in danger.'

'From what?'

'From the person we were talking about, Jayne Sutherland.'

Alex held back a laugh. Who knew with the **aware** exactly who was dangerous and who not?

'I see. Does she know why?'

'She wasn't clear. Something in her past I expect.' He turned towards the laptop as though drawn to it. He even took a step towards it. 'So, this is where it all happens, wonderful, I suppose I couldn't...?'

'I don't think so,' Alex answered, taking a step after George. 'It's best not to interrupt the storyline.' Concern swept over him. Something was telling him it was important that George didn't see what he had written.

'Of course, of course. Well, thank you for your time, and don't forget what I've said, will you? Most important, she said it was.'

Alex saw him to the door and returned to sit before his laptop, but he didn't raise the lid.

That was good of George to come round to warn him, even if there wasn't much he could do about it.

He had been kind, too, to introduce him to Lizzie. But what was it in Jayne and his past that was making people so jittery? It would be best to meet Jayne without some historical disaster hanging over their conversation. He imagined sitting down to a candlelit dinner, knowing she had killed a friend or even a lover. How do you even get over something like that? It would certainly be a conversation stopper, and as for a relationship… Maybe it would be a short-lived one. Literally.

He glanced at his watch and jumped up. It was time to get ready for their evening. It was only as he sat in the taxi looking out at the early evening traffic that he thought that maybe he should have rung Lizzie to let her know what was happening. Yes, he definitely should have. He wasn't good at the relationship thing.

CHAPTER TWELVE

Lizzie sat, hoping for a call from Alex, but nothing. Nothing except George Marlin ringing the bell, and she guessed what he wanted. It wasn't on the menu, not these days. She wondered what Alex was up to, maybe typing away, weaving a story. Did he realise what he could do? He seemed so naïve, so innocent. If only she could spend more time with him, instruct him, guide him, mentor him, then maybe everything would be alright. She then she also had a sense of dread, and it had stood her well in the past. But had Alex discovered it? She thought not. Alex, she thought, lived for two things, the present and the future, but then as a **dramatist**, he would. There was no altering the past, no matter what you wrote. You could channel the past, bring it to life again in a story for the future, but once it was acted out, that was it. What had been done was unchangeable. She toyed with her **phone**, torn whether to call him, but certain that the call had to come from him. He had to want her help so that she could guide him to write the narrative she wanted. But it seemed to be her lot to be alone; it had happened so often before until someone special came along, and here she was again. A never-ending trail of loneliness. If only Alex would get in touch. It could be so good. For both of them.

The taxi left Jayne and Alex at the restaurant and returned to the city in the search of more work. Politely greeted and seated, neither of them spoke at first. Alex had surprised Jayne by how quiet he was on the way over, lost in some distant land of thought. She had tried to make conversation, but it had been sporadic, and now she was dreading the evening. She looked around her, thinking how old-fashioned the place was. But the staff were all very pleasant, so she felt welcomed and not out of place. She went to talk, but couldn't think of anything to say. A beautiful occasion lost.

Alex knew he was being a poor companion, but the first glass of the Pol Roger champagne he'd ordered allowed him to throw away his cares and engage with Jayne. Whoever, whatever she was, he was going to give them both a good time Whatever had been said about her, she seemed harmless enough to him.

Jayne relaxed. It was the champagne that had done it, she was sure. Maybe Alex had been as nervous as her, just that he reacted to it differently. He started to talk, so she became more voluble, and he responded. It was going to be alright.

Alex looked across at Jayne and wondered what all the fuss was about. Here he was, sipping champagne with a perfectly ordinary woman who was excited at being made manager of a shoe shop. What was the problem with that? He was beginning to think that the **aware** thing was just a load of chat amongst those with nothing better to do. Oh, there was something in it, he'd felt it, but really it wasn't that bad.

Jayne warmed to Alex as the evening went on. And it wasn't just the champagne. He smiled so openly and seemed so natural. It was a pleasure to be with him. They talked about **awareness** but soon moved on to more important things. Her promotion, her cat, which she hadn't mentioned before in case he didn't like them, and her friends. Not one of her friends was **aware** and, given what happened in the group, it was probably just as well. Was it a decision on her part, conscious or unconscious? Or simply, that was the way it turned out? It was odd that she only realised this when talking to Alex; it had never occurred to her before.

Alex was interested when Jayne talked about her friends not being **aware**. It was the opposite of what he expected, and he wondered, briefly, if there was anything more sinister behind it. Did **aware** people shy away from her? Well, he hadn't, and they had history, it seemed, although not in the here and now. Not only that, but they were becoming more friendly as the evening progressed. They were holding hands whenever there wasn't anything to eat, and he caught a waiter smiling benignly at them.

When the taxi arrived to take them back, they cuddled up in the back seat. Then she kissed him.

And he kissed her back. And they fumbled around under one another's clothing. And then they were at hers. She didn't even think before inviting him in.

The next morning Alex awoke lying quietly in Jayne's bed, wondering if this was how Casanova felt, hopping from bed to bed. It wasn't something he was used to, but it wasn't at all bad. Either he was going to have to face up to sorting it all out, or life was only going to get more complicated. He looked across as Jayne gently snuffling beside him. She'd been quieter, less expressive than Lizzie, maybe more genuinely affectionate, and definitely less acrobatic. His time with Jayne had actually been mundane when he thought about it, boring even, so whatever George and his cronies thought Jayne was, they were probably wrong. Maybe they had another motive for keeping Jayne away from him. A raucous jangle erupted into the air, and Jayne leapt up and bashed the alarm clock next to her. She looked surprised to see him there.

'Oh, hello, sorry about that. I've got to get going to work. Sorry. It was a lovely evening.'

She gently pushed away his advances, jumped out of bed, and ran to the bathroom. He heard a shower, the sound of teeth cleaning, and then she was back, clambering into a dark blue suit.

'See, I get to wear a suit now. I had to buy one. The company doesn't provide it, they just said I can probably claim it against tax. Are you coming with me?'

He dressed quickly, ran his fingers through his hair, and they walked together, arriving at the shop so quickly that he hadn't even had time to think if he wanted another date. With a quick smile, she left him for her day's work.

He ambled through the city and trudged up Beechen Cliff to his front door. It was strangely empty without Jayne. He showered, shaved, toasted bread, which he buttered thickly, and then made coffee. The day was about to start properly.

He flipped open the computer's lid and settled down to work.

Amilie's mother took Jayne into a small room with a desk covered in papers, where she sat her down in the swivel seat that she normally occupied. Pushing away some papers, she perched on the edge of the desk, looking at Jayne, a frown clouding her face.

'I'm sorry, Jayne. I know this is going to affect your relationship with Amilie, but it's so important that I can't just leave it. I don't even know if you'll thank me in the end, and I have a feeling Amilie might not, but I can see where it will lead her if I make her **aware** *now. Her entire future depends on her concentrating on her studies, and* **awareness** *can and will interfere with that.'*

'Won't it interfere with mine then?'

'How do I put this? You're not as academic as Amilie, Jayne, but you're gifted in other areas. I

can tell that **awareness** is very strong in you, and although I haven't looked, I'm sure that it's backed up by past lives that have made you strong. Whereas Amilie, well, she's quite new to the path, with few lives behind her, she'll have a lot to learn.'

'But I don't know anything.'

'At this moment, that is what you think. But soon you'll realise just what you've inherited. Now, may I awaken your **awareness**?'

Jayne sat for a moment, her head down. Was it worth it? To likely lose a friend, just to gain this **awareness**. She wasn't sure. But then, maybe she'd lose her, anyway. There would be a barrier between them whatever happened now, her yet to be awakened **awareness** brooding, waiting. She looked up at Anne and nodded. 'Alright, I suppose you'd better.'

She heard Anne draw in a deep breath, as though she'd been holding on, waiting. And then she sighed. 'I think it's for the best. Let's start.'

The process took longer than Jayne expected. First, Anne asked her to close her eyes, then she went behind and she felt a light breath on her head, as words she would never remember were intoned above her. Anne asked her to place her hands in the prayer position, and then on her closed eyelids. She thought she saw symbols appear, just fleetingly, but she wasn't sure. Her eyes still closed, Anne walked in front of her, opened her palms, and traced symbols on them, then she closed them, and gently placed

Jayne's closed hands above her head. There was a pause. And then it happened.

It was as though a new world had opened to her, like a sea washing over her, a sea of vivid images. Images of times past that flowed over and around her, brushing past, leaving traces on her senses of memories she hadn't known existed. Sounds, smells, thoughts crowded in to enhance the images so that she felt completely overwhelmed, and she felt soft arms around her, supporting her.

'It's strong at first,' she heard, 'but it soon abates, and then it is up to you what you listen to, what you see.'

But it went on and on. There was no way she was going to remember any of this when, if, it finished. Maybe this was her life now, living in an ocean of memories tossed around until she broke. She felt tears creeping down her cheeks and was going to brush them away, but Anne held her hands above her head, even though pins and needles were creeping in.

She first noticed it was slowing when she made sense of some images. Not so much make sense of, but at least she could put them in some sort of framework. She knew it was her in many of the images, but she was not herself. She might be he, or even an animal, yet she still knew that underneath it was her and that she'd known it was her, even as she knew she was someone or something else. It was as she watched herself amble so slowly and painfully into a shop, she realised the simple fact that life was short and that she had lived so many lives.

'I think it's time to open your eyes now,' she heard Anne say as she let her hands go, and gratefully, she lowered them and opened her eyes. It was the same room, the same Anne looking earnestly at her. Had anything changed? Yet it must have done. It had seemed so momentous, so full of meaning, and yet now it wasn't there.

Alex sat up and stopped typing. It was as if he had been there, watching. His eyes filled with tears, as they had when he was **awakened**, and as Jayne in his story. Tears of **awakening**. Yet, like Jayne, he had wondered if anything had really changed within him.

He pressed save, and his words flew across the internet to be backed up on a remote server some-where to be, hopefully, preserved. That was it. For now. He'd do more in the afternoon, but what should he do next? The mundane needed attention, as it always did. The washing, the gardening, the… There must be… Lizzie. He hadn't talked to Lizzie. Would that be right, so soon out of Jayne's bed? He wasn't used to having more than one girlfriend. For ages he hadn't even had one. The hell with it. He would ring her.

CHAPTER THIRTEEN

They sat together, pint mugs at an angle, drinking in the amber coloured liquid from the taps of the Old Green Tree. Alex had run down Beechen Cliff, across the Halfpenny Bridge and through the city. If anyone could talk some sense into him, it was Mike, and with no thoughts of **awareness,** too. There was never much talking at first. There were priorities and other things, like writing, Lizzie, and Jayne, could come later.

'Eating?' he asked.

'Probably. You?'

'Yeh, it smells good.'

It was a small pub which could become over-crowded if there was a rugby match on, but today it was just right. An array of real ales, and a shed load of whisky, too.

'I'll have ham, egg and chips, you?'

'Beef platter for me, mate. You ordering?'

Alex stood up and ordered for them, adding a couple more pints as well.

'What are you up to?' he asked, since Mike seemed to enjoy drinking his holiday away. Which was fine, but…

'Haven't decided, but someone pointed me toward a charity shop that has a load of old books and music in it.'

'The Oxfam bookshop, I know it. Great place. I'll come along if you're going.'

'Where is it?'

He had to think. 'Lower Borough Walls must be about seven or eight minutes' walk from here, a minor road opposite M&S.'

Their food arrived, and all conversation stopped. When they'd finished, Mike was looking thoughtful.

'So, what happened to the girl then?'

'I was with her last night.'

'Serious?' He looked long and hard at Alex. 'Come to think of it, you look knackered.'

'I took her to Lucknam Park for a meal.'

'At their prices, you paid for a night then.'

'Cynic. It was a lovely evening, and I escorted her to work this morning.'

'Where's she work then? Bet it's a poncy place.'

'A shoe shop.'

Mike looked at him, then put back his head and laughed. 'Well, so much for your fancy **awareness** and all that stuff. It doesn't get you far, does it?'

'It got me into bed with an attractive girl last night. How did you do?'

'As it happens, I didn't do so bad. I was just going into my room when I saw this woman having trouble getting her key to work, so I helped her out, and the rest is history.'

'Spent the night together, then?'

'Well, no. But I know her name and she gave me her phone number.'

'Clearly swept off her feet by your charm then.'

'Ah, shut up. You going to show me where this bookshop is, or just sit there being an arse?'

It was on their way that Alex saw Lizzie, although he was sure she hadn't seen him. She was crossing the road in front of them, heading west towards the theatre, or any of the small shops and bars over that way. He wondered whether to call out, but by the time he'd made his mind up, she had gone. He tuned back into the rambling conversation that was Mike, and they walked on.

The shop was busy, it sold sheet music, maps and CDs, and was always popular. Mike wandered off to look at the CDs, and Alex sifted through the maps. Often, he came across an old map that sparked thoughts of some distant past and set his mind working on another story. Not today, though. He moved over to the section of old books. Some leather-bound, others more modern. They were an eclectic mix, but nothing he wanted today.

They walked back to Mike's hotel. Once Mike had gone, Alex wondered whether to see if Lizzie was in. He hesitated and then turned back up the hill towards the Circle. Maybe, and he had the book to show her.

As with most places in the city, it didn't take long to walk to Lizzie's, although being uphill it always seemed longer to go to her area. Bath ran downhill from the racecourse, past Lansdown, then into the city proper until you arrived at the bottom and the railway station. Or, as on this occasion, uphill from Mike's hotel, which wasn't far from the station. Because he dawdled, still not sure he should go, it took nearly half an hour to get to Lizzie's. He rang the bell and waited. Rang again and then gave up and walked back down the hill. It was as he was looking into a shop window, contemplating an extra shirt and jacket, that he saw her. She was walking down on the opposite side of the road in front of Jolly's. He hastened across the road. But she had increased her stride until she suddenly stopped, hugging a smaller figure. The small lady from George Marlin's. He stopped and watched as, arm in arm, they entered the Ivy. Well, at least he knew where she was going to be for the next couple of hours. He resumed his walk down the street and all the way home. Next time he'd ring her first.

CHAPTER FOURTEEN

Jayne walked back from Amilie's house in a daze. Her mother had said not to bother Amilie, so she had left with her head in another world, dazed and confused. She had gone there with so many hopes. But now she had less than before. She might have some new power, but she did not know how to use it. What was the point of that? Then there was the worst thing. Anne didn't want them to see one another again. She'd made it abundantly clear as Jayne stood on the doorstep. Amilie was to concentrate on becoming a doctor like her mother, and nothing should interfere with that.

Anger grew inside her. She'd never been an angry person before, but maybe it was this new power she had. She did not know what to do with it, though. She felt like hitting something, but there was no sense in that. What or who was she angry at? That was easy. Anne. She had stolen Amilie away. It was as simple as that. She could see her standing there, looking so studious and earnest, determined that her daughter would do as she wanted, determined that Jayne would not be a part of it. She felt her rage increase until it was almost unbearable. She turned to face Amilie's house, retracing her steps, seeing only what she wanted, Amilie's friendship. The anger built until she could only see red. She'd heard of that expression, now she knew it. She yelled, her arms thrown out at Amilie's house, all her anger released. It was as though something physical left her. It took her anger and left her spent, exhausted, and weak. Weird. That was all she could think of. She slumped down beside the road, her head in her hands, and wept. Wept for all she had lost, wept for whatever it was she had gained. There could be no going back now, Anne had said that. Now she was **aware**, *and she hated it.*

Alex stopped typing, because the more he typed, the more he felt for Jayne, and the more he wondered about the power of being **aware**. Was it a force for good, or its very opposite? Was it something he should turn his back on, or embrace? Did he have a choice? It was such an intangible thing that he wondered whether it existed at all. He did not know how to answer these questions, no idea at all. Would Lizzie be able to? Maybe Jayne. But he was being warned away from her, and by putting her name into the story he was now too close to her, let alone the night they'd spent together. Lizzie and Jayne, Jayne and Lizzie. What to do? He wondered about the short lady, first seen at George Marlin's, then with Lizzie today. It had felt as though George was guiding him away from Jayne towards Lizzie. But why? The small woman knew Lizzie and knew about Jayne. So what was her role, and how could he get in touch with her if he wanted? The answer came to him as he stared out over the landscape. He had to attend another of George's meetings, but again he did not know when they were being held, or if they would invite him. That left two routes. He had to understand more about Lizzie, and about Jayne, but Lizzie had to come first now. That was clear.

He saved his work and slapped the lid down, called a taxi, and twenty minutes later was outside Lizzie's house on the Circus. He checked his watch. It was touch and go whether she had finished her meal, and unlikely she'd returned home yet. Drat, he'd been too impulsive. He walked around the Circus, admiring the different types of columns that supported the building's porches. He'd heard that Wood, the architect, had formed a Masonic key using the Royal Crescent, Gay Street and The Circus. He must ask George he'd know. Now, George had directed him to Lizzie, and George wasn't **aware**, at least so they said, but he had a feeling about George. He shrugged; he was probably wrong. It began to rain, just light rain. He looked over at the house and kept walking. There must be another way. Maybe the ideas of **awareness** were laid out on paper somewhere, but he'd never seen them. Maybe there was an **adept** who trained others, but who and where?

He started at a touch on his shoulder and turned around quickly. It was the small lady whose name he still didn't know.

'She's waiting for you,' she said, turning and walking away almost as she spoke.

He looked across at the house. The door was open and Lizzie was standing there, grinning at him. He crossed over.

'Hello, you,' she said coyly, leading the way through. She shut the door. He turned to face her. They hesitated and then were in one another's arms. Clothing thrown aside, up against the wall, she yelled out. Then so did he. They sank to the floor. It was over too quickly. Nestled into him, she laughed.

'Well, that was quick, and there's me thinking you didn't care. You might at least have phoned.'

'I'm sorry, things got a bit heavy after, you know.'

'After the last time we screwed.'

'Well, yes. After that. I'm getting too involved in the book, too close to the principal character.'

She sat up, staring at him. 'Please tell me it's not someone called Jayne.'

He nodded. 'Yes. Is that bad?'

'It's certainly not good. Come on then, it sounds as though we have work to do.' She gathered her clothes up in a heap and led the way as he did the same. They walked into a beautiful kitchen with a clear ceiling, making it light and airy. She threw her clothes to one side, so he did the same.

'Coffee, or something stronger?' she asked, but didn't wait for his answer as she picked up a bottle of red wine. Its cork stuck in at an angle. Reaching into a glass-fronted cupboard, she lifted down two heavy handmade glasses and poured for them both.

'Cheers, I think we're going to need these, and more by the time we're finished. So, what exactly are you writing?'

'It's a story I started only a short time ago about a girl who has few friends at school. Her mother leaves with a lover, and the father is away working most of the time. Then her one friend's mother notices she has the potential to be an **aware**. She invites her round, and activates the **awareness**, but says she must not see her daughter again. That's about as far as I've got.'

'And the name of the girl? No, I know it already. You named her Jayne, didn't you?'

He nodded. 'I'd just met her, and it seemed natural. I often use the names of people I've known, but not ones from my present if you see what I mean.'

'A wise policy.'

'But was it wrong? Have I done something I shouldn't?'

'Well, let's see. We have to start at the beginning, don't we? Forgive me, but when we met, I thought you seemed, well, naïve about the whole **aware** stuff.' She looked at him closely and brushed a hand over his bare chest.

'I suppose I am.'

'You haven't explored your own life, have you?'

He shook his head. 'No. I have enough trouble with today let alone thinking about the effects of **awareness**, and to be honest, it scares me.'

'I suppose you think you might make the wrong interpretations. Well, that's certainly possible. Maybe it's best if we do it together, but you're going to have to face up to it, and the sooner the better.'

'What I am, and what I'm going to be?'

'Yes, exactly. Do you even know what a **dramatist** is? How powerful you are? No, I can see from your face what the answer is. Well, if you're running scared at the moment, you're in for a shock I can tell you because a **dramatist** is one of the most powerful roles in the aware world. There are people out there who would kill to be a **dramatist**, and there are people who would kill a **dramatist** to stop them from writing a story they didn't want. The question is, what do people want of you? Have you shown anyone the story? Even told anyone about the story?'

'Only you.'

She laughed. 'So, if anyone bumps you off it will be me then.' She looked at him. They were the same height, and she was looking straight into his eyes. 'But I won't. Not yet anyway.'

She looked down in surprise at their empty glasses and reached for the bottle to refill them.

'So, where to start? Logically it would be best to go through your **phone**, step by step, but I really can't be arsed to do that today. I've already had too much wine with Maggie, and what with that and the sex, it's all too much. So, what, my fine friend, we will do now, is to fetch another bottle and go to bed, where I will tell you all about the role of the **dramatist**, and why it is so important.' She kissed him and raised her eyebrows. 'Come with me.'

He thought they were going upstairs, but she opened a nearby door where a set of stone steps led down. Lights had come on automatically when she'd opened the door, and as he followed her the temperature dropped.

'It's alright, silly, it's only the wine cellar. I'm not leading you to your doom.'

There were racks and racks of wine, laid out by country and region. 'This calls for something reasonable,' she said, putting an arm around him. He felt her shiver. She walked to the middle of a row and plucked out a bottle. There were several missing from the row already. Maybe it was a favourite. There was a scrabbling sound from behind the rack.

'Bloody mice,' she said and led him back up the stairs. He was no wine connoisseur and had only a vague notion of what any wine label meant. He just knew what he liked. She uncorked it, smelt the cork, and poured for them both, then watched as he drank. It was lighter than he expected. Satisfied at his expression, she just said, 'Bed.' And led the way upstairs.

Her bedroom was a mess. Clothes scattered everywhere. She brushed stuff from a bedside table to put down the bottle and her glass and threw herself onto the bed. He did the same, and she laughed.

'Where to begin.' Her face was suddenly serious. 'A **dramatist** has had many lives, many, many lives, like an apprenticeship I suppose because until you have lived lives you can't write them, can you? No one knows how a **dramatist** comes to be, though. The role chooses the person rather than the other way around. Throughout my lives, I've known many **dramatists** and none of them like you. They were more knowing and more flamboyant, but that's probably because that's a type I attract.' She looked at him and smiled. 'You're an exception. You're unique, I'd say, and that's because you're doing it without realising what you are doing. You haven't done your homework, which is, I have to say, very naughty. But why, you might ask. Well, because what you write will come to pass. You're not writing history, you're writing people's futures. The Jayne you write about will come to be, and that might frighten you. I tell you it scares the shit out of me.'

'So, if I write Jayne a terrible death, then a future Jayne will too?'

'Yes, but the problem here is that you know a Jayne, and subconsciously you'll be putting aspects of that Jayne into your story. Eventually, it will be a Life of the Jayne you know.'

He frowned, swung his legs off the bed, and looked at her. Not at her long, taught body, but at her face, her eyes. She looked back at him.

'That's terrible,' he said. 'I don't want to write another word.'

'Oh, you will, because that is your life, and you'll find you have to do it, you just have to. There's no escaping it. Sorry, but that's the way it is. More wine?'

He shook his head, and she made a face before topping up her glass. Then, carefully placing the glass back on the bedside table, she reached for him.

'But that's for tomorrow. It's today now.'

CHAPTER FIFTEEN

'I've been thinking,' he said when she was awake.

'I'm tempted to say that's novel,' she answered with a sideways grin.

'If I write about people's futures, then they're going to want to influence that, aren't they?'

'Well, aren't you the bright one? Have you only just worked that out? That's why Marlin and his lot want to get their hooks into you. You could be their future lives.'

'And you?'

She went quiet at that, as he had expected her to. She shrugged.

'Yes.'

'Is that the only reason?'

'I'll be honest, it's certainly a driver, and Georgie asked me to find out more about you, and especially the Sutherland woman.'

'And?'

'Well, you're a surprise. **Dramatists** are usually up their own arses, full of themselves because they believe they have power, you see. Of course, they do, but a disproportionate number seem to get bumped off. I wonder why?' She was lying on the bed and had rolled onto her front, looking up at him, smiling sweetly.

'Are you saying I'm in danger, then?'

'Oh, stop being so self-obsessed. Of course, you are, as is every **aware** for one reason or another. You can't spend this **life** thinking about it though, peering around every corner. That's no way to spend a **life**. I looked you up.'

'You did?'

'On Amazon at first. You're what I'd call, prolific. There's a shed load of stuff in there. No wonder you don't have any time to find out about yourself.'

'I just roll with it. It's what I do, and I suppose I enjoy it.'

'Suppose?'

'As with anything there are good days and bad days, but for me, the good outweighs the bad by quite a margin.'

'Have you written stuff you haven't published?'

'Tons. Why?'

'Do you still have it?'

'Yes, probably, boxed up in the loft. I haven't looked at most of it for years.'

'So, how long have you been writing?' She looked him up and down. 'Let's say, twenty years?'

He shrugged.

'If you have, and if you've always been a **dramatist**, even if you haven't been an Awake one, then…'

'Then?'

'Then there will be people out there living the lives you've written for them.'

'Oh, fuck.'

'Yes. I think it might be wise if I were to have a look at all the stuff you've written, starting with the oldest.'

'Why? What's that going to change?'

'If I'm honest, I don't know, but I feel that I have to, which, for me, usually means that my subconscious **aware** self knows something, even if my conscious self doesn't.'

He shrugged and remained looking down at her. Her buttocks were tight and rounded, and…

'I still don't see what it's going to achieve, and anyway, there's so much stuff.'

'Then the sooner I start the better.' She moved as he'd thought only a gymnast could do, somehow flipping her legs over her head to stand at the end of the bed.

'How the…'

'Practice, darling, practice. There are two things I love in this world. No, that's not true. Two of the things I love are a flexible body and sex. They go together, really. I work one to enjoy the other. Capisce?'

'I suppose so. Do you work?' he said, looking around at the expensive devastation around him.

'No, darling, I don't. My dear darling departed father left his daughter with rather a lot of money. In particular, he left me this place. I love Bath, and I love this place, don't you?'

He didn't answer but walked over to the window, which looked out onto a well-manicured Italianate garden.

'You garden?'

'Oh, no, not at all. Ashley comes in to do that, he's a poppet. I prune things occasionally, but he doesn't approve. He always notices.' She was dressing as she spoke, just a sweater and jeans, nothing else. 'Come on, dress. We need to get to yours, don't we? By the way, where is yours?'

'I'm up on Bear Flat.'

'How delightful, it's ages since I was there. There's a park nearby with wonderful views of the city.'

'Alexandra Park. Yes, but it's so busy with tourists.'

'Right, call a cab and we'll get going.'

Reluctantly, he did so.

She sat cross-legged in the middle of his front room, while he watched her, sitting about-face on his writing chair, arms crossed on its back, head resting on his arms.

'I don't understand what good this is going to do,' he said.

'We need to understand if there are any problem cases that we can do something about.'

'But can we? I mean, are you saying that once I write a **life**, we can change it?'

'Yes, of course, but the person whose **life** it is doesn't know what's written until it's happened, do they, so if you've written something terrible then if we prompt them to make a decision that doesn't follow your plot, we can save them. Right?'

He was looking more worried than ever. 'Maybe I should just give up writing.'

She looked at him sharply. 'No. Definitely not, for two reasons, well three, I suppose. Firstly, if you don't write someone's **life** someone else will probably do it, now that you know the ramifications you might adjust the writing you do, and then you wouldn't have a job and you'd be poor. Oh, and given your success, you'd deprive people of a good read.'

'I think I'd put that last one first, at least I always have.'

She shrugged. 'Your choice. It's just as I see them now. I say, this is a juicy one, I might adopt this **life** for my own.'

He looked down at the thick sheaf of paper she was reading. 'I was nineteen when I wrote that. They never published it.'

'I reckon you should give it another shot, a different publisher. I'd give them all this unpublished stuff. Now you're a name, they'll probably give it a go. Only after I've read it though.'

'Coffee?'

'Alright, if you've got nothing stronger.'

'What do you fancy?'

'I'm not fussy.'

He went in search of a bottle and returned with one and two glasses.

'Chablis, I like that.'

'I thought you were going to teach me more about the **aware** world.'

'Mmmmm, this is nice. Yes, well, maybe this is more important. You know, people's lives at stake, but I suppose we could interleave some other stuff if it gets boring.' She paused. 'I didn't mean that your writing's boring, just that a break every so often would be nice.'

'When you're ready then.'

'Oh, come on, this one's good, give a girl a break.' She looked up at him with a smile he was getting to know. 'Bed after.'

In another part of town, Jayne was thinking about Alex, and that he hadn't been in touch. The evening had been lovely; it was so long since a man had treated her so well, and the sex afterwards was alright too. She hadn't had a relationship for a while, what with work and Vicki, but now she was in charge work seemed far less tiring. The paperwork hd come through now, and the pay was more than she'd expected. It called for a celebration, and she wanted someone to celebrate with. She rang him.

Lizzie looked up as Alex's **phone** rang.

'That'll be Jayne,' she said. 'I don't mind if you go. I think you have to. Just so long as you leave the wine. It'll give me a chance to read in peace. Don't you dare bring her back here.'

He arranged to meet Jayne at the Dark Horse. It wasn't his sort of place from what he'd been told, more cocktails than beer, but if it kept her happy. A taxi ride later, and he was meeting her inside.

'Hi there, how was your day?' he asked. She was looking radiant.

'Let's order, and I'll tell you. Mine's a pina colada. My treat, I'm in the money today.'

Alex had a Beefeater G & T, wondering why people paid a lot more for an expensive gin if they planned to drown it with an expensive tonic. No doubt they had their reasons, but life was too short to find out what they were.

'So, what happened?'

'The paperwork came through for my promotion, and she gave me far more money than I thought. I'm so happy, it's the first time I've ever felt valued in a job. How about you?'

'Oh, just turning out some old papers and writing.'

Luckily, she wasn't interested and didn't follow it up, though he wondered what she was interested in, apart from her own life.

'Oh look, I've finished my drink already. Would you get me another? Thank you so much, Alex. I thought we could just have a pizza after this, is that alright? The Real Italian Pizza Company is excellent, but it's back near the abbey.'

Right next to Mike's hotel, he thought. 'Of course, right next to the Real Italian Ice Cream Company.'

'You're going to say they go next door for the ice cream if you want it, aren't you?'

He wasn't, but hey. 'Of course. Have you advertised for your replacement yet?'

'Not yet. I'm doing that tomorrow. Now, drink up, I'm hungry.'

At the end of the evening, he was, frankly, bored. He'd heard a blow by blow account of every customer Jayne had dealt with during the day. Then there were her conversations with Amy, yawn, and finally, when he'd walked her home, the clear expectation of sex. He claimed a headache and heard about all the times Jayne had suffered a headache before he finally escaped. He wondered if the only danger she posed to the **aware** was that she might bore them to death. Surely there must be more to it than that?

A quick taxi ride back, and he found Lizzie exactly where he'd left her. The wine bottle was empty, as was another one she'd found.

She glanced sideways at them and looked up at him, shamefaced. 'Sorry. How was it? I'm surprised you didn't stay the night.'

'It was on offer, but I'd lost the will to live by then and pleaded a headache.'

'That bad? There's more to the girl than she's showing.'

'You could fool me. I don't want to go on with

this. I mean, what the hell is she going to do? Sell me a pair of shoes that don't fit?'

'Well, I don't know, but everyone seems to think she's a danger. Maybe George knows, although he's not supposed to be **aware**, just good at organising.'

'That's another one. I keep being told that George isn't **aware**, but that's not what I'm picking up. I think he's the same as you and me, just that he's able to screen it.'

'Interesting theory. I'll think about it, and I'll ask around about Jayne as well. One thing though, I hope you write her a decent **life**, it sounds as though she could do with one. Time for bed? Since you had to forgo your other offer, and I haven't tried yours yet. It must be softer than the floor.'

Jayne sat on her bed, Mylo, her assertive cat, on her lap. It hadn't gone as she'd hoped with Alex, and she was wondering what to do about it. She needed a man to make her world complete, and he fitted the role. She sat, trancelike, as she made her decision. She could not allow him to thwart her plans, could she?

CHAPTER SIXTEEN

'I have a problem,' Lizzie said, lying back in Alex's bed, a croissant that Alex had just run to the local store for resting on her flat stomach. 'One of my **multilives** is coming to Bath.'

'Eh?' Alex queried through a mouthful of pastry.

'We can't meet one another. I just can't take that chance.'

'Why not? What happens?'

'Well, if you meet someone, that's you, it's a **crossover**, and that's not good.'

'What happens? Do you spontaneously combust?'

'Don't joke! I don't know, I just know it's something you have to avoid at all costs. Fancy going away somewhere?'

'What? Now? Where?'

'I haven't thought yet, but would you be up for it?'

'I've got a friend on his hols in the city at the moment but we don't meet up a lot, and I can always bring my laptop, so I guess I'm free.'

'Good to know you're romantic. I'll have a think unless there's anywhere you fancy going?'

'I'd like somewhere hotter than here, and I fancy a bit of swimming. Is that something you're into?'

'Sounds like a plan. I'll check it out. Can I borrow your laptop?'

'I've got a spare one, I'll get it.'

'Don't bother, I'll just use the one downstairs.'

'Lizzie, it wouldn't be that you're going to sneak a look at Jayne's story, would it?'

'Of course not, the very thought. Oh, alright, get me the spare.'

He wandered off to reappear with a tablet.

'Try this, It'll be better in bed. It's charged up.'

'Oh!' She looked at him, shock on her face. 'Alex, we are going to have to get out.'

'Why, what's the matter?'

'Didn't you feel it? Someone's **scanning** for us, for me.'

'They're what?'

'An **aware** can try to sense where another **aware** is. They need to have something from the other person, or they can just do a general sweep to see if any **aware** are around. You've felt nothing?'

'No, though I wouldn't know what it felt like.'

'If they're **scanning** for me, then they'll have done the same for you because they'll sense another presence. So they'll know that two **awares** are together, but can only guess who we are unless they have something from either of us. Anything that we've touched will do.'

'Jayne?'

'How was she when you left?'

'A bit miffed at missing bed, I suppose, and maybe I hadn't been as attentive as she'd like.'

'So, it could be her, which is interesting because if she's showing her hand, she's desperate. Not the quiet inoffensive shop-girl anymore.'

'Your idea of a holiday sounds more attractive by the minute.'

'Last-minute deals, then. Fancy Tobago?'

'Where's that? The Caribbean?'

'Yep. I've been there before. You can't get any further laid back, liming they call it.'

'Sounds good. How do you get there then?'

'This deal's a direct flight from Gatwick. Hold on a moment. Is your passport up to date?'

'Years on it, I only got it renewed last year.'

'We could go, let's see, the day after tomorrow. What do you think? Give Jayne a chance to cool off, and my **multilife** will have time to sort itself out.'

'I'm game. Package deal?'

'Rex Turtle Beach; it's where I stayed before. It's a bit run down, but you don't need much out there, a shirt and trousers for dinner, shorts for lunch and swimming stuff for the rest of the time. Oh, and your snorkelling gear, though you could always hire.'

'Ticks for all those. I'm sorted. I've got sunscreen and defogger for the facemask as well.'

'Aren't you the prepared one? Look, if I pay…'

'Just give me your bank account codes, and I'll credit you straight away.'

There was a tapping of a finger on the glass. Then she scooted off the bed to get her credit card. More tapping, and then, 'Done.' She tossed the tablet aside and threw herself on top of him. 'Alex, you're wonderful. Not many people would drop everything to come away with me. I need to thank you.'

A couple of hours later and Alex had packed all he needed and found his passport and snorkel, which were hidden under a pile of detritus from a previous holiday. He had one large bag, and a shoulder bag with more pockets than looked possible. A taxi took them to Lizzie's, and she left him with a coffee while she checked she had everything too.

'I'm sorted,' she said an hour or two later. 'Sorry I took so long, I couldn't decide which clothes to take, and then which sandals, and then which cossies.'

'What do you reckon is the best way to get to Gatwick? Car?'

'Either the train into London, Underground to Victoria, and then train down, or, as you say, a car.'

'I'll hire one. A taxi would be stupid money.'

'I can afford it.'

'So, can I, but I just don't enjoy parting with… Oh, sod it, let's get a taxi, it's easier.' He checked the flight times with Lizzie, added four hours, checked the internet for a firm, got a quote, grimaced and paid. 'Booked' he said. She clapped her hands and kissed him and then stopped to look at him.

'Alex, maybe we should get away now. Go to a hotel or something?'

He shrugged. 'Alright. I'll find somewhere and then change the taxi.'

They left Lizzie's place within the hour. As the taxi drew away from the kerb, they might have looked across at the green in the centre of the Circus. Had they done so, they would have seen a figure sitting patiently there.

CHAPTER SEVENTEEN

Jayne Sutherland was late for work. It was the first time she'd been late as a manager, and it was serious because she was the one with the keys. Amy stood outside for nearly an hour, waiting and trying to raise her boss on the phone, without success. In the end, she walked over to Jayne's and banged on her door.

'Who is it?' It sounded more like a frail old woman than Jayne, and Amy nearly apologised and left.

'It's Amy, are you OK? If not just let me have the keys and I'll open up.'

'Amy, oh my, is that the time? Here.' The door opened a fraction, and a bunch of keys flew through. 'I'm so sorry, I'll be with you shortly.'

Amy ran back to the store, imagining a queue of irate customers, but when she got there, no one was waiting. Jayne arrived half an hour later, looking like death.

'What's the matter?' Amy asked, but couldn't get anything out of her, and Jayne remained that way all day, sending Amy off early as a thank you.

On her own, she mechanically served the few customers that appeared for the rest of the day and then shut up the shop. She didn't feel like going home, and after he'd rejected her bed last night, she would not be ringing Alex. It was up to him to come to her. So, she found a pub on the way home and went in. She hadn't intended to. It was a spur-of-the-moment decision, and having done so, she hesitated. There wasn't much room to move around and only one table with a spare seat where a bloke was sitting, looking equally miserable. She shrugged, bought a cider, and walked over.

'Mind if I…' He nodded, so she sat down. 'Been a bugger of a day,' she said, hoping for some distraction.

'Yep, you could say that. I've been trying to get hold of me mate, I've got a couple of tickets for the theatre, but I can't raise him.'

'What's on?'

'Oh, it's that Bill Bailey, you know, his comedy and music gig. I walked in, and they had two returns, so I snapped them up. Seems like a bad idea now.'

'I'll take one off you if you like,' she said, without thinking.

'Hey, that would be right champion, it'll be good to have company, though we'd better finish up here. It starts in thirty minutes. I'm Mike, by the way.'

As Jayne and Mike left for the theatre, George Marlin was just opening his front door to the small woman.

'Maggie, how good to see you, come in do. What brings you here?'

Even before she was over the threshold, she was talking breathlessly. 'The birds have flown.'

'What, both of them?'

'Took a taxi to a hotel a short while ago. I got its name off the driver while he was waiting for them if you want it.'

'Well, you are a wonder, what is it?'

'Gravetye Manor.'

'Do you know anything about it?'

'I haven't had a chance to look. I thought you'd want to know, so I came straight here.'

'So I do, Maggie, so I do. Let's look it up on the internet, shall we?'

They walked up the stairs to the next floor and into a study that looked out over the city and the countryside beyond.

'Now let's see, Gravetye Manor you said, ah yes, here it is, and very nice, too. Well, our young couple have the money don't they, what with her inheritance and his books. You know, Maggie, I quite envy them, everything I've got is tied up in this place.'

'You don't do too badly, George, and Gravetye looks your sort of place too.'

'You're right, Maggie, just look at the menu, and the way the restaurant with its glass wall is almost in the garden. Lovely. But that leaves us with a problem, doesn't it?'

'The Sutherland woman.'

'Precisely. I'd hoped that by putting Lizzie onto that author fellow, she'd keep him away from Jayne.

I just don't trust Jayne. She's the sort who would just blurt out the sort of things she gets up to. With those two away, who is going to be watching her? Keeping her in check. I don't like it, at least with them around we had her pinned down, but now…'

'What about David? He's prepared to do anything we ask him, without question.'

'Yes, that's a thought, although I haven't seen him recently, he wasn't at the last meeting.'

'He's on his own now, since his wife left him. He might be glad of something to fill the empty hours instead of the bottle.'

'Maggie, you always amaze me with the details. How on earth do you know all this?'

'I keep my nose to the ground, George, it's the only way. There are always people who know, and I make sure I know them.'

'Is it best if you or I talk to him, do you think?'

'Oh, you, George, he's a man's man, he'd like it from you. You have a way of making people feel important.'

'Very well, let's see, lunch tomorrow if I can get hold of him.'

'Excellent. You're good at this, George, a good organiser.'

'Err, how are you placed this evening, Maggie?'

'Well, since you're asking.'

'Excellent. Whisky?'

'A Laphroaig would do me nicely, thanks, George, with just a dash of water as usual.'

'You know, Maggie, what we need is a plan.'

'I thought we had one, George.'

'I mean a rather more long-term one. We're a pretty diverse bunch, you know, and people tend to do their own thing, without reference to anything, or anyone. I mean, who knew that those two would disappear off to a hotel? They didn't tell me, did they? I think it shows a lack of consideration for the group, don't you?'

'But of course, George. They should have asked you, shouldn't they?'

'Well, maybe not asked, but at the very least, they should have kept us informed. There're important things at stake.'

'George?'

'Yes, Mags.'

'You haven't said exactly what the important things are. I mean, we feel this Jayne is a threat, but it's not exactly specific, is it? Are you able to let me know a little more, perhaps?'

'Oh, I certainly can. It's her past, you see. Her work when she was with us. Who knows what she might say, and we have influential people attending, don't we?'

'Yes, I see.'

'We need to keep our little group safe, Mags, and she might be, could be, a threat to that. But we can be her saviours. We can keep her in the fold and ourselves secure.'

'Oh, George, how wonderful you are. Oh, yes, some more Laphroaig would be lovely, thank you. Come closer, won't you?'

Lizzie threw herself back onto the bed in a star shape.

'Oh this is lovely, Alex, a four-poster, you're spoiling me.'

With an effort, Alex refrained from saying that this was the only room available at such short notice and just agreed. 'Yes, spacious, a view of the gardens, and did you see the fireplace in the bathroom, not that it's used these days. Looks as though it has everything we need.'

They'd arrived just in time for the evening meal and had only just gone to their room.

'I'm not unpacking, we've got an early start tomorrow,' he went on, 'just an ablute.'

'Hey, I'm first, I want to wallow in the bath,' and she jack-knifed off the bed and ran as he stood watching. He listened as she ran the water and then sat on the bed, thinking. He wasn't sure how **awareness** worked, especially over distance. Could something or someone still scan them in Tobago? Or on the aircraft going there? Who knew? There must be a manual on it somewhere, surely. It was all so vague. Who was to say that Jayne was the problem, apart from just being plain boring, and wasn't that his problem, anyway? Who had determined that she was bent on injuring him, or anyone else? Who stood to gain from that?

He looked up as the sounds of splashing and singing came from the bathroom. She was certainly a character. And what was this about **multilives**? He had so much to learn. He needed to just stop and think, but life had been too hectic. Or was that the idea? He looked towards the bathroom. What was Lizzie's purpose? George had introduced him to her, but why? He shook his head. There was no gain from thinking like this. Lizzie was great company, and she would sort out **awareness** for him. It was best to forget everything else and just have a good time. He looked up and raised his hands in mock horror as a naked, wet, bubble-covered Lizzie ran into the room and splatted him down onto the bed.

CHAPTER EIGHTEEN

Mike lay on Jayne's bed, listening to her prepare for her day in the shop. It had been a great evening. They'd both laughed their way through Bill Bailey's performance and then found a restaurant that was still serving for a meal. It wasn't the greatest, but they didn't care.

'Just pull the door to when you leave, Mike, and I'll see you this evening,' Jayne said with a smile as she left. She was so pleased with finding a replacement for stuck-up Alex that she was happy to leave him there, even though she'd only just met him. He'd said he was staying at the Abbey Hotel, and that was good enough for her. Light of step and humming, she walked through the city to work. It was so different from the day before. It was wonderful. She saw Amy waiting at the door and waved. She couldn't wait to tell her all that had happened.

On the other side of the city, Maggie was making a full cooked breakfast for George. He had an Aga, and she still wasn't used to it so she was experimenting, putting the bacon in the oven to crisp it up while cooking the sausages and egg on the range. She liked George. He'd always been kind to her, although he did like his little schemes, which were often secretive. He was definitely a man's man. She knew he had other rendezvous he'd never told her about, but then, that's what men should do. She opened up the oven door, delighted that her idea had worked and that she could plate up a lovely breakfast for him.

He was waiting at the table when she walked in with it, holding up *The Times* as though in some ceremonial rite, which, she thought, it probably was for George. The salute to *The Times*. She giggled to herself and wobbled, nearly depositing his breakfast at his feet. He looked up, smiled, and folded the paper away.

'Ah, how wonderful, Maggie, it's not every woman who can master an Aga, you know. This looks superb.' He looked at her, puzzled. 'You having some?'

'It's far too much for me, George. I'll just have a bit of toast and maybe some marmalade, if that's alright.'

'Of course, it is.' He tucked in with enthusiasm. 'My, this is superb. Thank you.'

She went back to the kitchen, found the marmalade and toasted some bread. It felt good to please George, but did it mean anything to him? Maybe she'd never know. Maybe life would just go on like this, as it had for the last two years. Despite herself, she felt a sadness creep in as she chomped into her toast.

Mike was up and dressed, wondering what to do with the day. He was still in Jayne's flat and well, to be honest, being nosey. He'd looked through the drawers in her bedroom and was now wandering through the spare room. There wasn't much of interest. Jayne seemed to live a very simple life, and he was getting bored already. He'd tried ringing Alex, but the call had gone straight through to voicemail. He was just about to give up on his rummage around the drawers of a small desk when he saw a plastic wallet of papers. What made him stop and pull it out was the name, neatly typed at the top. *Alex Ash*. He flipped through the papers to find other names, George Marlin, Lizzie Westbrook, Maggie North, and loads of others. He shook his head. This was just weird. He was about to read the files when his phone rang. He answered quickly, hoping it was Alex and he could tell him what he'd found, but it was Jayne.

'Hi, you up?'

'Yes, I was just about to leave. How are you doing?'

'We're busy today, I'm not sure when I can get a lunch break.'

'Don't worry, love. Catch you later, yes?'

'Love you, see you this evening.'

Before he pocketed his phone, he went back to the papers and photographed each one. Just you wait, Alex, he thought, am I going to have a surprise for you.

Alex and Lizzie were at the airport and had just boarded their plane for Tobago. Alex was trying to get over his surprise at finding out that Lizzie had booked first-class tickets. He'd only realised it when she handed him the tickets, and they were one of the first to board. They now had the luxury of being able to lie down if they wanted to, albeit in single beds.

'You didn't say.'

'Surprise! I thought we both deserved a bit of pampering. I'll pay if you like.'

'No, that's already sorted, I put half the cost into your account, I just didn't realise that the hotel in Tobago was so cheap.'

'It was a deal. I just upgraded the flights. Anyway, here comes the champagne.'

Maggie was feeling happy. As a thank you for break-fast, George had invited her out for lunch at Chez Dominique. She'd never been there, had no one to take her, so it was exciting, both at the thought of the meal and George. She was wondering if he had become more serious about her and what that meant. She'd never found boys, or men come to that, attracted to her, so she had made a point of arranging life so that they did. Her parents had been virtual recluses. They never went out unless it was essential, and never for a social event, and they never had people coming round to see them. As a result, she had grown up with almost no social skills. She'd kept herself to herself through her education, although she managed a doctorate in an obscure field of biochemistry that virtually no one else understood. She worked from home for a large pharma, reviewing papers from around the world, but this didn't call for her to communicate with colleagues. But she did enjoy an interesting sex life, through advertisements, carefully placed, something she had expanded judiciously. She had only come across George because Lizzie had noticed her as an **aware** when she was in the library. Oddly, until then, she hadn't even known she was. Whereas most people had to be made **aware** by another, she had somehow bypassed the process. It thrilled her when Lizzie told her, for it immediately opened a whole unknown world to her, and she didn't have to communicate with anyone to access it. She read everything she could about the **aware**, picked George's brain relentlessly, and then tried to move on to Lizzie. Unfortunately, once she had spotted Maggie, Lizzie wasn't interested in engaging with her once she had introduced her to George, or she had too much else to do. Not to be deterred, Maggie made it her job to find out as much about Lizzie as she could. But she had failed. Apart from reading about her father's death, and how she inherited the house, and the money that went with it, there was little to go on. Until recently Lizzie didn't go out much either, although she soon noted that men seemed to come to Lizzie, a pattern she was familiar with. Alex was just the latest in an awful lot of men friends, which only made Maggie wonder how she did it. Maybe she cooked substantial breakfasts. Or maybe?

She had worked for and with George on the **alert**, the predecessor to the **aware**, they had started the group, nurtured it until it became what they both wanted, and Lizzie had worked with them too. It was then she understood that she and Lizzie had something in common, and as a result, it had become so much more than they expected, but not something that should be made public. Not something that anyone outside the group should know, and while Alex seemed to be around Lizzie longer than most, it was early days yet, and anyway, Lizzie had been asked by George to steer Alex in the right direction. But going away together? Well, that was taking it a bit far. It was almost like being married, although it looked to be a very nice hotel. She imagined George taking her away there. She would arrive in a chauffeur-driven car, alright, maybe a taxi. He would help her out of the car and escort her up to the front door, where a uniformed doorman would welcome her and offer to take her coat. They would have drinks, a sherry or a gin and tonic, and choose their dishes. Then, when they were ready, they would be escorted into that lovely garden room to eat, talk and admire the flowers. George would be so attentive and give her admiring glances. She sighed. It would never happen. Not to her. Just to Lizzie.

It was almost lunchtime in the shoe shop, and Jayne was wondering if Mike would turn up and take her out for lunch, even though she'd said she was busy.

It would be nice to show Amy that someone cared for her. Not that she hadn't talked all morning about him, and what a wonderful evening they'd had. It left Amy wondering how quickly she'd be on to someone else, given Alex's swift demise, but as long as her manager was happy, all was well with the world. She was used to Jayne's swift change of mood, and not just around "that time of the month". Maybe the current mood would be more permanent. She was also wondering what was going to happen to her career. She had been at the store for almost as long as Jayne, and in fairness, she was slightly older and had more experience of retail, just. It was simply that Jayne was better at catching their area manager's attention than she was. Somehow, she was in the right place when their manager arrived, always. It was uncanny.

Jayne looked at her watch. No Mike. Feeling deflated, she walked over to Amy.

'Which lunch break would you like, now or later?'

This surprised Amy. Since her promotion, Jayne had been in the habit of saying when she was going, leaving Amy to work around her. Galling. Maybe Jayne had realised this.

'Thanks, Jayne, I'll go now then.'

It was at that moment that Mike walked in. Arrangements forgotten, Jayne walked over to him, and after a whispered conversation said they were going to lunch. So much for a more considerate manager.

CHAPTER NINETEEN

Having arrived in the heat of afternoon Tobago, they grabbed their swimming costumes and rushed out over the short grass strip that separated the hotel from the sandy beach and the sea. With a squeal, Lizzie plunged into the water to find that the tide was out, and it was too shallow to swim. Alex was laughing as she floundered, and he strode over to lift her out of the water. It didn't curb her enthusiasm. She set off again, diving in when she was sure there was enough water under her. Alex followed, and they swam, splashed, and cuddled in the warm water. When they'd had enough, they simply stood, look-ing out as pelicans were diving for fish all around them. Sometimes a bit too close. As Lizzie had said, the hotel was old-fashioned but fine for this sort of holiday, where the buildings weren't so important. As long as the food was good.

'That's better,' Alex said, as Lizzie leapt up into his arms. 'I don't know about you, but I needed a break, and this looks just the place.'

'I'm pleased you said that. I so enjoyed it when I was here before. You must meet a few locals too, and we need to see who has a boat around for hire so we can go snorkelling.'

'No snorkelling off the beach, then?'

'Not much to see. I mean look, you can see baby fish swimming around your legs, but there's nothing very interesting unless we walk down the beach towards Blackrock where the remnants of the old quay are. If you snorkel along there, you can probably see an eel that lives in a crevice.' She made a swimming motion of an eel attacking Alex with an arm. Alex dropped her. When she surfaced, blowing water out of her nose, she went to dunk him, but he wouldn't budge.

'Bastard. I'll get you yet.' But she was laughing. 'I was saying that we'll need a boat. When I was here, there was a guy who had a jet boat that could run up the coast fast and get into the coves without damaging the coral. I'll ask at reception and see if he's around. Before that, there was a local who would take you out on his fishing boat. They strap a couple of outboards onto them, so they're still quite fast. He was a big bloke. He could lift you in and out over the side of the boat. No problem. The jet boat has steps at the back though, and it's much easier.'

'Sounds great. There don't seem to be many people here. I counted about fifty. Is it always quiet?'

'Until the weekenders from Trinidad come over, then it changes. They have a fast ferry service these days, and it's easy for them to bring their cars over.'

'Let's swim along the shore. Towards the bar first, Lizzie?'

'Trust you, is that because it's an all-inclusive deal?'

'Oddly enough, I'm happy just swimming at the moment, as long as you are. The water's warm, the views wonderful, I'm just letting my cares wash away.'

'OK, beat you to the fishermen's hut then.' She was off before Alex could ask where that was. He followed in her wake, content to watch her for a while, and then increased his strokes to draw level. Suddenly something caught him across his throat, and he struggled in the water. He dived and came back up to find Lizzie waiting for him. She was laughing.

'It's the fishermen's ropes. They tie their boats to the shore, but the boats are out there.'

She pointed to a series of boats covered in pelicans bobbing on the water a couple of hundred yards out. 'The ropes are just a few inches under the water. Still, you'll know next time.'

She was off doing a fast crawl. He ducked under the water and under the rope to go after her, fast. They went past the bar and kept going until they came to a large wooden building with colourful fishing boats drawn up on the sand outside. A few men, fishermen presumably, were sitting around by the building chatting and drinking. Lizzie had stopped and was pointing excitedly at something in the water. He looked down to see a stingray swim slowly past, Lizzie following a few yards behind and to the side of it. They swam along together until the stingray tired of them and turned out into the sea.

'That was wonderful,' he said. 'Absolutely magic. Thank you again for suggesting it.'

'You wait until later,' she said mysteriously, 'but before that, we have the sunset.'

They walked up onto the sand to a couple of spare sun loungers. Alex went to fetch a cocktail for Lizzie, and a gin and tonic for himself, and they settled down to watch the sunset. Fishing boats droned past, black shapes against the horizon, steered by a man standing at the back in front of the outboard, the boat's prow high out of the water. The pelicans had discovered a new shoal of fish and were diving right in front of them. It was absolutely magical. Lizzie held out a hand, and Alex held it. They sighed as the sun dipped below the horizon and sheets of red, orange and yellow coloured the sky.

'Just you wait,' Lizzie said, squeezing his hand. Sure enough, as the sun disappeared, the afterglow appeared, with more subtle but equally beautiful colours. Then it went dark.

'Show's over,' she said. 'I'm going to get ready for dinner. Coming?'

They walked across the grass and through the patio doors into their room, feeling that they really were on holiday. But as Alex looked into his rucksack, he remembered that his story and their home lives weren't that far away.

In Bath, Jayne was finishing for the day and locking up the shop. Amy had gone already, but Mike had arrived to escort her home.

'Where shall we go tonight, Mike?' she asked as she struggled with the last lock.

'How about the Old Green Tree?'

'That's that small pub where we met, isn't it? I thought we might go somewhere nicer.'

'They've got a whole range of real ales, and I haven't tried them all yet.'

'How about a restaurant? There's the,' she hesitated before saying it, 'the Olive Tree or the Ivy, if they have spaces.'

'Nah, they're overpriced fancy stuff, aren't they? If you fancy something more upmarket, there's a pub up the road I heard someone say was good.'

Reluctantly, Jayne agreed, and they set off. She noticed they weren't holding hands tonight, even when she nudged him several times. Maybe that had been a one-off. Maybe, having got his leg over, he didn't fancy her anymore. Disconsolately she plodded along beside him, as lost in her thoughts as he was with his, since he was still wondering why she had a file on Alex.

As Alex and Lizzie walked away from the restaurant, a shout went up from the bar.

'Quick,' Lizzie said excitedly, 'turtles.'

They raced over towards the bar, and then to where a guard was pointing. Out on the beach, they could see a little group of people and red lights.

'The turtle wardens watch out for the babies to stop the dogs getting them and to make sure they go towards the sea because the hotel lights confuse them. I expect someone will turn the spotlights off soon.'

They slowed down as they reached the group that had formed a horseshoe around tiny black shapes that were crawling down the beach. The wardens shone red filtered torches so that people could see without distracting them. Leaving flipper tracks behind them, the first babies reached the waves. While the waves were small for a human, they towered over the turtles, who plunged in regardless. Some made it straight away, swimming off, while the sea tossed others back onto the beach. Yet others were turning around to head for the hotel. Some of these the wardens turned towards the sea, others they put into a bucket.

'They'll release them tomorrow. They might stand a better chance then,' whispered Lizzie.

They stood to watch for thirty minutes or more and then strolled along the dark beach. The hotel spotlights had been turned off now. As they turned back, Lizzie gasped and fell to her knees.

'What is it?' Mike alarmed knelt next to her, but she couldn't speak. She was gasping for air, and tears streamed down her face. Alex put an arm around her and waited to see what would happen. There was little else he could do. Slowly, Lizzie breathed normally and clung to Mike. She looked up into his concerned face, distraught. It took some time before she could speak.

'Alex, something terrible has happened.'

'What? How do you know?'

'One of my other **multis** has died. I'm always connected to them, even if I'm not present. It was so sudden. So sudden.'

They remained kneeling together as Lizzie held tight and Alex hugged her. She was so still that he became worried and tried to see her face, but she looked up and blew him a kiss.

'I'm so sorry, Alex, I've ruined your holiday.'

'We're together, that's the main thing.'

'It's not so simple. I'm going to be in mourning now, I can't help it. I've been through it before, you see. I know what it's going to be like.'

'I'm here for you this time though.'

'I know, and I appreciate that, but I'll go into myself. I won't be any sort of company for you.'

'You'll be you. That's enough.'

She made to get up, but he beat her to it so that he could offer support. Together, she resting her head on him, they ambled up the beach to their room.

CHAPTER TWENTY

The next morning Lizzie slipped out of bed, into her swimming costume, and out to the beach while Alex slept. She walked out into the water, its morning chill stimulating, then she swam a slow breaststroke following the shore, looking at the quiet hotel. She soon returned to the beach to sit on a sunbed near a palm tree, watching as the sun rose and birds fed at the edge of the water where waves rolled gently in from a calm sea. Gradually people emerged. A few runners pounding along the sand, a gardener raking away fallen palm leaves, and fishermen rowing their net out into the bay. Still disturbed from the last evening, she strode down the beach, waded out, and dived in, pushing her body into a fast crawl. But the effort only kept her thoughts at bay for a short time. There was no other feeling like this. An overwhelming sadness coupled with waves of deep anger raging at the world. She knew who had died, and she knew where. But was she responsible? She would need to gird herself for when they went home because the 'where' was her Bath home.

She'd been a fool to use her home for her **multi** as she had called it, but it had seemed a good use of the space and there was nothing she could do now. She was already planning what she should do when they returned, and she was going to have to enrol Alex. He had been so kind, so supportive that she hated herself for having to do it, but it had to be done. He would have to be the one to discover the body. But the authorities, and yes, they would have to involve them, would want someone to identify the corpse. She hadn't thought of a way around that yet.

She ploughed through the water, from one end of the beach to the other, covering the entire width of the hotel's grounds each time. She wanted to hurt, she wanted to punish her weak body. Gradually, though, her strength left her, so she slowed to a stop, and then moved towards the shore until she could stand. As she did so, Alex ran down the beach and she waved to him. Her lover, and so naïve. He continued running out through the low waves to meet her.

'How are you this morning?' he asked.

'Bereft, I suppose, sums it up. Sorry. It hasn't happened often. I was unprepared for it. It's hit me hard.'

He hugged her and kissed her head. 'I'm here. I meant it when I said it, I'm here for you.'

She managed to smile up at him while thinking that he didn't yet know her plans for him.

'Thanks, Alex, you're sweet. I appreciate it.' She shivered. 'Sorry, I've let myself get cold, I'd better get out.'

They walked up the beach hand in hand, the low sun gently warming them as they went to get dressed for breakfast.

'I'm not sure I can do this,' she said, 'but I want to try. I won't eat much.'

They walked to breakfast together, to the self-service counters, Alex to get a cooked breakfast, she to find some fruit, they returned to choose a table and order coffee. They ate in silence for a while.

'Do you want to go back early?' he asked. She shook her head more violently than she intended.

'No. We weren't there, so we don't know, so we can't be back early. Unless someone else reports it, and we get a call. Then we have to go, or at least consider going. But that's unlikely because I don't have a cleaner or anything, so no one else is going to call. I know who the multi was now. There's only one person who is allowed to use my place while we were away. Anyway, I've checked on the others, and they're alright.'

'It must take some doing, living several lives at once. How on earth do you manage it?'

She shrugged. 'It was incredibly hard at first. I thought I'd made a mistake, and wanted to back out, but once I'd mastered it, I wanted more. I'll tell you how it's done one day if you want me to. After a while it becomes second nature, the **multi** pretty much runs its own **life**, and you drop in when you want to. Sometimes one runs into trouble and calls me, but rarely.'

'Does it mean that sometimes you're not fully in the one I know?'

'In a way, yes. You see, I am the key. I control the others, and if I die, so do they, but as you can see it doesn't work the other way around. I just mourn their loss. It hurts more than when I lost my dog when I was a kid, and that was awful. About the same as losing my father. Whichever way you look at it, it's not good. But I'll get over it, just give me time.'

'You just take the time you need,' he said earnestly. She reached across and squeezed his hand. It occurred to him that her **multi** might look exactly like her, but he didn't dare ask, not now.

'Thanks, Alex. I'll try to be an agreeable companion for the next two weeks, but, well, you know.'

'What would you like to do today, take it gently?'

'Yes, sunbathe, swim, read, the classic holiday combination.'

'I'll sit with you and tap away if it won't disturb you.'

'No, it'll be a comfort to have you there, and I won't feel guilty if you're getting something done. I expect I'll want to get out more soon, just to take my mind off things.'

Slowly they made their way back to their room and prepared for the day, picking up fresh beach towels and bagging a couple of sunbeds on the way.

Alex typed, occasionally glancing across at Lizzie as she tried to read. It seemed an age since he'd last addressed the story of Jayne, and it was difficult to get back into it. So much had happened, and it clouded his thoughts. He went back to Jayne, yelling at Amilie's house, distraught at the loss of her friendship and the imposition of **awareness**, even though she did not know what it was. He felt for her even as he typed.

Jayne slowly stood up, glared at Amilie's house, turned and trudged back to her own home. Home. A home without a mother and with a frequently absent father. Some home. As she went, she took stock of her position. She could leave school soon if she wanted; legally, there was nothing to stop her. She might not have great qualifications, if any, but at least she would have some freedom. Then she could go wherever she wanted, do different things, and maybe forget all about this **awareness***. But she had a feeling it wouldn't be as simple as that. She walked on autopilot, head turned to the ground, and almost bumped into the policeman standing at the end of the drive. She apologised and went to walk around him, but he called after her.*

'Excuse me. Miss Sutherland?' She turned to face him.

'Yes.'

'I'm sorry to bother you, but we need to talk.'

She noticed his car then, with its red and orange bands, and a female policewoman getting out of the passenger side. She walked over to join them, and it was the female officer who spoke next.

'Can we go inside, love? There's something we have to tell you.'

It was her quiet, concerned tone that caught Jayne,

brought a lump to her throat. She nodded and led the way up the drive, where she made a mess of turning the key in the lock. The policeman gently took the key from her and opened the door. She led them into the front room. It was a room of memories rather than of use. It was where her mother had always sat and hadn't been used since she left. She showed them to the settee and sat in her mother's big armchair. From it she could see out of the front window, the TV and, of course now, the police officers.

'It's about your father,' the woman said. 'I'm sorry, but we have some bad news. He was involved in a collision with a car earlier today and pronounced dead. I'm so sorry.'

Did she expect a reaction? Jayne felt nothing. She had loved her father once, but now? Nothing. An emptiness. A hollow in her soul. She just nodded. But despite everything, a tear trickled down one cheek. It was a tear for her, though, not for her father.

They offered to have someone stay with her, they offered to find her mother, and they hesitated about leaving her, but eventually, they did. But only after a social worker had arrived. Jayne ignored her, ignored the cup of tea she made and planned her life while she sat in silence. The house was probably hers now. She doubted her father had left it to her mother, and she knew it transferred to him with the divorce. He must have some money somewhere too, so she would need to find that. He was rarely home, so where had he been staying? A hotel? But doubts *were creeping into her mind. Did he have another woman? Had he always had someone else? Was that the cause of the breakup? She had to find out.*

'I've rung your school, to explain,' the social worker was saying, 'and we must find out if there's anyone who can look after you. Do you have any other family?'

'No,' Jayne answered. Maybe her mother might still be considered her family, but she wasn't going there.

'How old are you, Jayne?' She hadn't done much research, had she? This one knew nothing.

'Almost eighteen.'

'Oh, when's that? If you're that age you must be leaving school soon, and of course, you'll be your own person, you can make your own decisions.'

She had brightened considerably with this knowledge, as though realising that her workload wouldn't increase with a Sutherland case file. Bitch. The anger was returning, and Jayne strained to hold it back. She had to get rid of this woman.

'Well, I'm over sixteen, so I'm my own person anyway, aren't I? I'm over eighteen in a few days. Exams are in a couple of weeks. I'll do crap, but I'll do them. You can leave now.'

'Are you sure?' The bitch was almost out of the chair already, keen to get away, keen to get her case numbers down.

'Yes. I'm sure. I'll be alright. I'll find a solicitor to sort things out. Don't worry.'

With a few more solicitous remarks, they left, and Jayne slumped back into the chair. But she wasn't there long. There were things to do. She had little money of her own, and somehow she had to find out what her father had and how she could get it. She had a laptop her father had bought her a while ago and looked up a local solicitor. She wanted a woman. She found one and rang. They offered an appointment in three days, but after she told them what had happened, they agreed to see her as soon as she could get there. All she had to do was sort out a bus to get there. She checked her purse. There was plenty there for a bus, and a few days' food, although there was some in the fridge and the freezer. She was going to be alright.

The solicitor was kind, and not a stuffy old bat, as she'd feared. She promised to sort everything for her as quickly as she could, realising that Jayne was going to need some cash quickly. While Jayne was there, she contacted her school to let them know what had happened and found out where Jayne's father's body had been taken to. She was a little taken aback when Jayne said that she didn't want to see him, but somehow found out where he'd worked, and they sent someone to identify him formally. Then she cleared some appointments, which allowed her time to find out more about her father. The police had checked his possessions and found that his driving licence wasn't registered to the house Jayne lived in, but to one in the south of London suburbs. The one where they'd lived before he had lost his job. Except that he hadn't lost it. A pass clearly showed that it was the same company that Jayne remembered. Bastard. He had run two lives. Probably two women. Did her mother know? How had it not come out in the divorce settlement? She was more shocked at all this than she was at his death.

The solicitor looked at the original house deeds and found that they were in her father's name only. So she asked Jayne if she wanted to visit it. It was then that she broke down. Visit the family home she had loved before they dragged her to the small hamlet, away from everyone she knew, and to Amilie's mother and **awareness***. It was too much.*

The solicitor arranged for her to meet another solicitor local to her old home the next day, and she advanced her some money to make sure she had plenty for the journey. The police would deliver her father's possessions, including his keys to her, later that day.

Alex stopped typing. He wasn't sure he was right about all these procedures, even if they fitted the story. He shrugged to himself.

'Is everything alright?' Lizzie asked.

'Yes, I'm just not sure about some legal stuff in the story, but I can always check up on it later, or think of it as poetic licence. The trouble is that with the internet everyone's an expert these days, so I'll probably get some smart arse querying it.'

Lizzie chuckled, which was a good sign. 'I'm going to swim, then cream up and sunbathe. Want to join me?'

He walked back to their room, hid the computer away, locked up, and ran back to the beach. Lizzie was already in the water, watching him.

'We need to talk about **awareness**,' Lizzie said, making Alex give her a quizzical look. 'Put it this way. I think it would help both of us to talk about it. For me, it means facing up to what's happened, and maybe analysing it, and for you, well, it's what George asked me to do. He said you're a bit naïve, and to be honest, I think he's right.'

'I agree. I was told I'm **aware**, but that's about it. I just pick up bits and pieces as I hear them. I don't know how much I know, and how much I don't if you see what I mean.'

'So where to start. I suppose with a definition. What is **awareness**? This is where it becomes unclear because it means different things to different people, but at its core, **awareness** is an ability. It allows you to communicate with and influence others without actually saying or doing anything. It's as though you have a form of quantum thought that reaches out. Now, mothers, not that I am one, I've just been told many times, mums often feel this way when they have a child, especially a young child. There's an instinctive response if they're in trouble, even if they're not with you. Now before someone shouts at me and says that's not true for them, then I've also heard that it varies from person to person, a bit like

awareness. Some people are just **aware**, it's natural for them, others need some sort of ceremony to encourage it to work for them. Then you have many people who are **unaware**, some couldn't care less, and some have heard about **awareness** and either envy those with it or think that they have an advantage in life, or they're just up their own arses.'

'With me, my mother encouraged my **awareness** from an early age. Even before school age, she was drip-feeding **awareness** to me, so it became second nature to me. What does that mean? Well, I can **scan** someone and get a feel of what they're thinking, I can also get a feeling of where they are locationally, I can feed ideas and information to them subconsciously to change or bolster up their own opinions, I can—'

'One moment. Can we cover these one at a time? I'd like to know how you do them, and how I could do them too. I mean, I can some of it, but I'm sure there's more to it.'

'Sure. Let's start with **scanning**. Look at that man standing in the water. First, try to make your mind go blank. That should be easy for you.' She avoided the water as he splashed at her. 'Defocus your eyesight and think yourself in his mind. Take your time, it doesn't rely on an exact location, so it doesn't matter if either of you moves. Anything happening?'

'Not yet, but I'm getting a tingling feeling, so it might be, just slowly.'

'Keep at it. It becomes much faster and easier the more you do it. Try too much and you get a headache.

Even though I've been doing it for years, that can still happen if I have to do a lot.'

'Hey, it is happening. I'm getting images of his family, four children and a wife.'

'That's good because they're not on the beach.'

'I get a feeling that he doesn't know where they are.'

'Right, now suggest that he goes to look for them.'

'Eh, how do I do that?'

'Just imagine him walking out of the water and looking. Don't be too specific, we don't know where they are, they might not even be at the hotel.'

'OK, doesn't seem to happen though.'

'Keep at it. You'll be sending a weak signal, and probably not too well focused, so it'll take time. There you are.'

The man wasn't just walking out of the water, he was trying to run as fast as the water would allow him. Then he ran up the beach, across the grass, and off out of sight towards the far right of the hotel.

'Excellent. We'll take that as a success, even though he might have done that, anyway.'

'Right, so what's next, Lizzie?'

'How's the head? I need to check because it can be a strain at first.'

'Fine, so far. How about I try it on you?'

She laughed. 'And I wonder what you'd try to make me do? No, it wouldn't work, I've screens up that will blank an approach like that. I'll tell you about them another day. But let me see, I'll let you **scan** me, and then maybe some other people, just to see if they're **aware**.'

'Ah, I've done the checking for **awareness** before. Should I have done that with the guy just now, before I tried to influence him? I can feel it in people sometimes.'

'I'd already done that. I'm sure he's **aware**, so he's more suggestible. He didn't have any barriers up.'

'OK, don't say anything else, let me see what I can get.' He defocused his eyes and thought of Lizzie. Almost at once, he saw a black curtain, blood dripping down it. He opened his eyes immediately. 'Maybe I shouldn't have tried that.'

'That bad, eh, sorry I should have thought of that. May I ask what you saw?'

He told her, and she grimaced. 'Maybe we should give it a rest, I'm sorry.'

They swam slowly along the beach, each in their own thoughts, until Alex gestured at the bar. 'Drink?'

She hesitated. 'I shouldn't when I'm like this. It can get out of hand, but OK, as long as you promise to keep an eye on me. There's a chance that if I start, I won't stop.'

'Is that a side effect of **awareness**?'

'No, it's just the way I deal with things. Sorry.'

He reached out a hand, and they swam along one-handed, the other linking them until they were level with the bar, and then they let go, swam in until they could walk, and went up to the bar.

Then, sitting at a table looking out at the sea, they downed a couple of drinks, each in quick succession.

CHAPTER TWENTY-ONE

Jayne sat on her bed, dejected. Her time with Mike had been a disaster. He had taken little notice of her, and when he did, he was curt and, bluntly, rude. She was having trouble with Amy as well, who thought that they were friends rather than boss and worker. It had ended up in a row. Amy really shouldn't talk to her superior like that. Maybe she'd have to go. Maybe there was only one thing to do. She walked into her study, opened the top drawer, and took out a clear folder of papers. Maybe it was time to stop being Miss Nice Guy. Maybe she had to take more direct action. She didn't want to, but they'd made her do it, she'd had enough of being taken for granted by everyone. She looked at the pages she'd started, and the names that were on them. They were the people she'd dealings with, as it were, at George Marlin's, and those connected to the **aware**. Now, if she told George Marlin she was going to reveal what really went on at his soirees, she could have whatever she wanted. There was only one way to do this. She had to get him alone. But that would not be easy. It was that little woman who hung around him that was the problem. She was the one who had encouraged her to work there and hadn't wanted her to leave. Maybe she should approach the woman. But no, Marlin wasn't a strong character on his own. He relied on the little woman. She ran everything, her and that Lizzie. For a moment she wondered whether Marlin knew what went on, but she soon dismissed that idea. Of course he did. Didn't he?

Then she looked up. Alex was an **aware**, but he didn't appear to be clued up on it at all. He could be a way in. But had she wasted her chance? She opened her laptop and easily found his address in Bath. Noting it down, she thought about ringing him or texting. No, it would be better to see him in person, because then he was more likely to engage with her, and she could use her feminine charms on him. Satisfied that she had a plan, she decided she'd better sort her body out before she met him, and a bath would be the best way to start. She had to be at her most desirable when she met him again. Irresistible.

As she went to put the file of papers away, she noticed a smudge on the back of the folder. It hadn't been there before, she was sure. She checked her fingers to be sure, but they were clean, and anyway, the smudge was bigger than her fingerprints. Who the hell? Mike. He was the only one who had been in her flat. Anger flared. He would have seen the file as well. The meddling bastard. Her face reddened. Her anger was getting out of control, and she'd thought she had it under control. But this, this betrayal, it was beyond forgiveness. She tried her best to calm herself, deep breaths visualising her calm place, the sound of a river. Slowly she felt her anger subside, but she knew she would have to deal with it, and the only way was to remove the cause. Oh, no, not again, she thought, as her anger subsided to be replaced with tears. Would she never be free of this curse?

Later, after a bath, and a hair wash and dry, she put on the war paint with care and her best dress. Then she called a taxi to take her to Alex's house. It was time to take direct action, if only to save her from herself.

CHAPTER TWENTY-TWO

Alex and Lizzie were a little drunk, pleasantly so, as they went into lunch to find that there weren't many there. No doubt people had gone out rather than lounging around, which would explain the few people on the beach. They helped themselves from the self-service counters, found a table, and ordered drinks.

When they'd finished their meal, they made their way slowly back to the room, the sun high in the sky, and beating down on them. Time for a siesta. They stripped off and lay on the bed, the air-con cooling them down. But neither felt like sex. Too much had happened. Alex held Lizzie close as she nestled into his chest, and he gently stroked her body. It was a time to comfort, to soothe away the hurt and the anxiety. Anyway, he thought they still had the best part of two weeks to go. Shortly after, when Lizzie fell asleep, Alex sat up, retrieved his laptop and typed.

Jayne took the train to the suburbs of London and a place called Stoneleigh. It was fairly straightforward, the train from Bath to Paddington, a walk to the Underground, and the Circle Line to Water-loo and another walk into the mainline station for the train to Stoneleigh. She walked down the steps from the station to find a small row of shops and a church, which wasn't what she was expecting. A quick check in the newsagent's and she returned to the station to go back up the steps and then down to the other side of the tracks. Here was a wide road, with shops all the way down. She walked along it and soon found the solicitors. Thankfully, they were expecting her.

'Ah, thank you for coming to us, Miss Sutherland. I'm sorry you've had such a long journey, but it's best that we get things sorted for you. Your father was, how shall I put it, an irregular client. He came to us over his divorce and his will. That was all. But at least he arranged a will, eh? He was quite clear about what he wanted for you, and for the lady that he was living with. They didn't marry, for reasons I won't go into now. So he wanted to make sure that it was all laid out, and that there would be no mis-understandings. It's all quite simple.'

Jayne looked at him, not sure if he was expecting her to say anything, so she just said, 'Yes?'

'Er, yes. There are two houses, the one you live in and another, here. Well, he left the house you are living in, to you, as well as his house here, but there is a sitting tenant in that one. The will allows the lady he was living with to live there for as long as she wants to, which rather prevents you from doing

147

anything with it. However, and this will be of more interest to you, he left all his other worldly possessions to you. The principal areas of interest are his bonds, which are worth about £35,000, his premium bonds of £50,000 and his current account at the bank, about £5000. Now we must sort out an agreement with the lady living in the property here, because she'll be responsible for the bills now, and that includes maintenance of the property. Unusual, but that's how he wanted it. Unfortunately, there will be forty per cent tax to pay on the house, money, and our fees, so you'll end up with about £50,000, one house, and of course the house here which you can sell, eventually.'

'I see,' she said, wondering what should happen now. Fifty thousand pounds is very nice to have, but the business about the house was just confusing. Surely, if it was her father's, then it was hers now. Was she not allowed to even see inside it? To remember her childhood. Was this woman to take all this from her?

'What are my rights exactly, about the house?' she asked.

'The way it's drawn up, as the owner, you have the right to inspect the property, with the tenant's permission, of course. She might want to move, or maybe need a little incentive to move, but somehow, I suspect not at the moment. She has just lost her partner. I took the liberty of saying to her you were coming here, and she said that she'd be thrilled if you'd like

to drop in and see her. I think she's quite interested to see you. A link to the departed, as it were. Maybe you can be friends? Now there are some papers to sign, and I'd like your bank account details for us to transfer in the money your father left you when we receive it. Eventually, when we have completed probate. I think you'll be alright, but sometimes it can take a little while to get the money released, but I'll do my best. Now, is there anything else? I agreed with Mrs Sharp that I'd accompany you to see her if that's alright. It's not far.'

'I know,' Jayne said, 'it's where I used to live before we took on the other house.'

'Ah, yes, I'm liaising with your Bath solicitors to sort that one out. It should be a straight transfer to you. Unfortunately, we're going to have to sort out the tax situation though.'

'What do you mean?'

'Well, we have to establish which property was his principal residence. Tax will then be payable on the other residence I expect.'

'One moment, so I will have to pay forty per cent of the value of one house?'

'Er, yes, that's correct.'

'But the only way I could afford to do that would be to sell one of them.'

'Also probably correct. Yes, he has left us a minor puzzle, hasn't he?'

'Surely the tax people can't turn me out of my home, though?'

'Ah, that will come into play when it's determined which his principal residence is. It may well be the key factor. You are his daughter, living in his home, at least, one of his homes, and you are not yet eighteen, although you will be by the time this all gets sorted. A pretty little puzzle.'

'What's your view?'

'Well, maybe his lady friend cannot stay, because the Revenue will enforce a sale. I'm not sure until I can consult with them. Now, would you like to see the house, and meet the lady? I won't spoil things, but I might have an angle that will make her move on, but I don't want to say anything unless I have to.'

Lizzie stirred and opened her eyes. He saved his work and sat next to her.

'How are you?'

'Not sure yet, but I needed that. Were you writing?'

'A little more, it's slow going.'

'Maybe you should concentrate on that for a while, it'll give you a sense of achievement.'

'Possibly, but I want to be with you, make sure you're alright.'

'Oh, I'm alright, just, well, you know. I don't mind if you write.'

'We'll see. Another swim?'

'I don't think so. I think I want you. Come here.'

CHAPTER TWENTY-THREE

Jayne turned away from Alex's front window. She could see he wasn't there. She wondered if there was a back way and walked around into Kipling Avenue. About a hundred yards up, there was an unmade road that went behind the terraced houses. She strolled along it, trying to make out which was Alex's, but in the end concluded that even if she could work out which house was his, there was no way she could scale the fence. Her anger had abated now, and she was getting the familiar after-effects. She felt small and cold and afraid. Afraid of herself and for herself. This was no way to be. She took out her phone and called a taxi. A twenty-minute wait, but that would do. She walked back to the front of Alex's house and wondered whether to leave him a note, but it seemed pointless. Her determination had vanished. She was no longer riding into battle; she was just an exhausted, pathetic shop manager who wanted to go home and curl up in her bed.

The taxi took her back to her flat, and, after making cheese on toast, which she supplemented with a glass of white wine, she sat to watch the TV, her duvet over her for warmth and comfort. She had to get a grip of life before it really got a hold of her. The only way, surely, was to take control. Then she could steer in the direction she wanted, not the direction others wanted. She pondered this until she fell asleep, still in the chair, under the duvet, the TV softly talking.

She awoke, not quite knowing where she was. It was dark, and the screen was flickering at her. She reached for the control and killed it. Slumping back, she thought of going to bed, but couldn't be bothered. There were decisions to be made, but she wasn't up to making them. How she wished Alex was around. He seemed a sensible sort who would help her out. What was it with men? They were all over you one minute, gone the next. She'd heard others say it, so it must be true. But other women found decent blokes who stuck with them. What was wrong with her? But she knew. It was being **aware**, and the anger that often went with it. Who would put up with that? No one. Not one man. Nobody. She saw the wine bottle and took a swig. Why not? Mr Nobody would never know. Who cared about little Jayne Sutherland? Whether she lived, or she died, or she drank white wine from the bottle fully clothed under a duvet in an armchair. Not one person in the whole of the world. No one knew she was here at all. She was probably an illusion. A toast to the absent Jayne Sutherland, to an absent friend. Taking another swig, she closed her eyes. An image of Alex came to her, looking down at her, so real that it made her jump. Was he looking at her? Can an **aware** do that? Had he seen her before? Oh, lord, to think of the things he might have seen. No wonder he didn't want her. She was worthless. She took another swig, surprising herself that the bottle was empty. She had to check to make sure. Yes, empty. Should she get another? No. One's enough. More than enough. Better get some sleep. Yes. Work tomorrow. Amy tomorrow. What should she do about Amy? With that thought, her eyes closed, and a light snore came from her mouth. She was at peace at last.

The next morning, she awoke with the mother of all hangovers. It can't have been the wine. She often drank a bottle. It must have been the cheese on toast, either the cheese or the bread was off. She stripped off and showered. She was tempted to try a cold one, but chickened out. No one needed waking up that much. Quickly dressed, she went through her usual routine of grabbing a pastry and a coffee from the shop and hurrying across town. She froze at one point because she thought she saw Mike, but it wasn't him. The bloke wasn't bad looking though, and she wondered for a moment what he was like, but it didn't stop her. She arrived at the shop before Amy and unlocked the grill before unlocking the door. Then she pulled the grill down behind her. Time to enjoy her breakfast. It was odd that Amy hadn't beaten her, as was becoming usual, but it was nice to have just a little peace before the customers arrived. Not so much a calm before a storm, but peace before the carnage. She smiled at that. She'd tell Amy that, and Amy would laugh.

At nine she went and opened the doors and rolled the shutter up. Still no Amy, and no phone call. It was then that she realised she had left her phone behind. But Amy could always contact her on the shop phone. That would be better because her mobile signal was rubbish in the store, especially if you moved away from the door.

Nine thirty, no customers, and no Amy. What was wrong with the girl? There was stocktaking next week, and everything had to be ready. The company still did it the old way, pencil and paper. Black marks for the computer to read. It was out of the ark, but investment meant lower profits, so the system stayed the same. Like the back of the store. Which was a third world country compared to the shop the customers saw. One glimpse of the conditions back there, they'd never touch a pair of shoes from this shop. Maybe other shops were the same. What was that expression? Fur coat and no knickers. Well, that put her in her place. She was Miss No Knickers. She giggled at her joke. Where the hell was Amy?

Customers arrived, not neatly spaced, but in clumps. Three would come in at once, and those not served at once would tut away. What else could she do? She'd have to find a replacement for Amy. This wasn't on. Lunchtime came, but she couldn't go anywhere. It was raining outside, and it was driving people into the dry warmth the shop provided, not to buy but to browse and question. She had trouble keeping an eye on all of them. Thank goodness they only had one from each pair of shoes on display. She watched the three customers who she had provided with full pairs of shoes from the stockroom. The problem was that as soon as she went out to fetch another pair, she had to leave the shop unguarded. But there was nothing she could do about it. She had sales targets to reach.

By the end of the day, she was exhausted, and sure that she had lost at least one pair of shoes to an old lady who should know better. It was with enormous relief that she closed and locked the door and brought the shutter down, making sure it was locked too. But where could she go now? She had no one to go out with. She set off for home, and then with memories of meeting Mike, diverted into the Old Green Tree. He wasn't there, and the pub wasn't as crowded as it had been. The rain, probably. She ordered a cider and sat down. No one took any notice of her.

She'd have to get a temp in if she didn't turn up tomorrow. She couldn't continue like this. To be honest, she should have pushed on recruiting her replacement, but she and Amy were getting on so well it didn't seem right. But Amy was taking liberties now, and that was wrong, so she had to contact the agency, but they were so slow. There must be someone out there who wanted a job. The trouble was that the company expected managers to do so much. Maybe she could check where Amy lived and go round there. Was that against the law? All these laws said you mustn't intrude into the lives of employees, like not ringing them up when they're sick and asking them work questions. It was all very well people making these laws, but had they ever run a business? The police. Maybe she could contact them? They could go round and check, just in case she'd had a fall or something. But there was no knowing it was serious. She was probably skiving, ill, or had just buggered off. It was just after payday. That was probably the answer.

She went up to the bar for another cider. The barman was friendly enough but engrossed in a conversation with a bloke further along, and once he'd served her, moved back. She looked around. It was a quiet night here, and she could hear the rain hitting the pavement outside. A gust of cold, damp air swept in as a rain-soaked punter clattered through the door. She headed back to her seat to lose herself in her thoughts once more.

'Hi, mind if I sit here?' The guy who had just walked in was standing beside her. He looked alright, probably taller than her, with close-cropped dark hair and a heavily belted mac with water streaming off it.

'Of course,' she said with a smile.

'I'm Johnnie.' He placed his pint on the table and stripped off the mac, looked around for somewhere to hang it, but gave up, and dropped it on the floor. He held out a hand, and she took it. She noticed hands, Alex's had been soft, unsullied by manual work, but these, these were more muscular but not rough, with no calluses. Maybe he worked out a lot. His chest looked as though that was the case.

'I'm Jayne,' she said, lowering her eyes as she smiled. 'Do you work near here?'

'No, Bristol, but I live nearby. I get the train in. It's a wonderful service, only half an hour from door to door. You?'

'I manage a shop, over near the Abbey. I've been on my own all day. My assistant didn't turn up, so it's been hell.'

'Snap. At least with the assistant bit. Mine was supposed to run a load of figures for me, but I ended up doing it myself. If you want a job done…'

'Do it yourself, yes, that's right. Difficult in a shoe shop though, I have to keep going out the back to get shoes for customers, and some of them take off, taking the shoes with them because there's no one to watch the shop.'

'Well, that's not something I have to deal with. Sounds rubbish. Can't you get some extra staff?'

'I'm trying. Maybe a temp tomorrow, but they'll be difficult to train up if I'm on my own again. Anyway, enough of my minor problems, what do you do?'

'Me? I'm an engineer. I'm part of a team working on a new motorway. I specialise in sorting out the logistics these days, so once the design is agreed my team plans how the hell it's going to be built.'

'Wow, sounds important, and when it's done, you have a monument to your work.' He laughed, a pleasant laugh, not belly shaking like Mike, just pleasant.

'I suppose so. Planning works like a motorway is all about logistics. Divide it up into a plan, like a massive Gantt chart, that shows what gets done when, and who and what needs to be there to accomplish it, and how long it will take, and what will have to be done if something isn't completed on time. It's no good having cement turn up if there's nowhere to put it. Although to be honest, a lot of the day-to-day stuff gets handled on site.'

'That's a heck of a responsibility. You must be well qualified to do that.' She said, wondering what a Gantt chart was, but not liking to ask.

'A few years study, and a few years work. But that's all in the past now. Can I get you another one?'

She was feeling nicely pissed now, but… 'Yes please, my turn though, same again?'

She went up to the bar, happier now she had company, and that's all it was, wasn't it just company? This wasn't going anywhere. He wouldn't normally look at her twice. She took a sly look back at him. He was good-looking if harassed, but that was probably just his work. It sounded awfully important. Fancy getting something like that wrong. She took their drinks back to the table.

'Have you eaten?' he asked as she sat down.

'No, not yet. I just needed somewhere to drown my sorrows on the way home.'

'Shall we?'

'What, here?'

He looked towards the door. 'It's nothing special, the basics, but better than the rain, I guess.'

'Good idea then.' she looked at the blackboard. 'I'll have ham, egg and chips.'

'Great, I'll have the same.' He was off to order. No messing. She saw him look across at her, so she smiled, and moved her chair back, crossing her legs so he could see more of them, her skirt riding up. Maybe it would not be a rubbish evening after all.

CHAPTER TWENTY-FOUR

The next day and George was pacing. He became like this when he was worried, Maggie thought.

'I suppose you haven't seen Lizzie and Alex around town, Maggie?'

'No, George, I have seen nothing of them since the taxi. Why?'

'I was thinking of getting everybody back together for another soiree. It was enjoyable last time, wasn't it?'

'Oh, yes, George, and you lay on a lovely spread.'

'I hope people come for more than that, Maggie, the intellectual conversation, the company of like-minded souls. Then there's your entertainment too.'

'Oh, I'm sure they do. Mind you, I have noticed that numbers are dropping off lately.'

'Why's that, do you think, always the same faces? Yes, I was thinking that myself, although we got Alex Ash along last time. He added a bit of colour. People like to get to know authors and people like that. Mind you, we had an ulterior motive, didn't we?'

Maggie wondered whether to mention that the colour had been a bit muted when Lizzie took Alex away, but maybe George hadn't noticed that. She often wondered how much George did notice. He always said that he wasn't an **aware**, he just liked to encourage and support them, but she had her doubts. Although she could only pick up the slightest trace of **awareness** from him, she was sure he was hiding it, or at least something. If he was, then he must be a powerful **aware** indeed, after all, he had confirmed Lizzie's verdict that she was an **aware**. She'd promised herself to find out more, which was one reason she was here. Another was that she quite liked him. It was good to be in the presence of a powerful man, and he seemed to enjoy her company too, even if he was off in a world of his own rather too much for her liking.

'Maybe there are some others who would like to come? Do you know of anyone?'

'I'll have a root around the old address book. You know, Maggie, maybe now is the right time to rethink our gatherings. Widen the circle and increase our influence in this city, don't you think?'

'Why, yes, George, that sounds splendid. I'll have a think too, and we can draw up a list together, and maybe we can have the upstairs rooms redecorated. It's such a pity Lizzie isn't around, she can be quite a draw.'

'Er, yes, of course. You do that. Now, I was going to see someone for lunch today, and I'm damned if I can remember who.'

'Arnie Fellows. At Sotto Sotto, you said.'

'Ah yes. Good food, but difficult to hear what's being said in that place. At least that's what I've found. Maybe it's my age. It's in a cellar and I found I could hear bits of what everyone else was saying, but not the person in front of me. Never mind, Arnie could be useful. He moves in a different circle, artistic types, so he'll know people we don't. A good place to start our little campaign, don't you think?'

'You're absolutely right, George, and I'll see if some of my literacy group would be interested. I'm sure several of them are **aware**.'

'You are good, Maggie. A great support. Now, I must get on. I was thinking of getting some new shoes while I was out as well. This pair are getting on and they won't take mending again.'

'I was about to say you ought to stay clear of Jayne Sutherland, but maybe it's a good idea to see what she's up to.'

'Why? What's she got to do with my shoes?'

'Oh, you're becoming forgetful, Georgie. She works in a shoe shop, silly. I think it might be a good idea if you went to her first, then you've got a good excuse to be there. And then you can talk to Arnie about her. Here, I'll write the address down for you.'

'Right, will do. Cracking idea. Thanks again, Maggie, I'll be off now then.'

'Enjoy your lunch, and I expect to have a full report on Jayne Sutherland when you get back.'

She listened to the door shutting and looked out of the window to watch him walk along the Crescent until he was out of sight. Then she sighed and wondered what to do with her day. She had virtually moved in with George now. But she was still in the position of having most of her stuff in her own house some way away. Which was inconvenient when there was something you suddenly thought you needed, but it wasn't where you were living most of the time. Anyway, what to do? The literacy group she'd mentioned to George wasn't until next week, but there was always the tennis lot, although few of them were probably **aware**. It was difficult to find people who were **aware**, and good to mix in at a soiree, let alone those who would take part in the other attractions that she laid on, and she wasn't sure how much George understood about them. She'd have to give it some thought. In the meantime, it would be best if she went back to her own house. There would be the cleaning to do and a few more things to fetch back. Resolved, she went to change and face the outside world, hoping that George would be alright with Jayne. Nothing could go wrong in a shoe shop though, could it?

On the other side of town, Jayne was having a meltdown moment. Amy hadn't come in again, and nor had the temp she'd organised with their usual agency, and it was busy. Very busy. She couldn't keep track of everything and everyone, and she was sure that the couple who had been sitting nearest the door with two pairs of shoes to try on had done a runner. But there was nothing she could do about it. Harassed, she wasn't even going to be able to take a lunch break, as she ran from one part of the shop to another, into the back room and back, ignoring the jangle of the shop phone. There was only so much one pair of hands could do. It was then that the area manager walked in. She took one look and got stuck in.

'I'll take this side of the shop, you take the other,' she said. 'You look frazzled. We can sort that out when we've finished with the customers though.'

It was as she bent down helping an older lady that she felt that someone was watching her. She couldn't turn around to see who it was straight away, which was a pity, because the sensation died away soon after. Maybe it was just someone passing the door.

An hour later and the tide of customers turned, more going than coming, and soon it was just her and the area manager.

'Well, that was a rush. Good job I was here. Why are you on your own?'

'My usual hasn't turned up for a few days, and the temp's let me down, but I haven't had time to ring up for a replacement. Not that they'd be a lot of use without the time to train them.'

Looking at her hard, her area manager nodded. 'I think we need a chat. You need at least three here if not five given your turnover. Stock count's soon, isn't it, when's yours?'

'Just coming up.'

'Right, get me the date and I'll get a team in to do that, so you won't need to worry about it, and I'll see if I can poach someone from another branch. Probably two. Then when your usual girl comes back, you'll have the time to train new people. What's happened to your replacement?'

'The agency has found no one suitable yet,' she said, hoping that she wasn't colouring up. She hadn't even told them yet.

'Right. I'll make a few phone calls. I guess you haven't had time for a break, have you? As soon as I'm done with the calls, you'd better go, and I'll follow you. Alright?'

It was just as well Jayne didn't hear the phone calls.

The shoe shop failed to impress George Marlin when he looked in. He knew exactly what Jayne looked like and quickly spotted her kneeling on the floor beside an older lady. He looked around at the crowded store, decided it wasn't for him, and walked on. It was a pity because he'd liked to meet Jayne, just to see what they were up against. But there was always tomorrow. At least there was lunch to look forward to.

Jayne sat by herself on a bench in the centre of the city, chomping on a prawn sandwich. What a crap morning, although it was incredible how the area manager had dived straight in and helped. She hadn't had a go either, as Vicki would have done, but maybe she was more skilled than Vicki. There were some plus sides to life. Then there was Johnnie, who'd been nice in a quiet sort of way. It hadn't come to anything, but they had one another's phone numbers. So, who knew what might happen? She watched as a group of tourists followed a woman with the obligatory umbrella held high, as though she was praying for rain. Then another lot, and another. Bath attracted people from all over the world, which helped its residents You could get a Discovery card from the council, which gave free or discounted entry to places like the Roman Baths.

She checked her watch. Time had flown, and she'd have to run now. Drat. She was going to be late and the area manager would see.

George went down the steps into the restaurant and was pleased to see that Arnie had just arrived too. Shown to their table, George made a point of taking a seat facing out from the wall. With luck, Arnie's voice would bounce off it, and he could hear what he was saying. Arnie dived straight into why he wanted to meet. 'George, I hope this won't sound presumptuous, but I'd like to invite myself to those **aware** get-togethers you have. I know you invited me ages ago, and I never made it, but things change you know.'

'Love to have you along, Arnie. It would be great to see you there. Maggie and I were only saying this morning we should expand a bit.'

'Maggie? Is that the Maggie who was married to…'

'To Edward Snelle? Yes, that's right.'

'Well, well. Is she with you these days, then? I didn't realise.'

'A lovely woman, Arnie, and to be frank, wasted on the likes of Snelle. God rest his soul.'

'Cancer, wasn't it?'

'Yes, lungs, took two years for him to die, poor chap.'

'Well, if it's not one thing, it's another. How long have you been with Maggie?'

They looked up as a waiter hovered beside Arnie's shoulder to take their order, and George seemed to have forgotten the question when he replied. Arnie was too polite to query this, but he made a mental note with a wry smile to himself.

'We had an author chap at our soiree last time, Alex Ash. Heard of him?'

'Can't say I have. Famous, is he?'

'Certainly known. The thing is, we've come across a problem, and it seemed useful to have him on board.'

'What sort of problem?'

'There's a woman in the city who could cause a bit of a disruption. At least, Maggie thinks so. Jayne Sutherland. It's a cause for concern, and this author fellow was going out with her at the time. I set Lizzie on him to steer him away from her. He seemed naïve about you know what.'

'Do I? Oh, the **aware** thing, I get what you mean. Wise of you, he'll thank you for it.'

'Thing is, now he and Lizzie have legged it for some posh hotel in Sussex.'

'Well, good for Lizzie, she's a one. You been there, George?'

'No, I don't go to Sussex much, and it's out of my league, anyway. You?'

'Err, wasn't quite what I meant, old chap, but yes.'

'Anyway, since he's gone off with Lizzie, we don't have to worry about him and this Jayne woman. I went into the shoe shop she's a manager of before I came down here, and it was a right mess, people and shoes everywhere.'

'Buy a lot of my stuff online these days, saves me bothering with the shops. I can send things back if they're not the right size, or I just don't fancy them.'

'Ah, the food's here. Tuck in.'

Jayne was exhausted. It was the end of the day, and every customer had been served, and now every box of shoes stowed away. The ordering could wait until the morning. She turned to look for her area manager, to see her beckoning her over. She sighed. It would have been good just to go home to a hot bath. She walked over.

'I said we needed a chat, Jayne, so let's go into the office.'

Jayne followed her. Maybe she'd get a bonus for working so hard. Once they were sitting, and she'd been asked if she wanted a drink, it started.

'Jayne, to be honest, I was surprised to find you trying to work on your own when I walked in. You'll know as well as I do that it's impossible to keep an eye on the shop and fetch stock out, so we lose our stock that way. No doubt we will see the effects of that when the team comes in tomorrow evening. I might have been prepared to swallow that, because you clearly have a staff problem, with one member off, and a vacancy to fill. However, I contacted the agency, and they didn't even know there was a full-time vacancy here. Not only that, but they said that you only contacted them this morning for a temporary worker. Now, you told me that Amy had been off for several days, so why didn't you arrange something earlier? Something I find most hurtful because it was I who recommended you for the post of manager, is that you lied to me, on several occasions. I cannot work with someone who does that. How can I run an area if I don't know the truth of what is going on in each store? As a result, I have talked to Personnel and agreed that we are terminating your employment. They will contact you about your remuneration, P45 and so on. I don't think there's anything else to say, but if you have any questions, then now is the time. There will be a new team in here tomorrow that I've managed to gather from other branches. Frankly, that was something you could have done to cover your staff problems. Is all that clear?'

Shell shocked, Jayne nodded, a tear in her eye. But she didn't want to let this woman see it, and she had no answers that she could think of. It was true; she had lied. She stood, gathered her things, and let herself out.

CHAPTER TWENTY-FIVE

That evening Alex and Lizzie walked away from the hotel restaurant replete. A decent meal and a good bottle of wine to go with it. Just for the hell of it. As they walked towards the beach, a warden came running up.

'Turtle, laying over there, where the red lights are. Do what the wardens say and keep back so that you don't disturb her.'

Lizzie took off her shoes and went barefoot as they ran over to where he had pointed. There were six or seven people there already, looking at a massive black hump on the ground that was paddling sand with her huge flippers. She was a good eight feet long and four or five feet wide. Aided by the warden's red light and a full moon, they watched in awe as she dug a big hole, and then turned around.

'She'll start laying in a moment. Remember no flash photography, but I'll let you come up one by one to have a look when she's laying.'

The red light the warden shone just behind the turtle let them see first how deep she had dug the hole, and then the white eggs as they emerged.

The warden called them up one by one for a closer look.

'Like being in for your first in a teaching hospital,' said one woman, which raised a laugh, quickly suppressed by the warden.

It took her three-quarters of an hour for her to lay her eggs, and then, after a brief rest, she used her big flippers to paddle the sand back into the hole, turning around and around as she did so. Another forty-five minutes later, the hole filled, the sand around scattered to disguise her activities. She turned towards the sea. It wasn't far, only about twenty yards, but on land she was a cumbersome creature, and it took another forty-five minutes before she stood at the water's edge. They watched as she looked up at the moon, shuffled to take a slightly different angle, and then she was off into the sea. Slowly at first, as she walked through the waves, but then she was in her element, swimming quickly away.

'Her mate could be offshore,' a warden said. 'It depends, but she could mate with him again and come back to lay more. We just don't know.'

Amazed, they walked back along the beach, Lizzie barefoot paddling in the water.

'Thank you for this,' Alex said, reaching for a kiss, but he overbalanced and his shoes went into the water. Lizzie laughed, and together, hand in hand, they ran to stand at the bar. Time for a nightcap, and to see the flaming limbo dancer.

'Goodness knows what age he is,' Lizzie said, 'but he's been here all the times I've come here. He's still so supple.'

'This place is amazing I'm not surprised you've been here a lot.'

'My parents found this place when I was very young, about knee-high, I suppose. It was one of the few hot beach holidays where you didn't need injections then. So we came here every year after that. It's sort of special. But we haven't seen the best of it yet.'

He raised his gin and tonic to her.

'Thank you, you're incredible,' he said, and she curtsied.

'It's a welcome relief from the way I've been feeling. Thank you for your support, it's really helped. I'm not sure how I would have got through the last few days without you. I'd just be a ball of misery in my room. As it is, I'm laughing. Incredible. No disrespect to my multi though.'

'Is it the wrong time to ask how you create a multi?'

'Not now, another time, we're pissed and we're happy, it's best to leave it be.'

'True. Another day of sun and sea tomorrow?'

'Yes, and maybe we can look to see if the jet boat is still around. If the reception desk doesn't know, then the guys on the beach will, they know everything about everybody.'

'I've got my mask and snorkel. I'm all ready and raring to go.'

'It's great to have someone with me who appreciates this place.'

'Have you brought boyfriends here before then?'

'Oh, now you're fishing. Jealous? Yes, a few times, but you're the first to appreciate it.'

'The first sight of an all-inclusive bar, and that's it for some guys. I'm pleased you agreed to come with me, and I love you for it. I'm not saying more than that.' She kissed him. For a long time.

The next day, after breakfast, they looked through the brochures in reception, and Lizzie picked out what she wanted. Alex was looking at the rainforest tour, but she made a face.

'We can hire a jeep and do it ourselves. I know where to start, and it's an easy-going walk, preferably when it hasn't been raining. Also, while we've got a car, we can do the Rainbow Falls and the Argyll Falls. We can swim in both. Coldish water, but that's refreshing when you're hot. If we climb up the side of the Argyll Falls, we can stand under the water as it tumbles down, if you can stand it. Another day we can go to Jemma's Kitchen, a restaurant in a tree at the other end of the island. You can snorkel up there, but I wouldn't recommend it, the current can be fierce. That applies to a lot of that side of the island, the Atlantic side. Here on the Caribbean side, it's completely different, at this time of year, anyway.'

They went back to their room. Lizzie rang the number on the brochure and spent the next ten minutes chatting to the guy on the other end. She was excited at first, but then solemn, making Alex wonder what was wrong. After he heard memories swapped and arrangements made, she put the phone down. But Lizzie looked sad.

'The guy I knew had a heart attack and died on the boat. He was relatively young, it's such a shame. He was a lovely man. Another guy has it now, so I hope it will be as good for you. I talked about some bays we could visit, and the ones I thought best to start with. After a tussle, we agreed. They always want to take people to the nylon pool and Buckoo reef, but the reef can get choppy for the first snorkel of the hols.'

'It all sounds wonderful. Where were you thinking of going then?'

'If we go along the coast, there are lots of small, deserted bays. The ones I talked to him about are Cotton Bay and Emerald Bay. When I was last here, two semi-tame stingrays in Cotton Bay would swim through your legs and brush up against you. It was wonderful, their skin is silky smooth.'

'I remember when that guy got stung in Australia and died, though.'

'Yes, but didn't he corner it, so it felt trapped? I don't know, but these guys are really friendly, you just let them come to you. Mind you, when we were there a catamaran came in with a load of tourists. They got off to paddle, then one of them saw a sting-ray. He leapt for the rope that went from the cat to the shore and just hung there shouting. It terrified him. They all left soon after, leaving us laughing.'

'It all sounds good, Lizzie. I'm looking forward to it. How big is the boat?'

'I think he can take eight, max. There might be just one other couple if you don't mind that?'

'I don't mind at all; it just sounds fun.'

'Now, as for today, I just want to laze around again, if you don't mind. Sun, sea, drink, creaming up and reading, possibly in that order, except that the bar isn't open until ten.'

'Maybe you could tell me more about **awareness** as well, if that's alright, Lizzie?'

'Of course, I'd love to.'

An hour later they were sunning themselves on the sunbeds set out on the sand. Alex hadn't been a sunbather but, well creamed up, he was giving it a go. He'd taken a book from the hotel's borrowing shelves in the shop and was beginning a Ben Aaronovitch tale of a strange and fantastical London. There were only a few people on the beach, with the squeals of children showing that the pool next to the bar was being used. Bliss.

'I know what I could do with,' Lizzie said, sitting up. 'There's a lady who comes to the beach to do a wonderful massage, but I haven't seen her yet. Could you let me know if you see anyone like that, love?'

'I'll keep an eye out. There are so few people around she'll stand out.'

They lay back in peace.

Back in Bath, Jayne was distraught. No job meant no money, and her savings were not great. She'd used almost the lot fitting out the flat. So, she had to get another job. What reference would she get? She had a feeling that employers could only give references that said what your job had been, and how long they had employed you. It was the phone calls you never knew about that might be damning. But now she was in no state to do anything about it. She'd have to avoid the agency that the shoe shop used because she was sure that the area manager had said something to them. Just a hint would be enough for them to be wary of her.

She wasn't crying, she had gone beyond that. She just sat, head in hands, dreading the next stage. She knew what would happen to her, the anger, the over-whelming anger, and then the exhaustion, and the misery. There was no escaping it. What she needed was a plan, but at the moment it was beyond her.

Her phone rang, but she ignored it. If it was John-nie, she was in no fit state to see him. She looked at the number calling but didn't recognise it. She shrugged and let the phone drop. Picking up her coat, purse and keys, she left the flat, not knowing what the evening would bring, but it had to be better than being at home.

CHAPTER TWENTY-SIX

The police constable pushed at the door. He'd noticed it ajar earlier on his rounds, so it was likely it wasn't just a careless householder leaving it open. He stepped in and called out.

'Anybody there?'

No answer, so he went in further, walking along the entrance hall, peering into the front room to his left. He hadn't been in one of these properties before and was surprised to find the large kitchen diner at the front of the house, overlooking the Circus. He looked around, and there was a spacious drawing room overlooking a garden. Going into the room, he looked out at a perfectly manicured lawn. Turning, he made his way to the stairs and stopped. There was a smell he recognised. He went up the grey carpeted stairs two at a time. Everything in this house was white or light grey. First, he entered a bedroom, with a large dressing room and a small en suite, but could see nothing there. He swung around, the smell much more pungent now, and went to the other end of the house. This smaller bedroom looked out over the Circus and had a larger en suite. It was here that she lay. Head bludgeoned into oblivion, lying on the tiled floor as though she had been about to bathe, although there was no water in the bath. Retching, he ran down the stairs, reaching for his radio as he did so.

The police cordoned the house off as forensics, in their all-covering white suits, went through the house. They'd removed the carefully photographed body after they had marked its position, while Detective Inspector Torrey stood surveying the scene. As murders went, there wasn't a lot to go on. The owner of the property was Miss Elizabeth Westbrook, and they assumed that this was her. Assumptions, though, are there to be proven or abandoned. The next-door neighbours had said she was friends with George Marlin, a well-known long-time resident of the Royal Crescent. He would be his next call. There was no way of knowing if someone had stolen anything, although it all looked tidy. No drawers left open, nothing scattered around or just dropped on the floor, no obvious murder weapon either. He was waiting for his detective constable to check out Marlin's address, and then they were off, leaving the experts to their work. He ran a check on her relatives and emphasised to those going through the house what he wanted of them. He took one more look around, trotted down the stairs and out of the house.

The Circus looked to be a lovely place to live. A few hundred yards from the city centre, with its nightlife, entertainment and restaurants. It was also close to Victoria Park, although when he looked at the garden, he'd quite fancied sitting there for a while. But that wasn't happening because there was work to be done, and all for a salary that would never allow him to buy anything like this.

'Sir?'

Detective Constable Roger Deer had his uses. He happily ran from job to job with inexhaustible energy, developed through his love of the gym and the running track. He'd once been a full-time athlete, but an injury and a need to pay the bills had diverted him into the force. If Torrey had a gripe about Deer, it was his enthusiasm. There was just too much of it. If he was a mouse, he'd be rushing into every blind alley there was without forming a plan of action. As a detective, Deer had some way to go, experiences to encounter, people to understand. But he'd get there. He had no doubts about that. The fair-haired Deer was also taller than him, but he didn't hold that against him, much. He turned to Deer, who was standing expectantly, a thoroughbred awaiting the raising of the tape.

'George Marlin, heard of him?'

'He's been around for years, retired as director of a couple of companies, has quiet parties for people he knows, and I heard he had a lady living with him since his wife died, but I know nothing about her.'

'Very good, Deer. Well, we've plenty to fill in then. Do you know how he knows Elizabeth Westbrook?'

'Not sure. I expect she goes to his parties, but how they met, I don't know. Maybe the lady of the house knows her.'

'Fair point. Right, we're going there now.'

'The Royal Crescent. I know which house.'

'In that case, we won't get lost.'

They walked briskly across the Circus and along Brock Street, which led right into the Crescent. Less than ten minutes later and they were ringing Marlin's doorbell. A surprisingly short lady answered.

'Oh, sorry, I thought it was George back. He often forgets his keys. Can I help you?'

'We're investigating a homicide in the Circus, someone Mr Marlin, and maybe you, know.'

'Oh my God, you'd better come in, through there, in the front room. Can I get you anything, coffee, tea, water? But who could it be? I don't think we know anyone in the Circus. Oh, apart from Lizzie, and she's away with her man.'

'Lizzie, would be Elizabeth Westbrook?'

'Yes, George has known her for years, far more than me. I've just known her for as long as I've known George.'

There was the scrape of a key in the front door lock, the click of the lock, and before Maggie could move, George Marlin was in the room.

'George, these are two police officers looking into a murder in the Crescent. They were asking about Lizzie.'

'Lizzie? She's away, isn't she? You saw her go off with Alex. Who is it then, Officer?'

He had a commanding way of talking, thought Torrey, a manner used to command and having his word listened to. Also, he was sure he'd been drinking. Lunch, perhaps. Not that he had time for that himself.

'You say that Miss Westbrook is away, sir. Do you know where she's gone?'

'They took a taxi to a hotel, Gravetye Manor, it's in Sussex. They've only recently met, so we were so pleased that they hit it off so quickly.'

'Where does her companion live?' Deer asked. It wasn't the first question Torrey would have asked, but it would do.

'Over on Bear Flat, would you like me to write it down?'

'Yes please,' Torrey put in, 'and his surname if you know it.'

'Yes, it's Ash, he's an author. You might have heard of him. He came to one of my, err, our soirees recently, and met Lizzie there.' George wanted to get these men out of the house. He saw no reason for their being there since whoever had been murdered. It was unlikely to have been Lizzie unless Ash had committed some incredible duplicity. Sorry and all that, but we can't help. He didn't say any of this, though.

'Have you heard from either of them since they left?' Torrey asked.

'No, and I don't think we'd expect to. Two young lovers, away together for the first time in a luxury hotel. It's unlikely they're going to be in touch with us for a while, don't you think? They probably haven't even seen much of the hotel.'

Torrey was amused by the wistful expression on the woman's face. He checked himself and returned to business.

'Sorry, I didn't get your name.'

'Margaret North, people know me as Maggie, and I agree with George. I don't see how it can be Lizzie.' She looked thoughtful. 'You haven't identified her, have you?'

'No,' said Torrey, 'there are some who would say I shouldn't tell you that, but no. However, that does not mean that it isn't her. I suppose you don't know if Miss Westbrook let someone else use her house?'

'Ah, no, she said nothing,' George said.

'Now, I think that's all for now. Obviously, if you hear from either Miss Westbrook or Mr Ash, please let us know straight away.'

They walked back to the Circus. Torrey had left his car outside the building, and he motioned Deer to get in.

'Bear Flat next. While I'm driving, could you get the number of Gravetye Manor and ask them about our two lovebirds?'

'Are you thinking they didn't go, and that…'

'I'm not that far ahead. All in good time, step by step, Deer.'

'Yes, I see, sir.' He tapped away at his phone, and they heard a number ringing. He said who he was and asked about the two but met with a dead end. They would ring Bridewell first to verify who he was and then return his call.

When the return call came through, they went through the rigmarole of checking their names and numbers before telling them that the couple had only spent one night there, but the amount of luggage they had might mean that they were probably going on somewhere else. He didn't know where, but the taxi firm that had taken them there might. It took a while to find out which taxi firm had taken them, Airport Taxis, which was the best clue they had out of that encounter. Airport Taxis said that they would check and ring back.

They alighted and walked over to Alex's house. But, as they now expected, no one answered. His next-door neighbour, though, confirmed he was away, and he'd told him he was going to Tobago for two weeks. He'd met the young lady, very pleasant she'd been, but isn't everyone in Bath? They thanked him and returned to the car when the taxi firm confirmed what they had just been told. They sat there while Deer found out that Virgin flew directly to Tobago on the day concerned. After some more rigmarole, Virgin gave them the hotel as the Turtle Beach Hotel. Deer found their phone number and rang the hotel. They were seven hours behind UK time, so it was eight in the morning there. There was no concern about giving out information. The lady confirmed that Mr Ash and Miss Westbrook were indeed at the hotel and had just been in for breakfast. She'd seen them walk by a few minutes ago, and Miss Westbrook, who she'd known from previous visits, had waved to her. Would they like to speak to them? She could try their room later or send someone to look for them if they were out on the beach. Conscious of the mounting mobile cost, they thanked her and said that they would ring back later.

'Dead end then, sir,' Deer said dejectedly. That was the trouble with being young and new to this, thought Torrey. So much enthusiasm, so quickly quashed. He'd bounce back quickly, though.

'Our first one in this case. We'll have a shot at interviewing the owner by phone and see how we go. Did she let someone use her flat? Maybe someone broke in? Although, as you probably noticed, the place had a sophisticated burglar alarm, and it was deactivated.'

Deer was quiet. He probably hadn't noticed. But he'd remember that for next time.

'Back to the station. Time to write it up, and see if forensics has turned anything up. Then we make that phone call.'

A few hours later, Deer walked over to Torrey.

'Anything from forensics?'

'Early days, but they found little there. Blunt instrument but nothing more specific yet, but it hasn't been found yet. Any thoughts?'

'Not really. I think it depends on the phone call, doesn't it, and if she let someone else use the place?'

'Right, let's try them. I think we need to find somewhere quieter than here, though, and I want to record them. Let's grab a room.'

Turtle Beach reception answered their call quickly, but they couldn't raise anyone in the room.

'If you'd like to ring back in half an hour, we'll see if they're here. They may have gone out for the day.'

So they waited.

'It's odd,' Deer said. 'I can't put together what happened there. The victim was in the house with someone else. Fine, but there are no signs of them having been there any length of time, no detritus. They beat her around the head, so there's no way we'd recognise her face. No signs of blood, as far as we know, anywhere other than the bathroom. The front door left open. It's all inconsistent. Surely with that amount of damage to her head, she'd have bled onto her attacker. He would then have left traces of his exit. Then why leave the front door open? If he'd shut it when he left, the body wouldn't be discovered until the owner returned.'

'If he or, I suppose, she knew when the owner would return. Why now? Did they know the house was empty or was it just chance? I think we'll need another visit to the house. I have a theory, but I need to look around again.' Torrey played with a paper clip as he talked, which Deer found off-putting. He wanted Torrey to say more, but it looked as though he'd finished. As soon as the half-hour was up, Torrey phoned again. The hotel put them straight through to Elizabeth Westbrook, who was now waiting for them in her room. After introducing themselves, Torrey began.

'Miss Westbrook, we're investigating a death at your house in Bath. An officer was passing your house, saw the front door open, and, having checked the house for intruders, discovered a body in the bathroom.' He heard a gasp at the other end. 'We tracked you down, and understand when you went away, initially, to the Gravetye Manor Hotel. Now, I'd like to ask you several questions if I may.'

'Yes, yes, ask away. Oh, how terrible. Was it an intruder who died?'

'I'll get to that in a minute. First, does anyone other than yourself, have means of access to the premises?'

'No, not at all. I have two sets of keys, one I have here, one I have at home.'

'Do you ever lend those keys out?'

'Err, yes. If I'm with someone for a while, I some-times lend them a set, but it's not a regular thing.'

'Would you be able to provide me with a list of those please?'

'I'm not sure. My relationships have tended to be short term, and once they're over, well, that's it, I don't keep any details. There's no need to. Is there?'

'Everyone's different, but it would be helpful if you could think to see if you can remember any details, anything at all.'

'Right. Of course. I'm sorry, I don't want to seem unhelpful, but I don't think there will be much. Sorry. Sometimes I only have a first name, nothing else.'

'Whatever you can remember, then, it's all helpful. Now, were any of these friends females?'

'No. Only male friends.'

'So, just to be clear, you wouldn't expect any female friends to be in your house while you've been away, and no female friends had a key.'

There was a pause, during which Torrey looked up at Deer, raising an eyebrow.

'Sorry. I was just racking my brains. No, I don't believe so.'

Torrey mouthed to Deer. 'Lying?'

'So, are there female friends who you might not expect to be there, someone who has taken advantage of you, copied a key perhaps?'

'May I think about that, please? That might be possible. The thing is, I rarely invite people here. We go out to a café or a restaurant to see one another, so it's only really those I'm in a relationship with who come to the house. I was just thinking that maybe a year ago there might have been a couple of women who came round, but I can't remember who or why. If I mull it over, it's bound to come to me.'

'Any relatives?'

Another pause. 'Well, no. There's my sister, but she's never been to the house.'

'We don't have her down. Could I have her details please?'

'Oh, lord, I have nothing like that here. I'll look back through my phone when you've gone. There must be something there.'

'Her name?'

'Oh, Emily, oh lord, she married some time ago and I can't remember her new surname. I know, it's simple, Edwards.'

'And where does she live?'

'Glastonbury, but I don't have her address.'

'When did you last speak to her? You do talk, don't you?'

'Can you hang on for a few minutes, while I get my mobile phone out of the safe? She might be on there.' They heard her put the phone down, a male voice in the background, and then the beep of a safe being opened. 'Right, it's opening up now. Let me see, I'll try contacts first. There's only a few. If it's a man friend, they get erased when they're gone. Sorry, dear.' They smiled at one another as she pacified her current male friend. 'Oh, here we are, how silly of me, but it's not something I look up often, birthday, Christmas, that sort of thing, we're not close. Emily is now Edwin, not Edwards.' She read out an address in Glastonbury. 'Is that alright? Sorry, this has thrown me into a bit of a state, I'm not usually like this. Do you think it's her then? Is it Emily? I don't see how it could be.'

'We don't know yet. We need to make some enquiries but thank you, you've been very helpful. Now, is it possible that your sister has keys to your house?'

'Well, no, she shouldn't have. Let me think. Do you know, she did visit, just once, but it's quite a long time ago. I really can't remember whether she stayed, though. Oh, yes, she must have. They went to the theatre, her and her husband. I remember now, it annoyed me that they hadn't included me, but she said they wanted a bit of together time. She wasn't going to stay with me. She and her husband booked into a hotel, but there was some mix up, don't ask me what, and they stayed the night. I may have given them the keys so that they could get back in if they were late, or if I'd gone out.'

'Very helpful. So would they know the code for the burglar alarm?'

'Probably, if I gave them the keys, well, it would be sensible, wouldn't it? But it was so long ago, I can't be sure.'

'I understand. Now, I have your date of return from the airline. You are coming back then, I assume, no changes of plan?'

'Yes. Will I be able to go to my house? I mean…'

'I think if you could make other arrangements at first, it might be best. I don't know where we'll be with our enquiries then. Maybe at Mr Ash's house?'

Another pause, and a muttered conversation in the background. 'Yes, that's arranged. Do you want to talk to him now?'

'No, that can wait. I assume he hasn't left your side since you left your house?' Torrey kicked himself. Don't lead. Don't lead.

'That's right.'

'Then I think that's all for now. If there's anything more, we know how to get in touch with you.'

'But you didn't answer me, was it my sister?'

'I can't answer that at the moment. However, I'm sure the information that you've provided will help.'

'Can you let me know please as soon as you know?'

'I'll do my best. Thank you for your help and cooperation. Goodbye.'

Torrey sat back and looked at Deer. 'Well, what do you make of that?'

'I think it stressed her out, nothing more. I mean, you're relaxing on holiday, and hear a killer's been in your house, and then that it might be your sister who wasn't supposed to be there at all might have been killed there, blimey. It would stress me. The only thing that surprised me that she didn't suggest that she come back and support the sister's husband.'

'I was wondering if her memory was selective. Maybe she's had hundreds of men friends, I don't know, but it seemed odd, not to have any record of them. As to coming back, it seems to me they weren't too close, so I don't think it tells us anything.'

'Possibly, but not implausible. I haven't got a single thing about my past girlfriends. I don't know where they are, how to contact them or anything. I make sure I take them off social media, everything. I don't want to know who they're shagging now.

By the way, she didn't give us her sister's phone number.'

'Point taken. You're probably right. Let's call it a day and think afresh tomorrow. There's no hassle over the phone number, we'll sort that.'

'I'll get on to that, sir, we'd better talk to the sister. She might know something.'

'Off you go, then. Let me know how it goes.'

CHAPTER TWENTY-SEVEN

Lizzie and Alex walked back to the beach after the phone call, with a book and laptop in their respective hands. Lizzie was close to tears. She had cried and cried after the phone call, but didn't want to talk much.

'How can I explain what she was? I had to say, sister. I didn't know what else to say,' she chastised herself.

'Does she have your DNA then?'

'I don't know. I know nothing about that.'

'Look, Lizzie, I'm on your side, OK? Together we need to think out how this is going to play out. First, I need to understand more about the concept of **multis**. Then I can help plan a way forward with you.'

'You'll never understand. This is a female thing, Alex. A very female thing. I don't think I can explain it to you.'

'Alright, Lizzie, I don't know what's going on, I just don't have enough information. So, we can just get on with our holiday, and deal with the police when we get back, or we can try to work out something together. The choice is up to you, really.'

But Lizzie didn't speak. They lay down on their sunbeds and she lay there looking out at the horizon. Alex sighed, and, opening his laptop, typed.

The solicitor rang the doorbell while Jayne hopped from foot to foot anxiously. Meeting her dad's partner was daunting. He'd never shared her with Jayne. But then, how could he? He'd been living a double life. This woman had been looking after him while his wife was at Jayne's home, and continued living with her when his wife had left, and they divorced.

The door opened and Jayne's jaw dropped. How had her dad attracted a woman like this? She was stunning, and she had dressed to impress, at least to impress a man. A very low-cut top, and a skirt that wasn't much more than a pelmet, showed an enormous expanse of flesh. Her breasts weren't too large, but definitely on display, as were her long and shapely legs, supported by several inches of heel, which made her taller than Jayne. Long blond hair streamed down over her shoulders.

'Hello there, come in. I'm looking forward to meeting Jayne. Oh, there you are.' She came forward and clasped Jayne to her chest, while Jayne wondered about the possibility of suffocation. She led them into the house, a 1930s mock-Tudor detached, and far better than the one Jayne lived in. She left them in the front room while she made drinks.

Jayne looked around. There were photographs of her dad and this woman at the seaside in some hot country, given the number of palm trees. The ornaments on the mantlepiece were cheap souvenirs, and the furniture was new as well, but didn't look well built. Maybe it was all her dad could afford. What with running two families. She was teetering back into the room now, bearing a tray of drinks and biscuits.

'Best to get you sorted, since you've come such a long way. There's tea for you,' she said, handing a cup to the solicitor, 'and orange squash for you,' she handed a glass to Jayne, who felt offended at not being given a choice.

'Now, Mr Willowby, Jason, you're here to tell me how much I get from my dear departed, aren't you?'

Jayne's mouth would have dropped if she'd let it. The cheek of the woman.

'Yes, I suppose I am, Mrs Sharp. I do have the will here, and it all appears to be in order.'

'So?'

'Well, of course, Jayne here is his sole surviving relative, and, at her father's direction, inherits.'

'Yes, but what?'

'Everything.'

There was silence. Some silences are peaceful, leading to nothing more than the call of a bird, or a fish breaking water. This was the prelude to thunder.

'What do you mean, everything?'

'Exactly that. Everything he owned now belongs to his daughter. Although you may stay here as long as you want to. He said that.'

'But that cannot be. I was living with him, I loved him, I… No, no, you're wrong. I cannot accept what you are saying. I will get my own firm of solicitors and they will tell you that you are wrong. I was with him, so it's only right and proper that I inherit. What was his is now mine. With,' she smiled a sort of curled up smile at Jayne, 'a dispensation for his dear daughter, of course.'

Jayne wondered if this, to her mind, was about ten pounds.

'I'm sorry you feel like that, Mrs Sharp. To my mind, you are just incurring unnecessary expense, but of course, you are free to do as you feel best. Given the circumstances, I think we had better leave and probate will take its course. I understand you are married to Mr Sharp and have a joint interest in what was your joint home. Because of that, I think you will find, when you consult your solicitor, that you may have to leave this house and return to your own. If that is the case, we will give you due notice when to vacate this property.'

Diana Sharp stood up, puffed her chest out, and waved at the door. She didn't say a word. Didn't say goodbye, just slammed the door after them.

'I shouldn't say this, Jayne, but I didn't like her at all. I wasn't going to say anything about her husband if she'd been pleasant and reasonable, but I mean, how could I hold back? We will proceed as fast as we can with probate, which will be based on full possession of the property you have just seen, and *your home. I can't say how long it will take if she finds a solicitor who tries to be obstructive, but we will do our best.'*

'Thank you, Mr Willowby, that's very kind of you. I thought you handled her well.' They looked at one another and then collapsed in laughter.

'I'm sorry, Jayne, that's very unprofessional of me. But justified, I fear.'

Alex looked up, but Lizzie was still looking towards the distant horizon. Who knew what images appeared before her? What stories she might weave, or what the truth of the situation was. Alex shook his head and went on typing.

They talked on the way back, about how Jayne was going to manage, about asking the bank to release money for her keep, and about Jayne's future. She thought he was very practical and so keen to help. She'd encountered no one like that before, but maybe that was just because he was being paid to do it.

'What will happen next is that I will receive letters from the places where he has money confirming the amount and the account details. There will be a problem valuing the property we have just seen, but I can ask three estate agents to provide their estimates, and that will do for now. Tax is payable on the actual amount realised, not the estimates. Then I'll need another three estimates for the house you're living in.'

'Does that mean I must leave?'

'Not at all. We just need to find out how much it's worth for the taxman. I will apply to have some money released for you, but that's just for your day-to-day expenses.'

He left her at the station, and she waited for the next train. So much was happening she was losing track of it, and she didn't dare count on inheriting anything, let alone everything her father had. That was just too much to think about. By the time she reached home it was going to be late in the evening, with no time to do anything except fall into bed, but tomorrow she needed a plan. Life would not stop just because her father had died. Yes, a plan was needed.

'I fancy a drink.' Lizzie was sitting up, looking at him. He ran to the room to put the laptop away, having saved his work to the cloud. At least this place had good internet. By the time he got back to the sunbeds Lizzie had gone, and he saw her over at the bar talking to a man there. He took his time and sidled up to them.

'Oh, and this is Alex,' she said, as he approached, 'who's come with me.'

It was interesting, he thought, how much words can convey. Not a boyfriend, or anything that showed any commitment. But what was he expecting? They'd only known one another for what, a few days? It just seemed longer.

'Hi, I'm Dave, and I'm not with anyone.' The newcomer laughed. He was what Alex in his writing would call well built. Someone who could without a doubt look after himself.

Was it Alex's imagination, or was there a definite invitation being put Lizzie's way?

'Hi, have you been here long?' he asked.

'Nah, flew in today. Great place though, I love it here.'

'You've been here before then?'

'Oh, Alex, would you be a dear and fetch my wrap for me, it's colder up here.'

He did as he was asked, leaving the two of them together. Lizzie hadn't exactly been coy with men, and if they'd both been here before, then it didn't take a scientist to put two and two together.

He was certain when he returned to the bar with her wrap to find them gone.

CHAPTER TWENTY-EIGHT

Jayne woke to a rainy day and a headache. She took her time getting up, having a few cornflakes and milk for breakfast, followed by some toast. There was a vague memory of needing to do some work for school, but she couldn't remember. It was lonely in the house now, without even the possibility of her father calling. The postman only brought bills, and she put an elastic band that he had dropped outside her door around them, ready to send to Mr Willowby. What else was there that could she do now? Perhaps she ought to search for a job, but she did not know what she'd be able to do.

She looked around her bedroom, then wandered into her parents' bedroom. She'd never slept there, never wanted to. Opening a wardrobe door, she saw the remnants of her father's occupation. Her mother had stripped out all her stuff when she left. He had just a few old shirts, a suit, and a couple of tweed jackets that he'd never worn. She pulled them all down, checked the pockets, and made a heap on the floor. Moving from cupboard to cupboard, drawer to drawer, she removed every vestige of her father.

The haul wasn't great, but then how often had he been there? She fetched a roll of bin bags from the kitchen and filled four. Then to the bathroom. His shaver, toothpaste, small indications that he had once existed, thrown into a bag.

Then she came to what estate agents referred to somewhat optimistically as the third bedroom. It was hardly big enough for a bed and was where both parents had chucked anything that they didn't want but didn't want to throw out. It was a tip. She left it and walked downstairs, dragging two of the filled bags behind her.

The back room was where her father had once sat and read. She looked into the glass-fronted bookcase, shrugged, and left the books there. Maybe one day. That left only the kitchen and the small study. The kitchen had little in it since her mother had gone, just the food she needed for herself, so just the study to look in. This was where her father had once worked. His home office. She went back upstairs, brought down the two remaining filled bin bags and the roll of bags and set about the study. Most of it was out-of-date papers, work stuff, and bills. His desk drawer yielded a roll of banknotes. Ninety pounds, she counted, remembering that he liked to keep some cash for tipping tradespeople. Ninety pounds. A sign of when life had been different. Other than that, nothing was exciting apart from two small keys and a Yale key on a plain wire keyring. But she had no idea what they opened.

She wondered whether to give the clothes to charity, but the effort of getting the bags to the local Oxfam was beyond her, so she stuffed them into the council wheelie bin, and piled those that wouldn't fit next to it. There was a feeling of satisfaction about clearing the place out. It was beginning to feel like hers now, not a memorial to past times. Heartened, she went back into the house. It was going to get the biggest cleaning of its life.

Alex finished typing and looked up. He was back on the sunbed, but without Lizzie. He hadn't seen her or Dave at all, but he didn't doubt what they were doing. There was nothing for it but to get on with life. He got up, and took his laptop over to the bar, downed a gin and tonic, and got another. There was no one else there, and the barman was cleaning the place, so he walked back to the beach. It felt different without someone to share it with. He nodded to a couple of women walking towards him, but received little back, so he returned to the sunbed, and Jayne.

House cleaned and emptied of detritus. There was only one thing left to do, tackle the little bedroom upstairs. She hesitated and then ran up the stairs with her roll of bags. Here she found holiday clothes, suntan lotions, women's magazines, and old clothes her mother had discarded. Bagged. Two family photograph albums, which she spent some time browsing before putting aside, but toys she had long forgotten but brought back happier memories, were bagged. Then she came to what optimistically someone might call a strongbox. A locked metal box that wouldn't have survived the most unenthusiastic burglars' attempts to open it, although it would be easier just to carry it away. Thinking of the small keys she had found, she ran down to fetch them. The first wouldn't fit, but the second, with a bit of effort, yielded the contents to her.

It was just a load of papers, her passport, now out of date, which she didn't remember existing, birth certificates for her and her parents, old bank books, premium bond certificates in her name, and the deeds to the house she was in, and what looked like another property as well. She tried to make sense of it. It looked as though it was a shop in Bath, with a flat over it. There was no way her parents could have afforded something like that. Why hadn't they sold it when they split up? A set of papers attached to the deeds provided an answer. The property was partly occupied. The shop was now a café, and it looked as though its proprietor paid rent to her father. She wondered if her mother knew about it and if they had included it in the divorce settlement, but who cared, maybe it was hers now. She took out her mobile phone to ring Mr Willowby but had second thoughts and instead had a bath to get rid of the house's grime.

There was a sound of someone behind him and he optimistically thought might be Lizzie, although he dreaded the thought of her coming back. He wasn't sure he could face her. He should have understood from the start what she was like, the succession of short-lived boyfriends, her gay abandonment of one thing, one person, for the next. But it had been heady while it lasted. He twisted around to find an attractively slim woman looking over his shoulder. She gave a start as she realised that he'd seen her.

'Oh, sorry, I was being nosey. I'm terrible like that. I see someone doing something interesting, and I want to know what. I'm Penny.' She held out a slim hand, attached to a slim arm which led to a small, rounded face, curtained by short black hair. She was wearing a bikini on a well-tanned, nut-brown body.

'That's alright,' he answered. It wasn't his first thought. But then she was there, and Lizzie wasn't. 'Been here long?'

'Not long, just days, but there's only so much a girl can do on her own here. I'm making my way around the Caribbean, next stop Trinny.'

'Yes, it's not a place to be on your own, is it? I was with someone, but they've decided to sleep elsewhere. Where are you from?'

'London. Sorry to hear about your girlfriend, did you have a row? Oh, there's me again, it's not anything to do with me.'

'That's alright, we haven't been together long, and it seems she likes to swap around.'

'Wow, I couldn't do that. I just couldn't. I was with my ex for ages, and it was only when he took up a job in America that we split. I'm a homegirl, I didn't fancy moving. He asked me though, but still. Anyway, I was going for a swim when I saw you. Coming in?'

'I'll just stow the laptop and I'll join you.'

It was strange to find someone to share things with so quickly, he thought as he walked to the room. In all his years, he'd not done that. Maybe he was a boring, homely sort who didn't like change. His mind went back to the first meeting with Lizzie. It had all been about that other woman, Jayne, and talk of **aware**. Out here it was a world away, and he hadn't even thought of scanning people to see if they were **aware** or not. Maybe it didn't exist here. He locked up and went back to the beach to see Penny, arm raised, standing in the sea.

'Are you a writer?' she asked.

'Yes, I've had a few books published.'

'So, what's your name then? I might have heard of you.'

'Alex, Alex Ash.'

'Sorry, doesn't ring a bell, but then I'm into romances. When I'm not reading science journal stuff, but that gets boring after a while.'

'Is that your job, then?'

'I was in a lab, but I wanted to work from home, so now I read articles, and gut them for anything interesting. My precise goes to a company that publishes my work to those who haven't got the time to read all the articles. It means I can work anywhere, like you, I guess. What are you writing about at the moment?'

He struggled to answer. 'It's odd. I feel I have to write the story of a girl, but I don't know why. It's not the way I usually work, there's been no research, no plan, I just felt I had to do it, and it seems to write itself.'

'How odd. Are you enjoying writing it though?'

He had to think about that. 'I'm not sure. You see, I feel compelled to write it rather than wanting to write. It's different, almost as though it's beyond my control.'

'That's from a play. There was a woman who did all sorts of awful things while saying "it's beyond my control". Maybe your last girlfriend was like that?'

'*Liaisons Dangereuses*. I suppose there could be similarities.'

'People come here for the sex, you know, although usually, it's women and with the locals.'

'You?' Why did he ask that? It was asking for trouble.

She giggled and tapped his arm, recalling Lizzie. 'No, silly, I wanted the warmth, the sun and the sea, and this place has got it all, hasn't it?'

'Yes, it's good to get away from the rain, although I feel as though I'll get bored with sitting around after a few days.'

'We could go out. That's the trouble with all-inclusive hotels, they're like plush prisons and the outside world becomes something frightening that you don't want to venture into.' She looked up at him.

'I think I've got a boat booked tomorrow. It's something Lizzie booked, but I suspect she'll have forgotten about it. Would you like that?'

'Ooh, where does it go?'

'Some coves up the coast, they're supposed to be good for snorkelling.'

'I'd love to. I've got my snorkel, but it's still in my case, I hadn't even thought about it. If I'm honest, all I've done is work. Just a different location.'

'I'll give the guy a ring to see if Lizzie's said anything to him. Maybe sort out a different rendezvous so we won't be embarrassed if she's still going with her new friend.'

'That's thoughtful. Thank you. Come on, let's swim, my back's getting hot.'

They swam the coastline in comfortable silence, each lost in their thoughts. He, thinking how swiftly things had changed, she about an article she'd been reading, and how she could condense it. Universes moving in parallel in the same sea.

They'd done several lengths of the beach when she came out of her thoughts, and abruptly asked, 'Fancy a screw?'

He did a double-take. Did she really say that? Then, after a mental shrug of his shoulders, he answered. 'OK then, your place or mine?'

'It had better be mine in case your ex makes a sudden return.'

'I've got some condoms in the room.'

'OK, I'll wait here.'

He waded up to the beach and ran to the room. When he got there, he found that all Lizzie's thing had gone, clothes, cosmetics, even her case. It swept away any guilt he might have had as he grabbed a couple of condoms and ran back.

She wasn't where he'd left her, and he had a moment of panic before hearing her call out. She was standing on her room terrace, smoking a roll-up. He trotted over, and she offered the smoke to him.

'You like? It's the life out here, isn't it?'

He took a drag and handed it back. Yes, it was the local life, and he ought to just relax into it. He looked at her, standing there in front of him, and reached for her.

Later, they sat out on her terrace, beers in hand. She was quieter than Lizzie, who went about her sex with a zeal and athleticism he could never match, assuming positions that frankly he didn't see the point of. Penny was more self-contained, as though holding back, just in case. But in case of what? With Lizzie, you got her whole attention, if only for the act. With Penny, it was different. It felt as though she was thinking about something else all the time. She seemed to enjoy it, though, although he didn't dare ask.

As though reading his thoughts, she said, 'That was lovely. I needed it. We do, don't we, us humans, we need to have sex every so often just to feel calmer, not so on edge, to reset the world and move on. It's odd but necessary.'

'Yes, you're right, and I enjoyed it, too. You're lovely.'

She turned to smile at him. Not the tight open-eyed grin that Lizzie would do, but a soft happy open smile. How different people are.

CHAPTER TWENTY-NINE

It was raining in London as Torrey and Deer walked around the house in the Circus. Torrey wanted a close look at the garden. He'd neglected it before, and yet maybe it held the key to what had happened. They walked along the boundary first.

'Anyone could get out or in here, it's an easy climb over the wall.'

Deer walked over to a gate set into the stone wall. Using a handkerchief, he twisted the handle. It opened. They stepped out into an alleyway and walked along it to find a street of parked cars.

'Anyone could have parked here and then walked into the garden,' Deer commented.

'Or the other way around,' Torrey said thoughtfully.

They walked back and through the gate. 'Forensics must have checked the gate,' Torrey said, almost to himself.

'See if there's any CCTV, as well. Some of these places look as though they'd use it, and much of it is so small these days, we'd not see it.' Torrey was looking around and up at the building. 'It doesn't look as though she had any and we haven't seen a monitor.'

'They go to a phone or computer these days, sir. No need for a monitor. We'd need to have a look at the owner's phone.'

'Mmm, her again. Let's check the windows.'

They walked back through the garden, Torrey looking up, as though expecting a rope to be dangling down. They reached the back wall of the house, but the window was too high for Torrey to reach. He looked around at the ground.

'Interesting,' he said. 'Let's look inside.'

Once inside, he made straight for the ground-floor window overlooking the garden.

'Forensics have finished in here, haven't they?'

'Yes, they're all done.'

He walked to the window and tried the handle. It locked the window. He moved it back and tugged at the window's edge. It opened.

'So, they left the window open. A coincidence, or a deliberate act? Interesting, don't you think?'

Torrey was looking all around the window. 'It's not alarmed. The other windows have movement sensors on them.'

'Well, curiouser, and curiouser. Let's see, where's the movement sensor in this room?'

They looked but couldn't find one, but a sensor was covering the hall that led towards the room.

'I suppose it makes a kind of sense. Any burglar is going to have to go through the hall if they're going through the house. What have we got here, then? An open window. But anyone coming in or going out would have triggered the alarm. However, the alarm wasn't on. Why? Because the front door was open. Why? Someone moved the bits and pieces under the window at the back, so it would be easy to drop down and leave by the garden gate. One moment, I've had a thought.'

He almost ran back through the house, and outside, where he ran around looking. He spied a garden outbuilding and trotted over to it. He tried the door. It was locked, but the building had clear windows he could peer through. Satisfied, he stood looking at the house. 'I wonder?' he said and then turned to Deer. 'I think it's time we focused more on the sister. The local station wasn't able to rouse anyone.'

'Glastonbury, wasn't it, sir?'

'Been there before?'

'Yes. It was an interestingly different experience.'

'Right, yes, I know what you mean. Call them, see if she's there, or her husband.'

There was no answer, so they set off on the hour's drive, having let the local station know what they were doing.

The rain was still falling as they drove down a street of neat brick-built terraced houses. This was a world away from the Circus. Deer knocked at the door of number twenty-eight. They waited in vain.

'Let's find something to eat in town and come back later. They're probably at work. Or at least one of them will be. If we don't get an answer this evening, then we'll have to get the local station to gain entry forcibly.'

In Bath, Jayne felt so tired. She had tramped around the city, but nothing occurred to her, nothing that showed a way to a future. It was amazing how fast things could change. One moment she was happily working with a secure future, and the next out of work wandering the streets. They might be attractive streets, with beautiful architecture, but that soon palled if you had no job and no money.

'How much, love?'

She swivelled round to see an older bloke looking at her. Had she misheard?

'Eh?'

'How much? You know.'

'I don't know, so piss off.'

He gave her a filthy look and went away. Was she at that level now? Mind you, she'd heard it paid well. No, never, she wasn't going down that route, whatever happened. She was hastening back home when she heard a shout. Wondering whether she was doing the right thing, she looked around.

'Hi, stranger!' There was Johnnie, a smile on his face. She breathed a sigh of relief. But would he fancy an out of work shop girl?

'Hi, Johnnie, how are you?' Their one evening had ended by her front door with a polite kiss on the cheek. Nothing else. No apparent expectation of anything else.

'I tried ringing, but you didn't pick up, so I was coming to see if you wanted to go out.'

'Why not? Come on, it's been a sod awful day, and I'd love that. Where shall we go?'

A walk across town and they came to a little French restaurant that Johnnie knew. A glance through the menu, and she was happy. The food she fancied, and the prices weren't too bad either. She could relax.

'So,' he said, 'what's been so crappy about today?'

She nearly cried.

In Glastonbury, Torrey was looking concerned. There was still no answer at number twenty-eight. He called the local station. Half an hour later, a van parked nearby and two uniforms walked up. They asked for identification, and then knocked on the next-door houses, but no one had seen the occupants of twenty-eight, although there was no surprise that the lady of the house was away. She was often absent, and her neighbours had many theories as to why, which kept them busy for a while.

They took a ram to the door and entered. It was clear immediately that something was wrong. The smell was overwhelming. He was in the kitchen. Head stove in, but unlike the woman in Bath, recognisable. They called for backup and forensics from the station. Once they'd been, they walked around the house. It was a modest house, its occupants living modestly as well. They talked to the one neighbour who was in. The male occupant of number twenty-eight was an accountant at a local company and his wife a yoga and Pilates teacher. She'd once told them that she had classes all over the country, and they knew she was frequently absent.

Back in the house, bank statements laying on the dining room table showed a modest balance, and they paid their credit cards in full each month. Other than that, there was little to find. An ordinary couple. An extraordinary end.

Jayne and Johnnie walked over the Pulteney Bridge. The meal had been great; the wine had made them tipsy, and Johnnie had paid. He had been sympathetic, although she might not have told him the whole truth. He had made plans for her to set her on her way to a new job. She'd never thought of getting more qualifications and wasn't sure how realistic that was, but it sounded sensible, and sensible was what she needed to be now. They walked around the corner to look down at the weir, the great sweep of water churning down the river, and then turned away to the abbey, and through the city back to Jayne's flat. She went to kiss him goodnight, but it quickly became more.

'Come on, let's go in,' she said, slightly out of breath. 'It's warmer.' She unlocked the door and led him up the stairs.

CHAPTER THIRTY

They sat watching from Penny's terrace as the sun dropped into the sea, and then, so quickly, darkness fell. The lights came on to show a quiet, studious couple, both reading. Alex enjoyed her quietness. Lizzie was incredible, but in small doses, which might be why she swopped partners so often. To keep up the pace, she had to have new conquests or at least a swop of partners. Penny was her opposite. He hadn't been into her past; it hadn't seemed necessary; he was simply content to be with her. He was still marvelling that he'd been with three women in as many weeks, making his previous life appear monastic. They decided against eating in the restaurant and took room service instead. It seemed the best option, since Alex did not know what Lizzie was doing. Or to put it another way, he was sure what she was doing; it was whether she needed a break for fuel.

'Have you heard of **awareness**,' he asked, hoping it didn't produce an unsympathetic response.

'Yes, of course, we both are, didn't you realise?'

He just looked at her. Out here he hadn't picked up anything, never even considered…

'Wow.' Was all he could summon up? She laughed a natural laugh, a supportive, fun laugh, joining his amazement.

'Didn't you realise? It's why I stopped next to you. I was curious. I hadn't picked up on anyone else out here, and then, bingo, up you pop.'

'Do you know, I was thinking it was all a con, that people had been pranking me or something. Yet I know things have happened to me I couldn't explain any other way. You're a godsend, you really are.'

She was still smiling at him, and he felt strangely uplifted by it. She looked as though she cared, and it was a long time since anyone had looked at him like that.

'So, the question is, where do we go from here?'

She laughed again. 'Wherever life takes us, and tomorrow I believe it takes us on a boat ride.'

'Oh shit! I forgot to get the guy to change the pickup location.'

'Then, whatever happens, we deal with it. We're on holiday, just chill.'

'He's going to be here at eight-thirty, so we'd better go to breakfast early.'

'In which case, dare I suggest that your ex-friend is unlikely to be up, so no worries.'

'You're right.' He smiled across at her, reached for her hand, and nodded. Everything was going to be alright. Then he thought about the police and the murder. Well, that didn't concern him now, did it?

They were standing together with their snorkels and waterproof bags containing spare clothing and towels when the boat arrived, doing a doughnut to impress them, or just for the driver's amusement. Shane, their captain, was on his own. The boat seated eight when it was full, so with just two of them, they could spread out. In no time they were off, racing out into the bay, looking back to see the hotel shrink, and the forested hills above dwarf it. As soon as they hit the waves outside the bay it felt exciting, cutting through the waves, looking up at Plymouth and its sports stadium. After they had passed that Shane started swinging into more sheltered spots, shouting out the names of bays and back bays as they went. Then into the waves again.

'There were dolphins here yesterday,' he said, 'so we might be lucky. A pod of twenty or more, and little ones.'

They kept looking until, dolphinless, they came into a large wide bay.

'First stop, Cotton Bay. I'll drop anchor near to the shore, and you can either swim off the boat or wade in. See where the rocks come out on your left. If you swim along there, you'll see plenty of fish. And then to our right, out in the bay, there is a reef. You can't see it, but if you go halfway out by the rocks, and then swim across the bay, you can't miss it. But don't worry, I'll be coming in with you.'

Masks cleaned, defogger applied, and then washed out again. They shuffled to the stern of the boat, where there was a diving platform, and Shane pulled out a set of steps to assist them. Penny dropped expertly in backwards off the side, while Alex, admiring her technique, used the steps. Shane swam ahead, showing them all the fresh fish and an octopus. They completed the rock section and Alex, looking up for a moment. He found they had left the cove and were in rougher water, close to the rocks at its entrance. Another boat was approaching fast from the direction they had come. Treading water, he watched as a sharp-nosed speedboat sped past on its way up the island. He recognised the two passengers, sitting close together at the back of the boat. He was, he found, a little sad, as he returned to the underwater world. Lizzie had made other arrangements for her and her latest man.

Lizzie was enjoying herself as they swept along the coast, cutting through the waves, looking up at the tropical forest of the island. They saw a few isolated hotels, were told where the Queen's photographer, Norman Parkinson, once lived, and numerous bays and coves with no one in them. She had headed them for a little beach she knew as the pink beach. It was off the small town of Charlottesville and comprised a hundred yards of pink coral beach that could only be reached from the sea, and then only with caution. The coral sweeping out from the beach was close to the surface, and the sun had bleached much of it, or boat propellers had cut into it, but once in the water, it was going to be like visiting a fish village. She'd seen the boat she had been planning to go on in

Cotton Bay, although there was no sign of Alex. She hoped he was having a good time. He was a decent bloke, too decent. Dave? Well, there was unfinished business there, and it needed sorting.

Kitted up, they went into the water carefully. With so much coral so close it would be easy to cut yourself, and coral scratches and cuts took a while to heal. She headed out to the edge of the reef, sensing that Dave was following. She checked, and he came in beside her. It was then that she saw them. Barracudas. Not a danger, just menacing, with their large jaws, a show of teeth, and sleek bodies. It looked as though they were ringing the reef, ready for mealtime.

She reached out to Dave, but hit him on the head. The next moment she was being pressed down under the water. She struggled, trying to squirm her way free, but her snorkel pipe was being held under the water. She couldn't breathe. She felt her legs hit the coral as the pressure increased. Then, as suddenly as it had begun, it stopped. She felt muscular arms hold her up and her mask taken off. She took deep breaths, so relieved that she could take in air again, and she looked up into the face of their guide. She had never been so grateful to see anyone, and hugged him tightly. She didn't even think about Dave until they got back into the boat. He was there. Sitting calmly.

'You alright?' he said. 'Sorry, I'm not strong in the water, so I couldn't help.'

She looked at him, long and hard as their guide put some ointment on her wounds. They were soon on their way back to the hotel, and no one was talking.

After Cotton Bay, Alex and Penny went along the coast to Emerald Bay, where Shane hitched up to a white buoy in the middle of the cove, and they swam around its edges. This time Shane stayed on the boat, as the two of them watched a shoal of hundreds of squid hanging in the air, unmoved by their presence. An hour later, and they were back on the boat and heading back to the hotel for a late lunch.

It was in the evening that they heard the news. Lizzie and Dave were in Scarborough hospital. But there were no other details.

'I saw them,' he told Lizzie, 'they were in a speedboat going past Cotton Bay while we were snorkelling there.'

'Oh, you didn't say. Was it just the two of them?'

'Yes, with a driver, of course.'

'Oh.' She went quiet.

'I wonder what went on. Maybe the boat had an accident.'

They spent a quiet afternoon sunbathing and swimming, enjoyed their evening meal, and avoided the evening karaoke, to stroll the beach. The moon, full when the mother turtle had been laying, was waxing, but still bright, and the stars were so numerous that they just stood and stared. Hand in hand, they went back to Penny's place for the night.

The next morning, Alex dropped into his room on the way to breakfast with Penny. He stood in the doorway in surprise. Lizzie's things were back. Clothes all over the bed, which had been slept in, cosmetics scattered all over the dressing table, her case near the door. He swore, shut the door, and hastened out.

'What's the matter,' Penny asked, looking up at him anxiously.

'She's back. She's taken over the whole room. It's a tip in there.'

She put an arm around his waist. 'It's alright, you can stay at mine. Either bring your stuff down or just collect it when we leave.'

He looked at her, puzzled. 'We leave? I thought you were staying on after me?'

'No, you've got the wrong idea. I'm here at the same time as you. We're on the same flights. Would you mind talking to Virgin and see if you can change the seating? I feel it would be better if we sat together.'

'I'll do that from reception. Have you got your ticket handy?'

A quarter of an hour later, with Penny hopping up and down eager for breakfast, he walked over to her, smiling.

'All done. That was interesting. Lizzie had already changed the seats, so I was sitting with some unknown guy. She and David Makepeace are together now. She'd charged my credit card with his first-class fare because I'd booked the flights. They'd just added it on. I've let them know. They say it shouldn't have happened, and they'll be contacting Dave because they have his details, but not Lizzie's. He'll be in for a shock. I've swapped us over and paid the extra. You're in first class with me now.'

'Since I met you, I seem to be in for all sorts of surprises.' She reached up to pull his face down to her and kissed him. 'That's a thank you for the upgrade. It might be an interesting flight back though.'

'I wonder what happened.'

'It'll probably be the talk of the restaurant. Come on, I'm hungry.'

In the breakfast restaurant, which was next to the beach and close to the fishermen's building, they settled down to eat and watch the fishermen. They were pulling their net in. Alex had seen them take it out on another day, tying one end to a stake on the beach, and the row out in a large arc around almost half of the bay, to return to a point a couple of hundred yards up the beach from where they'd started. Now people were lending a hand to pull the net in, even tourists. There must be twenty people pulling with varying degrees of effort on both ends of the net as it came in. Seagulls dived around the net or perched nearby, and pelicans sat waiting their turn. Large brown birds swooped overhead.

'Boobies,' Penny said, straight-faced.

'Eh?'

'Brown Boobies. The birds, silly.'

The catch was landed and two men divided it up. The bulk was going into plastic containers, which were carried up to a truck, and tipped in the back of it. People were taking a fish or three, checking with the men, and then walking off with them. Favours being repaid or gained, they guessed. They threw some fish back into the sea to the delight of the noisy birds who swooped down onto them. Gradually it all calmed down, and it left only a few fishermen to sort out the net. Alex had been so busy watching that he hadn't noticed that Penny had slipped away and was now deep in conversation with a couple at another table. She returned, smiling.

'Apparently, Lizzie returned with a lot of coral cuts and scratches, and she and Dave aren't talking, which explains why she's back in your room. It's going to be interesting because I'm sure she'll try to swop the seat on the plane back now so she'd sit with you.'

'That's alright. I asked the airline to ensure that she can't change the seats again, and definitely can't do anything that affects my card.'

'What do you fancy doing today? To be honest, I'd rather not be around if Lizzie is likely to be on the warpath after you. Fancy hiring a car or a jeep, or something?'

'Sounds good to me. I'd prefer a car because it'll have air-con. I got caught before with that one, boiling hot day in an open jeep, and all you got was more hot air.'

'Great, we're of a mind then, Alex. Let's see what reception can do.'

CHAPTER THIRTY-ONE

Torrey sat looking at a list of Pilates and yoga courses that Emily Edwin had undertaken and planned, which was pinned to a noticeboard in the kitchen. They'd gone backwards to check with venues she had been to. Just in case they held a clue. But there was nothing. She had not attended any of the bookings. Not one. So, what was the list for? To fool her partner while she went somewhere else? With someone else? The CCTV from around all around the Circus was still being retrieved, and he was waiting for the results. The images were often automatically sent images to a cloud service, which might be great if they could get access to them quickly, but if the owner of the account didn't give up their password, then they had to apply for access, often to another country.

What had he missed? There had to be something. He ran through events in his mind; the alarm not on, the window that was unlocked and easy to push open, the access from the garden door, and the ladder in the outbuilding. Then there was Elizabeth Westbrook's absence in Tobago with the author Alex Ash.

She'd met him just a few days before, Marlin had said. Given the confirmed time of death, Westbrook was probably in a hotel in Sussex when the murder happened. So, who? The cameras might help with that, and since they were his chief hope now, he would have to wait.

Jayne had watched as Johnnie dressed and left for work, envious of his enthusiasm, and the simple fact that he had a job and a steady income. It was now afternoon. She'd wasted the best part of the day in self-recrimination and depression, so she had got no further in changing her life. But she had to do something, so with an effort, she levered herself out of the too-cosy bed and off to the shower. Not long afterwards she was sitting in the café downstairs, laptop out, tapping away, looking for a job. The café's owner gave a cheeky look at the screen over her shoulder as she brought her coffee to her.

'Had enough of shoes?' she asked.

'They had enough of me. They sacked me. But I need something so I can afford my food.'

'Oh, Jayne, why didn't you say, one of my people has just left so you can have a job here. If you want it, that is. I won't mind if you jack it in as soon as you find something better. It's the least I can do.'

'Really? Do you mean it? You're an absolute wonder,' she stood up and gave her a massive hug, 'that's so kind of you.'

'Careful, just remember that I probably can't afford the sort of wages you've been getting. I'm just a poor café owner with a lease to pay, remember.'

Jayne laughed. 'Oh, get you. I honestly don't know what to say, but just thank you so much. When can I start?'

'Now, if you like. I mean, I know you can work the machine and even do the swirly patterns on the cappuccinos because you were lovely and stepped in when I was ill one weekend, so you're ahead of most people. Here, have an apron, and I'll go sort the stock and the croissant oven.'

Jayne donned the apron with its café logo and, putting her laptop behind the counter, walked around the tables clearing and asking the punters if they wanted anything else. Then, having fulfilled their wishes, taken some money, and added beans to the coffee machine, she took a moment to herself. One door closes and another opens. Who had said that? Not that it mattered, it had just happened, and here she already felt happier than she had ever been in the shoe shop. Add to that, Johnnie seemed keen, and he was considerate, too. Life might be looking up. She saw a customer raise their hand and hastened over to her. Work could be fun.

Penny and Alex had a great day and returned in the dark to the hotel. They had driven to the rainforest where they had walked, and then to the Rainbow Falls, where they swam in the cool, fresh water. Then to the Argyll Falls, where a ranger accompanied them on the trail to the falls, hopping over stepping-stones until they saw the three levels of the falls. They swam in the bottom pool, then walked up to the top where Alex stood braced against the falling water. Not that he could do that for long. They continued their journey to the other end of the island, and Speyside for lunch up in Jemma's Kitchen tree restaurant, looking out at Goat Island, and Little Tobago.

'The guidebook says that Little Tobago is a bird sanctuary. Snorkelling's not recommended here unless you take a boat out to Angel reef between the islands. The current is too strong otherwise. There's a glass-bottom boat and they run tours, though. We won't have time today, but we could always come back,' Alex said as they tucked into their lobster.

'I'm stuffed already, and I haven't had pudding yet.' Penny laughed. 'I think a rain check on any other activity, I wouldn't make it.'

'Coffee, then? We can wend our way back afterwards. We could go the long way via Charlottesville or go back the way we came.'

Penny hesitated before saying, 'Would you mind if we went to Charlottesville? I've heard it's really lovely there. Is that alright? I know it's a lot of driving for you. I can drive if you want.'

'Sure, Charlottesville it is. Don't worry about the driving, I don't exactly have much to do tomorrow.'

According to Alex's phone, the journey from Speyside to Charlottesville would take fifteen minutes. It lied. It took more than double that. When they got there, Penny surprised Alex because she wanted to wander down by the fishermen. He followed slowly, looking out to sea as she walked over to the men who were sitting around a row of upturned boats. She appeared to be in deep conversation with them, and then she walked to some more before coming back to him.

'Well, that was interesting,' she said when she returned.

'What was?'

'I was asking if they knew what happened out near the reef yesterday. It was a bit of a longshot because you can't even see it from here, but I found two boats that were out there at the same time as our friends.'

'And?'

'Well, it's the talk of the place, mainly because the guy who owns the boat Lizzie and Dave were on used to live here.'

'So? Come on, I can't wait.'

'Basically, the skipper thinks that one of them attacked the other, but they weren't talking about it.'

'So, who attacked whom?'

'Ooh, whom, who's a writer then?'

'Penny. Stop it.'

'They don't know. The skipper saw some thrashing around, and he thought Dave was on top, but he wasn't sure. However, the fishermen were. They were cruising back to shore, saw the thrashing in the water, and the skipper shouting, and going out to help, so they went in as fast as they could, bearing in mind they had to be careful of the coral. They said the skipper had to pull Dave off Lizzie before he could help her. Then he lifted her out of the water and, after checking she was alright, carried her back to the boat while he let Dave sort himself out. Dave shot back to the boat, so he was already there when the skipper brought Lizzie back.'

'Wow, Penny. Sorry, Detective Penelope.'

'Come on, time to drive home. If your phone says it's going to take an hour forty-five, then it'll be more like three hours, and I want my dinner.'

'What! After the meal we've just had?'

'A girl's got to keep her strength up for the night time, you know, and you're a growing boy.'

Laughing, they walked back to the car and the drive back to the hotel.

There was no sign of Lizzie or Dave at dinner, as they ate their small portions. Despite all the bravado, it was a token meal given all they had eaten at Jemma's.

'So, they've had a falling out, by the sound of it,' Alex said, not for the first time.

'The big question is, over what? Over you? Sorry, but I suspect not. So, what is it? Are they just tired of one another? Who knows? We don't have enough to reach any conclusions, so I guess we'd better drop it. They quarrelled, hard luck, get over it.'

'OK, on with the holiday. Any thoughts about tomorrow, Penny?'

'Yes, a lie-in and a diet.'

'Ah, so you'll be running lengths of the beach then, through the waves.'

'Ha, ha, not a chance. No, seriously, Alex, a quiet day for me, will you be writing?'

'Sounds like a plan. Oh, look who's here.'

They watched as Dave entered and found a table by himself, as far away from everyone else as possible.

'Doesn't look entirely happy and did I see some scratches on his face?'

'I couldn't tell. Come on then, star watching, maybe turtles, and then bed. Or the other way around.' Penny laughed, grabbing his hand to haul him away.

As they went, Dave's eyes followed them. He did not look happy.

CHAPTER THIRTY-TWO

Jayne had decided not to mention the shop to anyone, but to see exactly what the property was like. It might just be a dump of a place, not worth having. The journey to Bath was going to cost her, but a day out would perk her up a bit. It took longer than she thought, but walking out of Bath Spa station, she was sure that she'd made the right decision. She hadn't been to Bath before, so she marvelled at everything. At the architecture of the station, the beautiful honey-coloured stone everywhere, the river, the weir, the Pulteney Bridge, the Abbey, she took it all in. So many lovely shops, and so many people here as well, and most of them were speaking a foreign language. She felt as though she had landed in another country.

She explored the side streets, exploring all the shops as she walked until she was exhausted. She checked the address of the property and asked a police officer where she could find it. It wasn't far. She slowed down, doubts creeping into her mind. This place was so magical she would love to be part of it. At last, she turned a corner and walked down the road it was on. She couldn't bear to look and instead kept her eyes straight ahead, knowing that it was on the other side of the road.

When she turned her gaze across the road, she gasped. It was a café, it really was. A wonderful, wonderful café. Then she thought, but it wasn't hers. Even if the freehold was hers, and that was debatable, the place was probably leased out, maybe for years and years. She was close to tears. This was so wonderful, and yet so unattainable. She didn't dare walk across the road. Instead, she walked away, into the city, went into a chain coffee shop, and had a panini.

What to do? She couldn't chicken out now, she had to do something. Should she get Willowby to sort it out? No, she'd been there, she would do this herself. Decided, she finished her food and more confidently returned to the café. There were only a couple of people in there apart from the owner, so she walked in.

'Can I help you?' The woman behind the counter was probably in her late thirties, and a little taller than her with short blond hair, her figure hidden by an apron with the café logo on. Jayne took a deep breath. She took the deeds out of her handbag and unfolded them.

'I hope so. My dad just died and left me the deeds to this property, but I know nothing about it.'

The woman gasped and just looked at her for a moment. Then she shook herself.

'I'm sorry. I wasn't expecting that. You took my breath away. Your father was Mr Sutherland?'

'Yes, did you know him?' The last thing she expected was the laugh that racked the woman. 'Did I know him? I'll say I did, and a lot of other women besides, no mistake. He was a bit of a one, your father. Sorry, but it's true.'

'Oh, did he cause you any problems?'

'No, exactly the opposite. When he moved on, if you get my meaning, he let me lease this place cheaply. Cash, so no tax for him. I've got the usual envelope ready for him out the back. But I have a feeling it's all about to change, isn't it?'

'Do you rent the shop and the flat then?'

'No love, just the café. He used to use the flat for his assignations. A different woman every time I saw him. I do not know where he got the stamina. I mean, he wasn't a big guy, was he? I wondered how he reeled them in, but then he got me, didn't he? He was just good with the chat. He looked after you, and then it was back to the flat, for you know what. What a man.'

'So, there's no one in the flat now?'

'Not that I know, and I would, wouldn't I. So, have you decided what to do with the shop? I'd like to stay, I'll be honest, I've carved a nice little trade out here, and your father's generosity means that I've paid off all the machinery and fitting out. Not that it will always be like that, but put it this way, I'm doing alright. Trouble is, I know what rents are like around here, and they're many times what I'm paying. I have to be realistic, but I don't think I can afford the proper rent for this place.'

'I don't know what I want to do, and anyway I need to get a solicitor to sort it out.'

'No, you don't.'

'Why?'

The woman looked at her before answering. 'Tell you what, have a sit-down, I'll get you a coffee, and then we'll talk.'

Jayne sat down next to the window and looked around. This café wasn't like the slick chain one she'd just come from. Rustic might be an apt description. They'd made the counter of old wooden pallets, the walls decorated with artwork made from coffee beans, and the furniture looked sturdy but very second-hand. It was a comfortable place to be. She came back out of her reverie as a mug of coffee appeared in front of her, together with a croissant.

'Right love, ready?'

'I think so. Is it that bad?'

She laughed. 'No, not at all. Now, people call me Jellie, instead of my full name, which is Angelica, Angelica Starling. Don't laugh.'

'I'm Jayne, Jayne Sutherland. Nice to meet you.'

'Same to you. Now this place,' she looked around the café, 'belongs to you. Isn't there anything on the deeds to show that?'

'I didn't read it. I just saw it was a deed and the address. That's all. Have I been stupid?'

'Of course not. You did what was natural. There's a story behind this, and I hope you'll thank me in the end. What you need is the key now, my dear,'

Jayne's mind leapt to the keyring and the three keys. Maybe the mystery was over. She smiled at Jellie.

'I think I might know where it is. When I was clearing out our house, where my dad and I lived, I found a keyring with three keys on it. The deeds were in there, so I reckon the Yale key might fit the flat.'

'Quick, let's have a look.'

They ran out of the café and to a door set into the stonework next to it. The lock had Yale written clearly on it.

'Looks as though you're in luck,' said Jellie. 'I've got a bottle or two in the café. I'm not licensed, but a couple of regulars ask for a bottle to be kept for them. By the way, if someone asks for alcohol, you come to me, because I know who they are. I don't want some council wally closing me down. Let's open one. It's time to celebrate.'

Jayne hesitated. 'That's so nice of you, Jellie, but I'd prefer to do that if and when I actually get in. I don't like to tempt fate.'

Alex stopped typing. He was sitting out of the sun on the terrace, while Penny sunbathed on the beach, just twenty yards away. As usual, there weren't many people around, although there had been a notice up in the reception area for a craft market somewhere up near the bar. A local woman had set up a stall, with lines of sarongs arrayed on a washing line giving extra colour to the beach. He'd seen Penny wander along to look, and then to the bar for a drink. If it wasn't for Lizzie and Dave, this would be idyllic. He went inside the room as his work uploaded to the cloud. Then he took out his bunch of keys, which had a USB attached, and copied it there too. This stuff wasn't enough for a book, but it would do for a magazine. It finished uploading. He clicked the link to release the USB and pulled it out. Then, hiding the laptop, he locked up and ambled down to see Penny. Time for a swim.

He approached the sunbed. But she didn't stir. Frowning, he reached out and touched her. She was cold. Too cold. He felt her pulse, but there was nothing there. Racing back to the room, he rang reception. Someone would come quickly, they told him. He raced back. Surely he was wrong. But when he got back, it was true. Penny was dead. His legs wouldn't support him, and he fell to his knees, his head resting on her.

They found him like this. The local doctor, the manager, the lady from reception, and later the ambulance crew. They moved him aside and checked. She had gone. They turned to why but could see no marks on her. They looked at one another while Alex sat still on the ground, looking dazed. Then, they called the police.

Torrey heard about it first thing in the morning when he walked in. The police in Tobago had called. Would he ring them back, please? It was important.

'Detective Inspector Torrey, who am I speaking to?'

'I am Henry, Herbert Henry. I am the superintendent of police here in Tobago. I have some unfortunate news for you. I talked to a man staying here, Mr Andrew Ash, and he said that I should talk to you. There has been a murder here. A Miss Penelope Vixen. She and Mr Ash were in a relationship.'

'I'm sorry, I thought he left with an Elizabeth Westbrook?'

'Yes, and she is still here. But things moved on. I understand that Miss Westbrook took up with another gentleman, and that after that Mr Ash moved on to Miss Vixen.'

'Things move fast in Tobago,' Torrey mused.

'Indeed. Now Miss Vixen is dead. Likely poisoned.'

'I see. Do you have anyone for it?'

'Well, Mr Ash is under suspicion, because he says he could see Miss Vixen all the time, which is most strange until we understood he is a writer, and all the while he was typing a story, and no doubt engrossed in that. He is taking the blame for allowing her to be murdered, but I believe he is completely innocent. Nonetheless, we must keep him in mind.'

'Yes, of course. Is there anyone else in the frame?'

'Not really, but some strange goings-on. Mr Ash told us about Miss Sutherland, and it appears that her new boyfriend seems to have been involved in an altercation with her. That may have been a failed murder attempt.'

'What's the name of the new boyfriend?'

'David Makepeace, provided by Miss Sutherland. He seems to be missing.'

'More and more interesting.'

'Yes, which was why it would be useful if we shared the information that we both have. Perhaps I could send you a photograph of each of those involved here, just to check that we have the right faces against the right names.'

'Of course. That would be much appreciated. I'll give it my immediate attention. On that point, you're seven hours behind us, are you not?'

'Indeed. It is one o'clock in the morning here, the number you have is my private phone, my home.'

'Oh, I'm so sorry.'

'Don't be. This is part of my duty and I accept it gladly. My wife maybe not so much, but that is something one gets used to, am I right?'

Torrey laughed. 'Yes, Superintendent, you are right. Well, I'd best not take up any more of your time. I'll await your photographs later.' He gave him his email address.

'That will do for now. They will be with you later. They are at the station, so it will be a few hours yet.'

'Anything you have will be appreciated. Thank you for contacting me, it's very helpful.'

'Oh, don't thank me, thank Mr Ash.' He signed off.

Torrey sat still for a few moments, wondering how this might affect his investigation.

Alex slept badly, which wasn't a surprise. The hotel had said that he could continue to use Penny's room if he wanted to, Lizzie still being in his, or rather their, room. He was sure that if someone had poisoned Penny, then he would have seen them. So why hadn't he? He got up, put some shorts on and went out onto the terrace. Sitting where he'd been typing when Penny died, he had a view of the garden, with small circles cut out for plants. Three palm trees delineated the end of the garden and the beginning of the beach. At the edge of the beach were four permanent palm roofed umbrellas. Penny had placed her sunbed near the second from the left, just out of its shade, so she could sunbathe, and then pull the bed into the shade when she'd had enough. The other umbrellas had not been in use. People had churned the sand up around her sunbed when they came to help, so there was no trail of neat footprints to her sunbed. The route from the sea was more interesting. From the sunbed the sand was flat for about twenty feet, then it rose slightly, where the waves came in and deposited sand. Then the beach sharply dipped about three feet before it sloped gently to the sea. It would have been possible for someone to swim up to the beach, and, crouching, run up the beach, unseen. A climb up the steep slope and they would have had twenty feet to reach Penny. Would he have seen that? Would she? He shook his head. While he was sure that he'd kept Penny in his sight at all times, he had to admit that he had been typing, and sometimes absorbed in the story. So, yes, it might be possible. He'd only thought about someone walking along the path in front of the rooms before, but this more covert route changed that.

He walked barefoot down to the water's edge and looked back. It would be easy to count the palmed umbrellas from right to left looking from the sea, and so work out which one Penny had been next to. There would no doubt have been a reconnaissance trip beforehand. Who had he seen? Unfortunately, the answer was no one. He looked around. A hundred yards to his right now the hotel grounds ended, and while the seashore continued, the land gave way to a public wooded picnic area. There was nothing to prevent someone walking out of this and along the beach, because, as he'd learnt, all beaches in Tobago were public. The number of potential routes for a killer were increasing. The police had talked to all those who had been on the beach around the time of the murder, so there was nothing he could add to that. But then he remembered. She had walked to see the wraps, and then he had seen her walk up to the bar for a drink. Had there been anyone else there? He couldn't remember, although he'd felt foolishly peeved at the time that she hadn't asked him if he wanted a drink. He'd been a fool. All this stalking about, when the answer had been obvious all the time. He must talk to the police.

Mournfully, he walked up the slope and back towards the room. The police had taped off the umbrella and surrounding area where Penny had been, so he stood and paid a silent homage before returning to what had once been their bed. Before settling down, he put through a call to reception to ask them to contact the police.

CHAPTER THIRTY-THREE

Jayne loved her first day in the café. Her feet were used to her standing on them all day, so no problem there, and every single customer had been lovely. Working with her new boss was easy. A laugh. They complemented one another, working seamlessly to keep customers served and everything tidy.

'Jayne, you've been a lifesaver,' her new boss said as they were cleaning down the coffee machine. 'You've made my life so much easier, and I've loved your company. Thank you so much.'

'I've enjoyed it too, the entire experience. Do you really want someone permanent?'

'Jayne, I'd love that, and I think I can afford it if your salary expectations aren't too high. Sorry, but I have to be realistic.'

'That's alright. I'm happy. Just let me know what you can do, but I want to work here. Now, do you have time for a "My First Day" celebration?'

'I'd love to. But I have a husband and two children who will want to be fed soon, so, you see, I need to be home. I'd like to try another night, though, when I can arrange a break from my womanly chores. I shouldn't complain. They pull their weight, but they like their routines, and Mum suddenly disappearing for a night out doesn't feature.' She paused. 'Do you know? Sod it. They can sort themselves out, they're old enough, and I haven't had a night out for years. Let's go for it. But I'll ring Tom first.' Phone call made, they locked up, and headed into town.

At four in the afternoon, Torrey received the photographs from Superintendent Henry. There was nothing remarkable about them. The characters he knew were Elizabeth (Lizzie) Westbrook and Alexander (Alex) Ash. He gave Penelope Vixen and David Makepeace to Deer to check out. Henry had asked if he would like passport details of all the guests at the hotel, but he passed on that for the moment, although he had no other leads to follow. On an impulse, he emailed Henry to say that he'd changed his mind, and could he please send them? Henry had been diligent. Within the hour, he sent over the passport details of all of those staying at the hotel and asking if there was anything else that he could do. Torrey, unable to think of anything, thanked him.

At six he chased Deer to see if he'd got anywhere, and receiving a negative, he went home. There would be plenty of late nights to come, and a break from churning over the images of the two dead bodies would be welcome. There was no loving wife to go home to, no woman to be with at all. He hesitated as he left the Bristol police station. He would have liked to be based in Bath, but consolidation meant that there was no full-time police station there. He decided to walk to Temple Meads station and take the train to Bath. Since the London express was pulling in as he walked onto the platform, he was there in twelve minutes. It was, without doubt, the gentler and more beautiful of the two cities. Once upon a time, before he joined the Force, he'd messed around with watercolours. Maybe he should try them again? But unfortunately, he found that after a day's work there was no way he could concentrate on anything like that, so he'd taken to punishing himself in the gym.

He wandered through the city, watching as with evening the party animals emerged, groups of scantily clad girls on hen do's taunting groups of men looking for a drink, mixing with couples strolling, maybe making for a restaurant. Two universities and a college kept the age of the population younger than it might otherwise be and the atmosphere livelier. He strolled at peace with the world, noticing a few familiar faces, both good and bad. He saw George Marlin, accompanied by the short woman whose name escaped him, as they made their way into a restaurant. The woman from the shoe shop, with a café owner, looking around, maybe for somewhere to go. As a police officer, you noticed these things, the activity, who was with whom. It was like being back on the beat, and he wondered why he didn't do it more often. In some ways, he'd lost the pulse of this place, too focused on particular crimes, not on the whole.

A shout behind him made him turn, but it was only a group messing about. He walked on up the hill, only realising where he was heading when he arrived. The Circus was as beautiful as ever, the architecture, the soft honey-coloured stone, the central island with its trees and bench. He walked into the centre and sat there. He was looking directly at Elizabeth Westbrook's house. There was nothing remarkable about it, apart from its inner secret, nothing to see. He wondered whether to walk around the back, but dismissed it. He was, after all, out for pleasure. He stood, turned and went towards the Crescent, looking into a restaurant and shopfronts on the way, then into the Crescent itself. It was interesting how different each of the illuminated interiors was. Some, maybe rented, displayed a mess of cheap furnishings, others opulent. A panoply of lives. He walked away, down the hill and through the park, the railway station on his mind. He had achieved nothing except still his mind, but that was enough. Sometimes you had to take a break before you could move on.

He wasn't sure why he turned back, it didn't matter, something was puzzling him. His subconscious prodding him into action without revealing why. Returning to the Crescent, he ambled along to George Marlin's house. Marlin held events for some elite club, he'd heard Deer talking about it, but what was it and what did it do? He was looking for a clue at the house, a brass plaque of something, but of course, he was being daft, and there was nothing like that there. It looked as though he'd have to make an appointment and return. He was just about to walk on when a voice behind him said, 'Not tonight, old fella, it's next week.' He turned to see an elderly man resting on his stick. 'Made the same mistake myself last month,' he went on, 'walked all the way here for nothing. Still, my daughter said it did me good. Maybe it did, maybe it didn't, but I did it again tonight. I'm Gavin.' He held out a hand that Torrey grasped.

'Actually, my business was more official. I was here to ask Mr Marlin about the society, the **aware** I believe it's called. I wanted to know more about it.'

'Oh well, if that's all, then I'm your man. I could do with a drink though, fancy one?'

They found a local pub, Torrey bought a beer for himself and a double scotch for his new friend, who was keen to address the subject.

'George didn't set his soirees up. It was his lady friend, Maggie. You'll see them about the city a lot these days, but back in the day, his wife was still with him Not that a little thing like that stopped the pair of them. I reckon they started these soirees to let them see more of one another. It's supposed to be about **awareness**. They say that there are two types of people, the **aware**, and the **unaware**. Well, it sounded intriguing, so when I was at a loose end after my Rosy died, I went along to one. A friend of mine had mentioned it, he'd been twice, and thought I should give it a shot.'

'What was it like?'

'Oh, it's just a fairly civilised drinks party. I say fairly because some couples sneak upstairs for a bit of fun, but that's all controlled by Maggie.'

Torrey raised an eyebrow.

'You have to pay your subs, and they're not cheap. Then there's the drinks kitty, and a room is extra, which you book through Maggie. I've known Maggie arrange a partner for a gentleman, or a lady come to that. She doesn't tell George about that. He's quite straight-laced, is George, wouldn't like it at all. He'd think they had turned his home into a knocking shop, which of course it is.' He laughed, and Torrey joined in, wondering if it was worth a raid. Probably too small. All the participants would claim they were just friends enjoying one another's company, and they would treat the very idea of money changing hands with disgust.

'Anyway, where was I, oh yes, now there is a more serious side to all this, the **awareness**. It puzzled me, I can tell you because as soon as someone said I was an **aware**, I felt that I was. I felt I saw more around me, anticipated people's actions, and became a better person at interacting with the world. It was why I kept going, to keep up my confidence that it was real. Of course, George didn't say that it existed. Very cute is George. He claimed he wasn't **aware**, so how could he tell if you were **aware**, that was something only an **aware** could do. So, people came, they massaged one another's egos, they came for companionship and they came for sex. An ideal combination.'

'So, you still go?'

'Oh yes, for the sex of course,' and he laughed so much George worried about a heart attack. 'The sex, of course, yes that was it. If you want to get into that game, you must catch Maggie on her own, or I've heard she has a special phone for that. I reckon she's making a little fortune all for herself. A little bird told me Maggie paid her £500 to go with some guy, and the guy told her he'd paid Maggie more than double that. Yes, a nice little earner.'

'The next one is next week, you said.'

'Same day, next week, at eight o'clock. Should I look out for you there?'

'I think I'm busy that evening, but probably another month.'

'Oh, yes, another would be grand, thank you.'

Torrey obliged and set their revived drinks down after a brief trip to the bar.

'What sort of people go there?' he asked. 'Anyone I'm likely to know?'

'Maybe. Maggie is very careful. I've heard she keeps details of all the members on her computer, little snippets from here and there. She'll say it's so that so and so's wife or husband isn't invited while he or she is enjoying themselves. But I reckon she has a few words, and they pay up if you get my meaning.'

'Blackmail?'

'Yes, I suppose so, though she'd probably see it as an incentive for her to be careful. I mean, she could accidentally reveal some unfortunate's misdeeds to interested others, couldn't she? Mind you, the editor of the local rag goes along, so maybe he could arrange something for her.'

'You mean he'd get the juicy gossip if someone didn't play ball with Maggie?'

'I couldn't possibly say that now, could I? But I'm sure some would.'

'A writer I know said he'd been, seemed to think it was all kosher.'

'I saw him, and I heard what Maggie whispered to her companion, not George, I hasten to add, when he left. The words "lamb to the slaughter" come to mind, an innocent abroad. Shame, he seemed a likeable lad. I notice George directed him to Lizzie, so he'll soon be up to his neck.'

'Lizzie?'

'Lizzie, Lizzie, oh, what's her surname? It'll come to me in a minute. Yes, seems a big fan of George's but she spends a fair bit of time on her back for Maggie. She'll have that author eating out of her hand soon enough. Lizzie Westbrook, that's her, she's got a place in the Circus, so she can't be doing badly, can she? Wonder if it all comes the same way?' He was laughing again while Torrey smiled encouragingly.

'You seem to have noticed a lot, Gavin. What did you get up to?'

'Me? Oh, I'm too old for all that. I just enjoyed observing, which was another of Maggie's little earners. For a bit of money, you can go upstairs, shortly after or even before the couple or couples taking part and look through a mirror or a peephole. She's very careful who she tells about that, very careful. I probably looked too old and past it for sex, so she sidled up to me one day and mentioned it. It cost, though. Several hundred just for a view.'

'So, did you?'

Gavin looked sideways at him before answering. 'Just the once, just to see what happened. It was Lizzie with some bloke Maggie said worked at a bank. Put it this way. Lizzie was as enthusiastic and athletic as I was told to expect. They both looked as though they enjoyed it, though he looked a bit knackered afterwards.'

'Well, it all sounds as though I ought to go along sometime. Do I have to get invited by someone?'

'Maggie's the key. Here, she gave me some cards. You might as well have one. If I see you in a room, I promise not to tell.' He was laughing again.

Gavin told tales of the **awareness** initiations, but they were all along the same lines. He was right. It was a knocking shop, with added **awareness**. George Marlin disappointed Torrey, he'd expected more of him, and the more he thought about it, the more he was sure that George was just turning a blind eye.

'Of course, Maggie likes her turn, too, but she likes threesomes. You pay more if she's involved, and to be honest, she's bloody good. I don't know where she learnt her tricks, but, well, she knows it all, with knobs on. Alright, I see you looking at me. Yes, I've watched them more than once.'

'Interesting. You reckon she's done this sort of thing before then?' Torrey was tiring of the tawdriness of the whole thing.

'Oh yes, you don't get to run something like this without having tried it before, trust me. She's first class is Maggie and knows it.'

Somehow it didn't gel with the small, round-faced woman he'd seen, but he trusted Gavin. He excused himself but bought Gavin another scotch to thank him for his help, which put a smile on his face.

As he walked down the hill and to the train back to Bristol, he had a lot to mull over. If Lizzie was on the game, and so was Maggie, then what new insights did that bring to the murders? It might be an additional motive for murder, but if her then why not Maggie? Then why kill Lizzie's sister? Mistaken identity? He boarded the train, still reeling from his conversation and the snapshot of the city's other life. So, he thought he knew it all, did he?

CHAPTER THIRTY-FOUR

After a quiet morning, Alex settled down to write. He had paced the beach too many times, trying to make sense of the scene. But nothing came to him. Yet there must be a solution. Maybe Superintendent Henry had solved it already? Pleasant as he was, he suspected that Henry had not. He replayed it all in his head again, but it made no difference. So, writing would have to be his escape, even if his mind wouldn't settle to the job. He made a mug of coffee and tried.

Jayne made her way back home, her mind in a whirl. As if by a miracle she was suddenly the owner of three properties. One already in her name, two she might have to fight for. It was incredible. Walking from the station back home, yes, she still thought of it as home. Nothing was certain yet, but she felt a lightness she'd never felt before. She had met someone new, made friends with her, and found out that they had a common interest in the property. Amazing.

She turned her key in the front door and walked in. Someone had been here. They had tipped out the bags she had put in the hall. Drawers opened and left open. She gave a little cry and rushed up the stairs. She had left the keys on the bedside table beside her bed. They had gone.

She slumped down on the stairs and sobbed. How hopes raised so quickly could be washed away on the next tide. Did she have no rights to anything? Was she so worthless that people could just walk in and do whatever they wanted to her? After a while, she stopped and rationalised her situation. It was unlikely that whoever had taken the keys, and she had a good idea who it was, would also know about the Bath shop. All she had to do was get a locksmith to open the door. She could show him the deeds to prove her ownership. Her breath slowed down, and she looked again at the mess, shaking her head. How was she going to sleep now? Anyone could come in. Which was a thought. How had they got in?

She ran downstairs, going from room to room, checking the doors and windows. The answer was obvious. They had broken a small pane in the dining room at the back of the house, and that had let an arm come down and open the bigger window. There was a draught coming from both now. It was her fault; the windows were double glazed, so it was possible to lock every window. Now she had seen the window key somewhere. The kitchen drawer. She ran out there. They had pulled the drawer open, but she could see the window keys were still there. Thank goodness for that.

She spent the next ten minutes walking around, locking every window. The broken pane was annoying, but not essential. With the big window locked, they'd have more of a problem getting in, but it looked as though they'd been through the place, anyway.

Tired, she rang the police, but since there was no one on the premises robbing it, they couldn't say when they might be able to come out to her. So, she made herself a meal and settled down to watch TV. Tomorrow was another day.

Alex gave up, put the laptop away after saving his work to the cloud, and wondered what to do. The answer was simple. He checked a leaflet and picked up the room telephone.

'Hey, man,' Shane, their boat captain, answered cheerfully. 'How you doin'?'

'I wondered if I could hire the boat again, just me this time.'

'Hey, I'm so sorry, I heard what happened to your lady. That's a bum deal. I'd love to help, but I'm all sorted for the next few days. Tell you what, though. There's another fast boat to rent, not as good as mine, of course, but I might get it for you tomorrow. How would that be?'

'That would be great. Thanks, Shane. Just let me know.'

Alex sat on the bed, wondering what Lizzie would make of this. But who cared, she was nothing to do with him now.

The phone rang. 'You're in luck. Tomorrow, pick up from the beach at ten. You'll have time for a relaxed breakfast. Good luck.' He had gone, and he hadn't even said who would take him out the next day. Happier, he retrieved his laptop, walked out onto the terrace to type. It was an odd feeling. There in front of him was the spot where Penny's life had ended. The spot where he had missed her murderer. He wasn't sure he could do it. To sit and look out at it all. But maybe that was exactly what he had to do. To type and yet let his subconscious play with his memory. There might be something there.

The next morning was bright and sunny, which was exactly how Jayne felt. She raced through her breakfast, having just toast and marmalade. Then made for the station. She hadn't checked the train times, so she had to wait a while, but the train turned up, eventually. At Bath Spa, she couldn't run down the stairs. There were too many people, but once through the barrier, she made speed to the coffee shop. There she had to wait until Jellie was free so that she could ask her to ring a locksmith and see if they could come out urgently. Jellie provided her with a second breakfast and a cappuccino while she waited.

The locksmith took nearly two hours to arrive. He checked the deeds, her bank card, and her credit card before he dealt with the lock. He didn't drill it out as she'd expected. He had a little kit of oddly shaped metal prongs which he wiggled into the lock, and after just a few minutes it was open. As he showed off his work, she asked him if there was a lock that was more difficult to open, and he laughed. It seemed that just about any lock could be picked. Half an hour later, her credit card a little more loaded, she was the proud possessor of a new Yale lock, and a mortice lock, and a feeling that the property was now safe. She wondered whether to wait for Jellie before going in, but the café was so busy that she went into the property by herself.

The door opened onto a set of stairs which ran up beside the café, and she could hear Jellie chatting away, and the hiss of the coffee machine. They ended in a closed door. She took a deep breath, plucked up courage, and pushed the door open. She gasped, and then laughed more than she'd laughed for many years, maybe ever. This was where her father had spent his money. Diana Sharp, eat your heart out. This was the opposite of the plain house where she and her father were supposed to live, and the house he had left her to live in. This was him, not those.

She wasn't sure that she could live here long term, not in its present state. It looked a bit, well, it looked like somewhere a man would bring a woman where he intended to have sex. It wasn't exactly a long-term home. She looked around, bursting into sobbing laughter at the black silk sheets, and when she looked into the bedside cabinet, the sex toys, even handcuffs and ties. Oh, shit, wait until Jellie saw this. Oh, lord, had Jellie seen this already? Maybe she had been here. With him. It was beyond belief, and yet this was her father. Her father! The kitchen, though, was beautifully equipped with all the latest shiny gadgets, complete with a well-stocked wine rack. As for the coffee machine, it rivalled the one downstairs in its complexity. In the cupboards were all sort of exotic spices and herbs she didn't know her father knew how to use, and she certainly didn't. There was a whole array of coffee beans in the cupboard above, and she wondered if they had been supplied from downstairs. Had she upset Jellie with the news of her father's death? She hadn't seemed upset.

She set about a systematic search, starting with the lounge. It had a huge TV and a sound system she'd never know how to operate. The pictures on the wall were modern splashes of colour that did nothing for her. There was no settee, but two cuddle chairs. There was a clear expectation there. A thought that sent her into a fit of giggles. His choice of DVDs wasn't hers, and most of them weren't likely to end up in a charity shop either. Really, Father. Back to the bedroom, and she went through the wardrobes. A different man from the one she'd known was in here. The flash suits, all good brands; the same applied to the shirts that must have cost him a hundred or two each. As for the shoes. Blimey. Not a great number, just expensive, and probably handmade for him. She picked up one shoe to feel the leather, and something fell out. A wallet. Stuffed with cash, nothing else. One way of avoiding Diana finding out what he was

*spending, and the taxman how much he earned, but
then that was how Jellie paid him. Very conveniently,
he had it all worked out. No doubt restaurants and
other amusements were paid for in cash as well. She
flicked through the notes. She gave up at eight hundred pounds. It was something between that and a
thousand. How much did Jellie pay him each month?
She had no idea what the rent was for a shop in Bath.
Shit. It was raining money now. There was one more
room. A small bedroom used as a study. A laptop sat
on a cheap melamine desk, a good printer was close
by. There was a filing cabinet, but it was locked. The
last key! But of course, she didn't have it, not that
it mattered. It opened when she pulled the handle.
There were just files there, work files. She shut it
again and went downstairs to see Jellie, carefully
making sure that she had the new front door keys
with her before pulling the door shut.*

Alex stopped, saw people heading for the bar, and,
after putting the laptop away, joined in. There might
be sad looks, consolatory speeches and sad toasts, but
hopefully not Lizzie or Dave. It was time for lunch
anyway, and he didn't want to stay in the room for
that. A couple of drinks first should set him up nicely.

Two gin and tonics later, and he had met two
blokes who wanted to tell jokes that he just didn't
get, and a woman who had probably been drinking all
morning or hadn't sobered up from the night before
and thought that the death of a partner meant he was

up for it. There were all sorts of people in the world, and he happened to be with this lot. He wasted no time dispatching his drinks, excused himself, and bolted to the restaurant. Quickly because he heard the patter of flip-flops following him. The drunk woman was on the chase. At the desk where he had to book in for lunch, he walked straight past and whispered to the woman who should book him in. After a swift glance at the flip-flop woman behind him, she took him to a table and rapidly removed the second set of cutlery. Shortly afterwards, he could hear her fending off the marauder. He smiled and whispered a thank you when he saw her next.

He sorted out lunch with the speed of an Olympian, so that, refuelled, he was on his way before flip-flops had started. It was strangely rewarding and relaxing to walk away. He walked back past the bar, and, seeing it deserted now, grabbed two more gin and tonics in the plastic cups they provided for take-away. Was it time to write some more, or for a siesta? But he knew there was no way he was going to sleep. His brain would just replay Penny. Penny alive, and Penny dead. He felt tears welling and was glad that their stress-reducing hormones might help. He let them come, didn't fight them, just let them flow down his cheeks. With everyone at lunch, there was no one to see, no one to say or do anything. He just wanted to be alone with his memories. Most of them, anyway. And yet he wanted to remember her at the end as well. How she had run down to the sunbed, waved to him, how he had watched her cream up, how she had stuck her tongue out at him as she had run to the bar for a drink, and then how she had flopped down, never to get up again. He stopped. What was going to happen to her body? What about her family? Was he even going to a part of her last journey? He drank the two drinks down without a pause. A fresh fall of tears cascaded down his face as he unlocked the room door and crashed onto the bed. One way or another, he had achieved the sleep he needed.

CHAPTER THIRTY-FIVE

He didn't know where he was when he awoke. There had been dreams of death in which he was always the observer, unable to do anything about what was happening. At one point someone had strapped him to a chair while assailants rampaged along the beach, massacring everyone in their path. Bells were ringing out. Then it came back. Shit. He didn't have a hangover, but then it was only four gin and tonics. Well, six if you counted the two that they brought to the lunch table. He looked at his watch. Nine exactly. In the morning. The boat. He scrabbled up and checked that he had everything ready to go. He'd been good after the last trip and had repacked his kit. Time for a quick breakfast. He opened the patio doors and understood at least a part of his dream. A small herd of cattle was making its way along both the beach and the hotel garden, and one of them had a bell around its neck that bonged as it went. It gave him something to smile about. He wasn't going completely mad.

Nine twenty-five and he was back in the room picking up the bag, hastening out to the beach, locking up behind him. The boat was already there. The sharp bowed speedboat that Lizzie and Dave had been in when they had their incident. He walked down to it and paddled through the sea to take the proffered hand to wrist grasp that helped him into the boat. His skipper was a quiet man, who patiently took his time making sure his boat was neat before they set off. He had already decided where he wanted to go. The same pink beach that Lizzie had visited.

The wind in his hair they swept along the coast, past the features he had already seen, but his brain hadn't taken in. A small bay where he'd been told that once a hotel way above it had featured a piano, and hummingbirds that fed while you had afternoon tea. Another hotel that looked as though it belonged in some eastern land sat high above them, a lone angler casting from the shore. On to Englishman's Bay, which had a small shack at the back of it, and then another hotel that looked as though Robinson Crusoe had built it. Behind all this was the forest. It brought back memories of Penny as they'd made their small incursion into it. It had been a civilised trail, with other groups around most of the time. The most exotic bird they'd seen was a large king-fisher, but it seemed wonderful at the time, and he remembered he had pulled her in for a kiss. Little things. But now their importance was beyond any measure. Priceless.

Suddenly the boat veered out into the open sea.

'Dolphins,' his skipper shouted. He tried to remember the man's name. He had said it as he'd clambered aboard, but he hadn't fully heard him. Ajax? Unlikely unless they were off to fight a mighty warrior and rescue the body of Achilles from the Trojans. Perhaps not. He concentrated on looking out for the dolphins. After a few minutes powering away from the coast, the engine cut back, the boat swung to starboard, and there they were. A wonderful pod cresting through the waves. Then more, alongside, so close he could almost touch them. It was the biggest pod he'd ever seen, entire families running beside them. They ran together for a while, and then as if by command, they turned away, off out into deeper waters. Alex turned to the skipper and gave a thumbs up.

'Fantastic. Thanks for that. I'm sorry, I didn't catch your name.'

'AJ' was all he said, as he returned to the wheel to take the boat back towards the island, increasing pace, the boat bouncing on the waves. As they returned to calmer waters, flying fish leapt from the waters, and a flight of pelicans flew past. Another world.

Past two wide bays, where he'd read that the English had trapped a pirate fleet in one bay and attacked them, their blood drifting into what was then termed Bloody Bay. Next, they were approaching a small island just off the coast. The boat skirted around the island and then slowed to a crawl. Alex looked over the side and saw why. AJ was weaving through the coral, which was incredibly close. Just below the clear waters, he saw shoals of fish darting in and out. It truly was a fish village. AJ dropped his anchor in a small area of slightly deeper water, a gap in the coral, and waved at the shore. There a strip of pink beach ran for about two hundred yards along the coast, and about twenty feet back to where it met the cliff which was covered in vegetation.

'I don't think you need me in,' AJ said, 'but be careful, the coral's always close, and you heard what happened to the lady I took out.'

It was the opening Alex had been waiting for.

'Not really. What happened?'

AJ gave him a look and a slight frown before answering.

'It was strange. When I picked them up, they seemed a together couple, you know, cuddling up in the back there. I thought it set us up for a pretty good day. As we came down the coast here though, their mood seemed to change, so that by the time we stopped here, and they were preparing to get out, they were snapping at one another. Nothing too bad, just like a married couple, pissed off with one another about something. They got in and started by going off in different directions. The woman over there,' he waved to the left of the beach, 'and the bloke stayed close to the boat. Then the woman shouted something. I think it was barracuda, and the man went over to her. There's often barracuda around here. They're OK, the worst they'll do is try to nibble your toes, but I suppose if you're not used to them, they look more frightening than they are. Anyway, he goes over, and I was watching, just in case. You have to in this job. People are always doing daft things. He gets over to her. He was looking down, head with his mask on in the water, and as he approached her, she stood up, and it looked as though she threw her full weight onto him. If she'd been heavier and stronger, she would have pinned him down. As it was, he thrashed around and threw her off, which is probably when she scraped herself on the coral. Then the guy turns on her and pushes her down. He even bent her breathing tube. So, I went after him. I think he saw me coming and backed off and got back to the boat as fast as he could. I pulled the woman up and brought her back to the boat. That was about it. The bloke just sat in the back, silent. The woman. I sorted as best I could, and then I brought them back to the hotel. I heard they went to the hospital later. She didn't go near him, she just sat up near me. I could do without daft stuff like that. It gets all around the island, and it's not good for business.'

'Wow, that was awful. Were they arguing or something?'

'Nope, nothing I heard, anyway. Some unfinished business they brought with them. At least they survived. I hate to think of the publicity if I'd lost one or even both of them. Fancy a roti?'

He upped anchor and took the boat over to the left of Charlottesville, where there was a sandy beach and a beach café. Alex gave him some notes, and he ran off for food. Ten minutes later, they were tucking into roti. After lunch, AJ took his boat to the opposite side of the bay to the pink beach, and Alex snorkelled around, mainly looking at the plethora of squid there. Then they were off, and motoring back to the hotel, a smoother, faster journey than on their way down.

They returned to the hotel at the end of the afternoon, and Alex made straight for the bar, downed a couple of G & Ts, and took a couple more back to the room. Still no sign of Lizzie or Dave. He walked tentatively past the fatal sunbed, no longer cordoned off by the police, without too much of a problem. It was when he walked back into the room and saw the amount of Penny's stuff that only now, he realised he'd have to pack, that he broke down. It wasn't as bad as the previous day, and with a heavy heart, he began sorting her things out and packing them. He wondered what was going to happen to it. Maybe the hotel had it all sorted. Then who had informed her relatives, parents, siblings, whoever? The thoughts whirled around his head as he sorted through her stuff.

Then he found his book. Well, not his, but a book he'd written a couple of years ago. How odd. And then the files. Three of them. He became more cautious now. The police hadn't come for them, but maybe they would, and he wasn't keen on explaining his fingerprints all over the files. The rest he could explain. He went to the toilet, fetched a couple of sanitary bags, and used them to handle them.

There was a file on him, one on Lizzie, and one on Dave. What the hell had been going on? At the bottom of her case, wrapped in a dress, was the answer. A full identity in the name of Janice Weston, Investigator. Penny had been entirely fictitious. A myth, a dream, and yet so real. There wasn't much in the files. He looked at his file first. It was just basic information that she could glean from the internet, with pencilled notes about his likes and dislikes, and about the **aware**. One thing was clear though, it was the **aware** she was investigating, and Lizzie in particular. In Lizzie's file were detailed notes of her life. As a high-class prostitute. Dave's file was comparatively sparse. He had served in the forces and drifted when he came out. Various jobs, but also a bit of crime. Convicted of burglary and possession, but the sentences were minor. Maybe they took his army record into account. The last two years were blank, with pencilled question marks against them.

That was it, nothing else. There was no note of who had asked for the investigation, or what triggered it. He took out paper and pen and copied anything he thought relevant, and then returned the papers to the case, neatly re-wrapped in the skirt.

He resumed his browse through Penny's things, ending up with her handbag. There were the usual cards, a bit of cash, lipstick, and an asthma spray, and then there was a bunch of keys, with a USB stick attached. He took them out, opened up his laptop, and plugged in the USB. He waited a few minutes while Bitdefender did its stuff and then copied everything down into a new file. Then he backed up to the cloud. He uncoupled the USB and replaced the keys in the handbag. He checked everywhere, but he couldn't find a laptop.

After downing the last of the gin and tonics, he went to reception and asked them how he could contact the officer who was dealing with the murder. The receptionist gave him a long look, maybe wondering if he was about to confess, before saying she would ring the police for him and direct the call to his room.

Picking up another couple of drinks from the bar on the way back, he sat in the room, waiting. There was no call. Instead, a smartly dressed police officer arrived at his door. Maybe they thought he was about to give himself up. Especially as he noticed another officer outside the door.

'Henry, Herbert Henry, Superintendent of Police, how may I help you today?'

'I was packing up Penny's things when I found several items that might interest you.' He showed the items. 'There's a book I wrote, some files on another woman and man staying at the hotel, Lizzie Sutherland, and a guy called Dave. As well as those, there's a USB attached to her keyring.'

'Well, thank you, Mr Ash, that is most kind of you to call me. We were planning on checking her things today. Nothing happens quickly here, not like in your country, I guess. I will see that this is all taken care of. I will arrange for all of Miss North's luggage to be removed. We will, of course, carefully assess it, and store it pending its return to her relatives. Most kind.' He stepped out of the door and a tall young policeman stepped in.

'Is it just the big bag and the handbag?'

'Yes, I have found nothing else of hers. Though,' he said, with sudden realisation, 'I haven't tried opening the room safe.'

'Excellent. Then I will wish you a good day and thank you again for your assistance. I will have the hotel send someone along so that we can see inside the safe. For the record, I am liaising with an officer in the United Kingdom. Mr Torrey. Perhaps you know him?'

'No, I haven't had the pleasure.'

'Ah, very well. I will leave you to write some more. Perhaps about our beautiful island?' He gestured towards the open laptop.

'Yes. Although it's difficult in the circumstances, I try. Oh, I nearly forgot. Have you interviewed the skipper of...'

'Indeed, we have, indeed we have. I understand you had a good time out with him enjoying the beautiful coral waters near Charlottesville. He told me you'd been, and what passed between you. He's my brother-in-law, so we talk often. It's a small island, especially the way people talk. My problem is that when they don't know something, they make it up, but in this case, no problem. We are, as they say, on the case. Good day to you now, Mr Ash.'

Feeling exhausted by the encounter, Alex sat out on the terrace. He no longer felt such an attachment to Penny or whoever she was. Maybe the other identity was her false one, or maybe both were false. He would let Superintendent Henry sort that one out. He sat in a dream, staring out at the sea, unwilling or unable to continue Jayne's story. Sometimes there was just too much shit going on.

CHAPTER THIRTY-SIX

Torrey looked at the long message he had received from Tobago, shaking his head. It had come in during the night and was first on his email list. The case was getting more intriguing by the day. He walked over to Deer and handed it to him.

'I'll send it to you, but I thought you might like to have a hard copy first. Old habits die hard. As soon as you've thought about it, we'll get together and sort out the next moves. Any ideas welcome as usual.'

They got together half an hour later, when Deer walked over, coffee in hand.

'Want one?'

'Normally, yes, but I've had so much already, it wouldn't help. Thanks, though.'

'It gets even more interesting, doesn't it? I mean, just having some private detective involved is worrying. What did she know we don't?'

'Yep. Tell you what, before we even talk about it, would you board it all up, and we'll talk in front of the board. I'm visual, so looking at a load of emails and reports doesn't do it for me.'

'Will do. Can you give me an hour? I've got something else going on, and I need to make a couple of calls.'

'Sure. I'm in the same position.'

Just half an hour later, Torrey took a call that changed all that.

'Deer,' he called across the office, causing others to look up. 'Glastonbury think they've found the murder weapon. Coming?' A cheer went up, causing Torrey to smile. Policing may be too much admin and not enough actual policing these days, but a hunt was a hunt, and everyone appreciated a win. Even if a small one,

They were soon in Torrey's car, heading back to Glastonbury.

'What did they say?'

'Not much, only that they're sure they have it and would we like to be in on it, or sit on our arses in the office looking at paperwork?'

'Not much else we can get from that, then. You going to the rugby at the weekend?'

Bath had a great rugby team, which was playing Wasps at home on Saturday. The problem with that was that extra police would need to be on hand to deal with the numbers flooding into the city, especially when they turned out and the best part of 15,000 people headed out, often for the pubs. It was a subject that covered most of the journey time to Glastonbury.

'Anyway, obviously, we'll win,' Torrey ended with.

'Are we going to the station or the house?' Deer said.

'To the house. They want to show off their success.'

They pulled up outside. There weren't as many vehicles around as Torrey had expected. Maybe all the excitement was over. They walked up the drive to be met by a smiling woman.

'You must be the Bath contingent. You've missed the small amount of excitement, but I can show you what we have before it's disturbed and taken off to the Lab. I'm Detective Sergeant Linda Harrison.'

'DI Torrey and DC Deer. We were here a few days ago. We had number twenty-eight opened up and found the body.'

'Of course, well we have some news, come this way.'

They walked behind her, into the front garden, through the house, and out through the kitchen. Then she stopped as they stood on the garden terrace.

'We kicked ourselves we didn't see it earlier. Spot the murder weapon time.'

Torrey just looked at her.

'OK, see that line of short poles that have been used to mark out, I don't know, a new flower bed or something?'

'I see them.'

'The murder weapon is third along. There's no way you'd spot it normally because it all looks so ordinary. The poles that have been used are iron, they might have bought them at a boot sale, or something, they're not particularly for garden use. Let's have a look.'

They walked down to look at it.

'We've already had it out, and all the analysis is being done. This isn't the actual pole, we found it behind the shed, it's only here for scene reconstruction.'

'I wouldn't have spotted that,' Torrey said. 'How did it get found?'

'One of our constables. He was just looking after the place, probably a bit bored, and saw brown stuff and scraps of hair on the pole, right near the ground. He had the sense not to touch it, but he called it in and bingo.'

'Excellent work. What I think we need to do now, is go back to the scene of the murder and see if there's anything similar there.'

'It's been good to meet you, sir. Let us know how it goes.'

They said their goodbyes and set off back to Bath.

There was no parking in the Circus, or nearby, which left Torrey cursing, so he double-parked and left Deer to sort it out. Striding up to the front door, he let himself in, turned off the alarm, and headed for the garden door. Once outside, he looked around. There were no comparable poles. He strolled around the garden, circling, working from the outside in.

Nothing. He looked at the outbuilding. The last time he was here it was locked, but since then someone had broken in and then fitted a shiny new padlock. He checked the keys on the ring he'd signed out, picked what he thought was the most likely. It fitted, and with a quick twist, the padlock opened. He hefted it off, pushed back the hasp, and opened the door.

It was a lot neater than his shed. The ladder he'd seen when he looked through the door was still there, resting to one side. An upmarket lawnmower stood in the centre, with a rack of tools along the back wall, shelves on the other two sides. He started with the ladder, checked it over, lifted it, put it down. Nothing. He looked at each tool, though he was sure someone would have done that. Nothing. On to the back shelves. They were just basic self-assembly metal and could probably be bought at a garden centre. He couldn't see onto the top shelf, so he wheeled the lawnmower over, and stood on that. Now he could move individual items and see the actual shelf. He faced several open-topped plastic boxes and some old looking cardboard boxes. He wasn't too interested in these yet. He wanted to look around them, not in them. Any weapon would probably be longer than they could contain. He stretched up and moved them around by lifting the first one down to the floor, giving him room to slide each one over. Nothing behind the first, the second, third, fourth, fifth, sixth. Nothing. He replaced the first box, but at the other end of the shelf. Next shelf, same process, only he could do away with the mower. Right to left, he made his way along. Nothing. The same process, the same result with the other shelves. He stood, lost in thought. It had to be around here somewhere.

He walked out of the building and stood looking at it. Then he went in and brought out the ladder. If you have a ladder to hand, why not use it? Might have been the murderer's idea. It was one of those ladders that unfolded, but he just stood it against the outbuilding wall, steadied it, and went up. There, lying in the gutter, was a metal pole. It was likely that rain had washed much of the blood off, but there were hairs and other stuff on it. He climbed down and shouted at the sky. 'YES!'

After forensics showed up, Deer arrived, having at last found a place to park the car. They walked through the garden and then the house, re-familiar-izing themselves with it all.

'How do you see it?' Torrey asked.

'It looks to me as though someone comes along the passage at the rear of the house, opens the garden gate, takes the ladder from the shed, and opens the window, which had been left unlocked. They run in, do the deed and exit the same way, placing the murder weapon in the guttering and restoring the ladder to the outbuilding. Oh, and they opened the front door to confuse us. Yes?'

'I don't know. In theory that might work, although the outbuilding would have to be open. I'm going to have to give this some more thought, it doesn't all add up.'

'Sir, I've got a meeting in thirty minutes. Would you mind if we went back now?'

'Sure, where's the car?'

It was back at Manvers Street carpark, a fifteen-minute walk.

CHAPTER THIRTY-SEVEN

Jellie was busy when Jayne walked back into the café, so she just sat on one of the sturdy seats and waited. She was safe now. No one could take the flat away from her, although she still had to deal with the awful Diana character. But then she had a solicitor to do that. How could her father have taken up with a woman like that? But then he hadn't had he? He'd dealt with her as he had with her mother, and every other relationship; he'd kept his options open. If she was harsh, then she might say that he ran away and had been running from day one. Running away from responsibility and commitment. Although he'd been committed to himself alright, and fitted out for himself, no one else, a one flat ego trip. She thought back to the way he had fitted it out. Not luxurious, but expensive, certainly. While she was going to have to change a few things, she still had to think about the future and how she was going to earn a living. A flat wouldn't run itself, and she'd noticed a few bills lying around, and since she owned the property, she was going to have to pay them. She owned the property. She couldn't believe it. The cash she'd found covered the immediate future. After that, though…

'Well?' Jellie was standing next to her. 'What's it like now?'

'I think best seen rather than described. It must have cost him to do it out, though perhaps not to my taste. When are you free?'

'Not until we close. Unless you let me go up while you cover here.'

'Well, that might ruin your trade, Jellie. I've never used a coffee machine. I'm willing to learn though if you like, then I can help from time to time.'

'Now that's an offer I can't refuse. Would you like to start now?'

Jayne joined Jellie behind the counter and was provided with an apron that had a white coffee bean emblem on the front and was, of course, coffee-coloured. Jellie then took her through the intricacies of the machine. The loading of the beans into one compartment, and the milk into another, the cleaning out of the little coffee pan, and how to fill it up and tamp it down. She learnt which button to press, and which lever to pull, and watched as the brown liquid glugged its way into a cup of foamy milk to form a lovely fern pattern. Not that she could do that, not yet. Hers looked more like a pregnant teddy bear. An hour later and she was being told about the fridge, the freezer, the stock cupboard, cleaning, and the various types of pastry in the glass-fronted cabinet. This, of course, required an obligatory tasting session of the ones she did not know.

'Well, that about covers it. Happy?' Jellie enquired.

'I think so. I'll only find out the things I don't know when I encounter them now.'

'Right. You jump in the deep end, and I'll run up and see what you have upstairs. If you get stuck, you know where I am.'

Without waiting for a reply, she held out her hand for the keys, which Jayne gave her with a grin, and ran out of the door. Jayne heard the click of her lock as it was opened, the slamming of her door, and then the thump of footsteps up the stairs as Jellie raced up. She turned her attention to the café. There were only three tables occupied, and they all seemed deep in conversation, coffee or tea, and cake. She looked around the counter. It was made of marble, not good for dropping cups on, and wiped it down. There wasn't much more to do apart from waiting for Jellie to return.

Jellie stood in the flat and sobbed. How could Jayne know what had happened between her and her father in this flat? He would never have talked, and she was the only other person who knew. All she could do now was mourn his passing. Tentatively, she went to the right-hand bedside drawer and reached for the back of it. They were still there. Her love notes to him. He'd kept them despite all the other relationships he had going on. Once, like all the others, she had thought she was the only one, but it didn't take long for disillusionment to settle in. About a month, if she remembered correctly. And *she did. She didn't need to look at them. She remembered every word she had written, and at the time she meant each and every one of them. Now? Even now, she probably did.*

She had told him he ought to put the flat into his daughter's name, that way she would avoid death duties and would be provided for, whatever other properties and assets he had, and whatever other claims there were on them. She was sure there would be other claims. She knew him too well by then. A wife or someone else who felt they were secure, tucked away no doubt. But she was the one who had acted as a wife should have done and stepped in to protect his offspring.

There was no point in looking around the flat any further, she knew it intimately. He had told her what he liked, given her the money, and she had furnished it. But that was after. When she knew him too well. Were they friends then? Friends with benefits was the latest term, wasn't it? Yes. Friends with benefits. That fitted it exactly. But who had it benefited most? Him.

With a last look around, she took the notes away and left, locking the front door after her. Now she had to face his daughter, and that was altogether a different proposition, but not an unpleasant one.

'It's interesting,' she said as she entered the café, to see Jayne working the coffee machine for a couple who had recently entered, 'very interesting.'

'That's one word for it. I mean, for him, well, I'm sure he loved it, but for me?'

'Oh no, it would never do. Tell you what, would you let me help? I used to design rooms, once upon a time, and I'd love to be involved.'

'But of course, I'd love it. I've never done anything like that, so you'd be welcome. In the meantime, I need the solicitor to get a move on and sort out his other half, or rather, the bitch he was living with. She's got a husband too, somewhere.'

'Ah, what's she like?'

'You don't want to know.'

'But I do.'

'Well, her name is Diana Sharp. She has pointy features, long legs, a short skirt, and pushed up showy tits. Heaven knows what he saw in her. She wants his money, no more, no less, and even though there was no mention of her in his will, she's instituting legal proceedings to challenge the will. Who knows what will happen? I'm not sure I trust my father's solicitor, but then I don't trust anyone at the moment. Meanwhile, I'll make a start finding a job, so that I can deal with the day-to-day expenses.'

'Oh, no need, you can work here, I could do with a...'

'Jellie, that's very sweet of you, but I need to make my own way. I hope you don't mind. I'd love to help out from time to time if you need me, though. I'd love that.'

'Of course. Independent. Like your father. I hope we can be friends though.'

'Yes, that would be lovely. Did you and father ever, you know?'

*Jellie nearly wept in front of her. Her lip wob-
bled as she composed herself, hoping Jayne hadn't
noticed. She hadn't, because a customer had called
her over to provide more tea. When she returned,
Jellie had sorted herself out.*

*'I'll be honest with you. Yes. But he wasn't exactly
a man to get tied to one person, was he?'*

*'No. He wasn't. But in the end, he did right by me,
and I can only judge him by that now.'*

*'Yes, live with the positive, it's what I try to do,
and sometimes those thoughts play out, and all that
you hope for comes to be.'*

He stopped typing. The language was more emo-
tional than usual. Maybe it was the influence of a
film he'd been watching. Who knew what influenced
a writer if the writer himself didn't know? Perhaps
the characters just took over the narrative. Maybe he
should stop this and try another book for the younger
readers. But no, it needed to be finished. He had to
finish it.

*'Yes, you're right. The positive. I'll remember that.
Tomorrow I'll have two jobs to do, solicitor and
work, and I'll do my best to be positive about both
of them. I have no idea what sort of work I can get,
I've few qualifications.'*

*'Probably shop work of some sort, love. At least
it'll be a start. Then, maybe, if you do get more
money, well, you could see about getting some more*

qualifications. You'll see that when you're more set-tled and you have a few years behind you, you might find that studying comes more easily. It could change your life.'

'I was useless. But, maybe, we will see. I always envied the ones who got good marks and did it so easily, or at least it appeared that way. Now, I really must sort out my new life upstairs. There are things I need there, so I'll have to do a quick shop. Thank you so much, Jellie, for everything. You've made things so much easier for me.'

'You don't know how happy that makes me feel, Jayne. If ever you need anything just drop in. Oh, and here's my phone number.' She took a card from behind the counter and handed it to her. 'Any time, I mean it. Now we need to sort out payment for your work.'

'Jellie, no. It was only a few minutes, don't be silly.'

'I'll tell you what. Because you might pop in from time to time to help, you can have free coffee and a morning pastry on the house. No arguments. It's the least I can do, and it ensures I get to see you.'

'Oh, Jellie, you're so kind, but I warn you, I can't resist an offer like that.'

'Good, that's settled then. Now you'd better go and stock your flat with the things that you want, rather than the things your father thought he needed. Oh, before you go, I've got the rent money for you. It was £1000 a month, for the shop and the cellar. I'd better tell you that the true rate is more than double that. I don't want it to come as a shock if you see

something like it in an estate agent. Er, you can close your mouth now.'

'Blimey, Jellie, I had no idea,' she took the proffered envelope. 'That sounds like an extraordinary amount of money.'

'It'll keep you going. I'm not sure what he did about tax, but I declare it through my accountant, I have to. If you want her name, I'm happy if you want to use her as well. Whatever it'll take the pressure off a bit. Look, your father was good to me, so don't think bad of him. I would never have been able to keep this business going if he hadn't helped. Good luck and let me know how you get on with the solicitors.'

That would do for now. Another day, another few pages. The story went on. But could he? Of course, he could. Let's face it, he'd attracted three women in as many weeks, even if at least one of them had an ulterior motive, so life couldn't be all bad. Except for the murders. And the deception. And… Oh, sod it. It was time for another drink. He'd been in this place for over a week now, and the ease with which alcohol was available would normally concern him, but not now. He walked slowly, and maybe a little unsteadily, along to the bar, the way Penny must have gone, and waited to be served, the way Penny must have done. He looked up at the barman and asked the question that was burning away in his mind. But Henry had already been there. Henry knew what had happened. The question now was why?

CHAPTER THIRTY-EIGHT

Torrey stood inside a cottage in a village a few miles out of Bath. It belonged to Janice Weston, who indeed was a private eye. She lived on her own, and at first glance, she was the tidiest person Torrey had ever known. Everything had a place and was in it. First, he had contacted her parents, who lived in Bristol, then collected the keys from them. They had been distraught but agreed to him looking around her cottage. They had seen very little of her for a while, which usually meant that she was working on a case.

The cottage would have had a front room and a dining room, but someone had knocked them through to make one room, which was dominated by an enormous desk on which were three computer screens. These linked to a standalone PC under the table, and a laptop. He'd had a look and seen that they were both top of the range. They were gaming versions, far more powerful than you might expect. Also plugged in were three ten terabyte external hard drives. Her internet matched the setup and was provided by a specialist company. It ran at 500mbs, just a little faster than the thirty he had at home. There were no papers left out, but there were two double-doored safes with keypads where presumably she kept all that sort of thing.

The room was done out in muted colours, with light blue rugs on the floor matching the curtains. There was a bookcase, almost all fiction, and an easy to operate sound-system with B&O Bluetooth speakers. At the far end, a door led to a kitchen that had been enlarged so that it extended into the garden. She didn't appear to be a great cook. There were no recipe books, but the new space had allowed her to make a kitchen diner. The kitchen table was clear glass on a wide squared-off tree trunk that had been stripped of its bark and the wood treated. A book lay open on it, a guide to Tobago. Pre-trip research. But what had made her go there? What had made her get to know Alex Ash? Which of course tied into the key question of why was she killed, and by whom?

There wasn't anything more to be gleaned downstairs, so he went up the stairs to find two bedrooms, a bathroom and a toilet. The bedrooms were incredibly neat and tidy, pedantically so. There was nothing on any surface, and in the drawers and cupboards, she had regimentally stored everything. He hadn't yet found any personal papers and assumed they must be in one of the safes downstairs, and he'd arranged for someone to come and open them. Which made him think of the house security system. It had been professionally installed, every entrance covered, and it had caused the police team that had turned up to deal with it several problems, and the neighbours a few headaches as they couldn't stop it going off... until they took the drastic step of cutting wires. Even so, their movements were being watched by the cameras that were placed all over the place, and no doubt sending their pictures off to the cloud and a server or servers in remote parts of the world. He just knew that the safes were going to cause a problem, too. They also had a team coming to sort out the computers. He wanted to be assured that if they did anything, their storage wouldn't be wiped.

He stood for a moment, looking out into her small garden, neat and tidy of course, at the fields that it backed on to. There were a couple of horses grazing there, and it occurred to him that maybe this was what his family had missed, being on an estate in Bristol. A family before his wife had died. A world apart. He heard sounds downstairs and went down to find Deer looking at a door in the kitchen.

'Cellar do you reckon? It's locked.'

'Try a shoulder, it doesn't look too strong.'

A few minutes later and they were in Torrey holding onto Deer, who nearly fell down the steep steps on the other side of the door. There was a light switch there, and they cautiously made their way down. It was just a wine cellar.

'She knows her stuff. No wonder she locked the door,' Deer commented as he scanned a few bottles.

'Like our lady in the Circus. I suppose it's too much to hope that they knew one another. Two private detectives? No, not likely is it?'

They retreated up the stairs and stood looking at the computers.

'Just like our workplace, eh?' Deer said.

'You wish. Not that we'd know how to use all this kit. She'd run rings around us.'

'But she got killed. Puts things into perspective, doesn't it?'

Deer shrugged and looked as though he might try to switch something on.

'Better not touch anything, it might have to be done in a certain order, or everything gets wiped, and we don't want that.'

'Did the IT guys say when they were coming?' Deer asked.

'Nope, just as soon as they can. I'm hoping that will be today. But I don't want to leave this lot alone, it could be too valuable. Too valuable for someone to want to leave it intact. If word gets around that she's dead, all sorts could crawl out and decide to make sure we don't get to know what she knew.'

He tapped away on his phone for a moment and then turned to the window as a green van drove up.

Alex woke early. This time his sleep had been dreamless, or at least he didn't remember them. It was probably because recent activities had exhausted him. He slipped on his swimming shorts and opened the patio doors. This was the sort of time that Lizzie used to be up, and he hoped that wasn't the case today. He had no desire to renew the relationship. He had a feeling that she didn't have friendships with men after a relationship. It had to be full on or nothing. With Dave presumably out of the picture now as far as she was concerned, maybe she'd be on the hunt, if only for some semblance of protection.

He couldn't see her, so he ran to the sea and braced himself as he ran into the waves. Not that they were big, just a shock to his early morning system. He swam the length of the hotel a few times and then waded back out of the sea and onto the beach. There were the tiny tracks of baby turtles heading down, and they sent his memory reeling back. How much had changed in a few days? He trudged back to the room to make coffee and maybe to write, maybe not.

Coffee made, he thought about Penny, or whatever her name was. The USB. He hadn't looked at it. Maybe he should. He picked up his laptop and set it on the table outside the room, next to the coffee. He took a deep breath and, opening up the laptop, tapped on the first file under the USB header. It asked for a password and he swore. Of course, it wouldn't be that easy and he knew so little about Penny, there was no way he was going to guess it. He closed the file. It wasn't worth guessing. It might erase itself and other stuff on the laptop as well. He wondered whether to upload it to the cloud and decided against it. He didn't want it corrupting that as well.

There was only one thing to do. So, he started writing.

Jayne walked to Bath Spa station and took the train back home. Back home. Where was home now? The home she was travelling to had been violated and didn't feel safe now. She nearly turned around and went back to Bath straight away, but instead, she turned the lock to her old home. She walked from room to room, just to make sure there was no one there. Her heart was in her mouth as she entered each room, but nothing had changed. No one new had been in to wreck the place. She went to the small room, where she knew there was a suitcase, took it to her bedroom, and began to fill it. Bath was going to be her home now. A decision made easier by the break-in. She emailed the solicitor to instruct him to sell up as soon as he could. Her life could then move on. Johnnie wasn't part of this. He might be gone next week or even the next day. This was for her. No one else. It was time for Jayne Sutherland to stand tall and be herself.

An email pinged on her phone. The solicitor reporting that he had heard from Diana Sharp's solicitor and would be responding. He also said that he would arrange a sale with a local estate agent as soon as he was able. She texted back to ask him to arrange for someone to clear the place of everything that now remained and to have it cleaned.

Job done, she wondered what to do next, and thinking of nothing, she called a taxi. With a heavy case,

*a couple of bags, and money in her pocket, she was
going to take the easy route back to Bath, where she felt
welcome, and for once in her life, happy. And wanted.*

He knew what was going to happen next, but didn't
feel that he could write it. A block. Maybe he should
start a new story and run it in parallel? He could see
people heading for breakfast, though, and that seemed
a better idea, so he packed up and followed them. As
he sat enjoying his bacon and eggs, and a black coffee,
a shadow fell over the table.

'Mind if I sit here?' Lizzie was back. He said nothing, so she sat down opposite.

'How are you, darling?'

'Lizzie, is this really appropriate?'

'What's wrong? You're alone, I'm alone, seems
sensible to me.'

'My friend was poisoned not that many hours ago.'

She shrugged. 'Sorry, and all that.'

'What happened to Dave?'

'Gone, with, I'm told, the police looking for him.
Do you think he had something to do with your friend?
They reckon he might try to steal a boat and make for
Trinny, but I don't see it.'

'Why not?'

'He wouldn't know what to do with a boat.
Anyway, what would he do there? Make for Argen-
tina? No, I reckon he'll try to make it back to the
UK. He kept saying he had almost no money, which
was probably true, so he's stuffed.'

'And you?'

'I knew you'd get around to me, eventually. I'm alright, thank you. As you've probably heard, I caught some scrapes and scratches on the coral, and they say they'll take a while to heal, so I'm covering up. It really is a bore. Would you like to see them? Back in my, sorry, our room?'

'No, Lizzie, I wouldn't. I have got a day's writing ahead of me, so I'll keep to that. Thank you for the offer, though.'

'Always the gentleman. I appreciated that, but it leaves you open to those who aren't. Men and women. Don't you think?'

'I suppose the only answer to that is, you should know.'

'Ah, claws, at last. They do exist then. Alright, I'll leave you in peace for now, but you are the only person I know here now. We'd make a good couple.'

He finished his coffee, stood, and after tucking his chair in, walked out of the restaurant. Outside he could see the pelicans diving and the fishermen bringing in their nets. A different way of life from back home, but unfortunately back home had followed him here. He unlocked and went into the room, almost surprised to find everything intact. How strange it was to feel on tenterhooks all the time. Whatever Lizzie said, he had a feeling Dave hadn't gone that far and might well be close by. On this island, there was plenty of cover, and even the tropical forest was not far away. Whatever Dave did, though, he couldn't hide his white skin and likely a lack of money.

He picked up the laptop and went onto the terrace, but his mind was all over the place. Lizzie had driven into it like some rebel tank and occupied his mind with pictures of her body that erased Penny. Penny, or Janice, or whoever she was. As equally false as Lizzie, just in a different way. Maybe he ought to talk to Lizzie if only to find out more about the **aware**. He'd almost forgotten about them with everything that had happened, but in less than a week's time, he would be back where he'd started and have to face it all again.

He spent the morning musing, sunbathing, drinking gin and tonic, and dipping in the sea from time to time. He could see Lizzie when he went in. She was, as she'd said, covered up in a sarong from the beach seller, sitting on a sunbed under a palm tree. Once she waved. Just once.

At lunchtime he walked along the path by the beach, and, as he'd guessed, she moved to walk with him. Together they walked along without a word said. He couldn't say he was lost in thought, he just avoided both thought and conversation. They walked into the restaurant and sat at the same table. She went to get her food, and he followed. It was only when they had both eaten that she spoke.

'I never answered your question about **awareness**, did I?'

'No.'

'You know it's all a con, don't you?'

He looked up at her.

'It is. Nothing more than a bloody great con, and they sucked me into it.'

'Marlin?' he asked.

'Oh, George,' she laughed, 'he hasn't much idea what goes on, or if he does, he's a bloody good actor. Small fry. Just a venue. That's George Marlin.'

'So?'

'Do you mind if we move away from here? I need a smoke if I'm going to get into this, and a drink or four.'

They walked back towards the room, by way of the bar. She fetched a small bag of rolled cigarettes, which, when she lit up, he recognised the sweet smell of cannabis. A drink, and a smoke later, he realised how tense she had been.

'I got into it when I was invited to a soiree, as he calls them, with a friend. You know my idea of a friend now so I won't beat about the bush. I met him, we screwed, and the next day he rings and asks if I'll go with him to this party. So, I went. At first, it was all very tame and well, you've been there, you've seen them. Then they started talking about **awareness**, which I was interested in. At least I was interested until Maggie taps me on the elbow and drags me off. She said she knew all about me, and what I liked, so how about it? I honestly didn't know what she was talking about, so seeing me looking puzzled, she takes me upstairs and shows me. There were six of them, and one of them was the guy who'd brought me. Full sex, six of them. Do you know it actually shocked me? Hard to believe, isn't it, but honestly, I'd never even thought of anything like that then. But there they were. My friend for the night had recommended me. Bloody cheek.'

'Maggie reeled me in. She said it didn't have to be that way, just one bloke at a time, and she'd make sure she vetted them. It tempted me. Then she said it was £500 a time. So it was a knocking shop, not a nice little club. I demurred, and she upped the rate until she got to £800, but it wasn't the money I was interested in, it was the variety. Before you say it, I know you've already realised that. I didn't agree to anything that evening, but I mulled it over.'

'Then, surprise, surprise, who should appear on my doorstep the next morning, but Maggie. It wasn't just the sex she was selling, it was the whole **aware** package. She thought that I would be the ideal person to come into partnership with them, with her really, but she kept saying them. I was to chat blokes up, sell the **awareness** thing, brush up their egos, enrol them, get them to buy an expensive phone, and then slowly assess them for the rooms upstairs. If they showed interest, I was to put them Maggie's way. She has a stable of about a dozen girls, not all working at the same time. I'd got used to the idea, as I'm sure she knew, and so I said alright, I'd give it a go.

Awareness doesn't exist, only in your mind, but if enough people say it does, then it becomes real.

There was an entire language to learn, an entire world of spin. I started, and it sucked me in. I mean, I had a new and willing partner every night if I wanted. I know it's not for everyone, but it was for me. I loved it. The selling bit I wasn't too bothered about and Maggie could see that, so she soft peddled with me, but the punters enjoyed my company, enjoyed me, so she wanted me there. I never had more than one guy in an evening, although I experimented with a girl or two, but it wasn't for me, and I could drop out of any evening if I wanted.

There was the occasional evening when Maggie was a bit insistent, and one of those was the time you turned up, and you had money. She said that you'd need careful handling, but it would be a coup for the group if you joined. She also wanted to keep you away from Jayne, who was one of her girls, because she thought she might tell you what was going on. That's how it played out, but I enjoyed your company, so it became a bit more. I don't know if I should say sorry or not, but maybe you should take it as a compliment that you lasted more than anyone else.'

He raised an eyebrow, and she laughed and held his arm. 'Men and their egos. Let's put it this way: you lasted longer than any other man for a long time. OK? I do actually like you, and I mean this nicely, because you are, well, a bit naïve. There's an innocence about you, that, I'm sorry, I've probably eroded a bit.'

'I was beginning to accept that **awareness** was a con. It can't have been just George Marlin who was behind it. Even my parents believed in it.'

'Yes, I know. No, it's not just Marlin, it's at least nationwide, probably further, I just don't know. It's still a con, a front for other activities. That's where Dave came in. He's part of the bigger picture, and it's not pretty.'

'Enforcement?'

She gave a slight frown and a sideways look. 'Yes. How did you know?'

He'd thought about what he would say now and was ready. He wasn't going to bring Penny into this.

'He looks the type, and then AJ told me what happened on the boat. You're in trouble, aren't you?'

She went quiet, looking down at her covered legs. 'Yes,' she said.

CHAPTER THIRTY-NINE

Torrey was getting impatient. He was sure that the whole of his investigation depended on the computers and safes that were in Janice Weston's house, but so far, his experts hadn't cracked them. They were talking about taking a blowtorch to the safes, and as for the computers it was like defusing a bomb, so they said. If they made one false step, everything would be wiped, never to be seen again. She had all sorts of ways of preventing access, none of which he understood.

They were back in Bath, and he was musing over the house in the Circus. Suddenly he stood up and called to Deer. 'You free for an hour?'

Together they walked towards the Circus, having already signed the keys out.

'Something is bothering me, and I don't know what it is. Something I've seen, but not understood, and when we saw the setup at Weston's house it was ringing bells, but what bells exactly I don't know. My subconscious, I suppose. I'm hoping you can help.'

'Can you put any frame around it, narrow it down, sir?'

'No, not really, but see if you can think if there are any inconsistencies between the two places. It's something to do with that.'

They arrived at the Circus and let themselves in. It all looked familiar now. Taking each room in turn, they just stood and wondered. It was on their second time around that Deer suddenly said, 'Internet. Computers. There's nothing. Not a modem, nothing. Was she really that IT illiterate? She doesn't strike me that way.'

'You're right. Absolutely right. But why? I mean everyone I know has a modem these days if only to download movies. There's something we're not getting with all this. Let's have another look around now we know what we're looking for. It's not as though there are no providers here, lots are offering a high-speed connection. It's bloody odd.'

They walked from room to room and out into the garden.

'I still don't get it, there's got to be something else,' Torrey said, looking around.

'Search me, sir, maybe we'd better see if anyone else at the station has an idea.'

'It's not that sort of thing. It's something here, something that should be obvious that we're missing.'

'One more time around?'

'Come on then.'

They went back to the station, Torrey racking his brains, but the answer eluded him. What with that and the length of time it was taking to crack Janice

Weston's security, it was a frustrating day. It was about to get worse.

They rang him just after lunch. He went ballistic. They had gone for the heavy arm option to open one of the safes. The interior had combusted, and they expected that nothing in it had survived, but they were continuing with their work trying to open it. On the plus side, opening one might let them see how it had been constructed, and help them open the second one.

He rang IT and laid it on the line. Maximum caution. This woman had the best systems going, and it really would be a good idea if they did not screw it up. Or words to that effect.

He heard that they'd put in a complaint afterwards. When it was all over.

Alex woke up early again, in his own bed, or rather in Penny's, but with no one else in it. Lizzie had suggested they sleep together in the room they'd booked, of course, but in a half-hearted way that wasn't like her. He wasn't sure if it was her injuries or her fear of Dave coming back. Maybe both.

As the day before he went for a swim, up and down parallel to the hotel, the pelicans quietly sitting on the fishing boats moored off-shore. He was used to the ropes that stretched into the shore by now and knew when to look out for them, diving under, or just lifting each rope as he came across it. He slowed and watched the shore. There was no one apart from the leaf sweeper out yet. That changed as he watched while he slowly breast-stroked his way along. It wasn't Lizzie, but a couple from near her room who ran down to the water hand in hand and squealing into it, splashing each other and then swimming. A honeymoon couple, maybe.

He turned and kept going. Maybe she wasn't coming out? Maybe he shouldn't care? After half an hour or so, he walked back up the beach, shaved, and made himself ready for breakfast. How odd it was that he should now want to see Lizzie, to talk to her, to understand more. Especially since it was quite likely she was just telling him a story, something to keep him around, keep his attention on her. Something to keep him from the truth, whatever that was. Maybe she was simply coming clean. Who knew? But if he heard what she had to say, then he could judge, come to his conclusions. If he didn't, well, it was lost, whatever it was.

He went to breakfast, and still, she wasn't there. Wasn't there again today, I wish that girl would go away. A rhyme from the past. He went through his routine, brought the laptop out to the terrace, and typed.

She'd settled into the flat now, but in a desire to be independent, the hunt for a job went on. Maybe she should think about getting some qualifications. She had some money now, and some coming in each month from the café. Maybe it was time to try. There were two universities in Bath, but what they offered was likely beyond her. She had brought over the laptop her father had given her with her last haul and opened it up. Tapping in "courses in Bath UK" she watched a list come up. Her heart skipped as she saw one, something she had never even dreamed of. It was for a cookery and baking school. Baking. She could be a baker. Maybe she could bake things for the café. Wow. It didn't have to involve lots of textbooks and writing stuff, it would be making things, things that people wanted. It was a revelation. Excited, she ran with the open laptop down to see Jellie, but the café was busy, so she retreated. Maybe later. What to do next? Ring them. She ran back up the stairs and sat down. There were several courses at different places, and it looked as though an introductory course would cost about £200, or a five-day course for almost a thousand. She needed to talk this through with Jellie, she really did. She was out of her depth now. Moneywise she could afford it if they'd have her. Even before she found a job, she had the cash she had found, and the thousand pounds Jellie had given her. There would be another thousand next month, too. She could afford it if she was careful. She also had to go through the bills that her father had left her. She couldn't give them to Willowby to offset against the estate because he was the last person she wanted to know about the flat. After Diana Sharp, that is.

Her mobile rang, making her jump. No one rang her these days.

'Hi, poppet, the masses have gone. I'm free now. Did you want to talk?'

Did she! She ran back down the stairs.

'Are you busy?' Lizzie was beside him, and he hadn't noticed her arrive.

'I can stop if you want to talk. Have you had breakfast?' he said, closing the lid of the laptop.

'No. I had a fever. The doctor has been and given me antibiotics. Some of the coral scratches went septic. He cleaned them up and thinks they'll be alright now. You?'

'Yes, I swam a few lengths, not far. I started writing as soon as I came back from breakfast.' She was subdued, he thought, not her usual self.

'I wondered if you'd like some company. Just to talk, nothing else, I'm not up to it.'

Was it only Lizzie who thought that he'd immediately want something else? It was just the way she thought. Sex first, anything else second. He was becoming used to that.

'OK, pull up a chair. Would you like a coffee?'

She nodded, so he made them both one and went back to her. She had drawn up a chair so that it was at ninety degrees to him.

'Was there anything particular you wanted to talk about?'

She shrugged. 'I felt we sort of left it hanging last time. Maybe I ought to say more.'

'You said you were in trouble.'

'Yes. I want out, and they don't want that. Dave was supposed to convince me. They thought I was running away, and they sent him after me.'

'So, you hadn't been here before, with him?'

She laughed. 'No, nothing like that, but he knows what I'm like. I tried to convince him I was harmless.'

'Do you want to say who wants you back?'

'More like what. There's an organisation that looks after the **aware**, a sort of brand management if you like. I found out that it was pushing drugs, not in Bath, yet.'

'It's criminal then?'

'Yes. It probably started quite innocently, but it's definitely criminal now. Dave thought that someone was onto him, someone he thought he recognised, and he panicked. I think he tried to kill me, back on the reef. But AJ sorted it out. Dave just said he was thrashing around because he couldn't swim, but that was a lie. He's an excellent swimmer, and anyway, he was holding me down and pushing my breathing tube into the water. I know what he was trying to do. But something has spooked him now. Maybe he's paranoid, I don't know, but he's done a runner. I think I said, he doesn't have much money, so I don't know what he's going to do. Whatever, I need to be careful now. In case he comes for me. He's a bit unpredictable. Sorry.'

He shrugged. What the hell could he do? Apart from providing company and a listening ear. Should he ask about Penny? There seemed little point since he was sure that it was Penny who had spooked Dave. One of them killed her. It was just a question of which.

'That's alright. I'm here, I'm listening. Is there anything else?'

She looked at him as she did when she was after something and gave a slight toss of her head. No, Lizzie, "that" was definitely off the list. But then her face turned serious, little lines appearing, and she gave a little shiver. He wasn't sure if she was acting, but he thought not.

'No. I'm just frightened.'

'How about the police?'

'Here? I doubt if they've got the manpower to do anything. I mean, it's a poor island.'

'Not so poor. Trinidad has oil. Although I heard Tobago sent money back to them because they thought the extra money would change their way of life. That might be nonsense of course, but someone told me that.'

'The doctor thought that seawater might do my legs good, not today, but maybe tomorrow, once the cream he put on has had some time to work. Would you come with me?'

'Along the coast here? Of course. It's an easy swim if we avoid the fishermen's ropes, and you can swim in your depth. No problem there.'

'Thank you. I can't, you know, to thank you.'

'That's not necessary. I'm just helping a fellow human being. Not every bloke wants sex for every little deed you know.'

'It was the way I was brought up, but you don't want to hear about that.'

'If you want to tell someone, and that helps you, then tell me. As I say, I'm here, and here for you. Let's face it, I don't have anyone else to talk to now.'

It was harsh, and he saw her wince. But the hell with that, he had feelings too.

'Thank you. I don't think anyone has ever said that to me before,' she said as she placed a hand on his.

He thought she was going to lean forward to kiss him. She certainly moved that way. Maybe it was something in his reaction that warned her off, so she just rocked gently on her chair and smiled at him.

'We don't have many days left now, do we?' she said. 'Then we'll be winging our way back to Gatwick, and Bath, and whatever awaits us. It seems so far away, and yet. We've brought it with us, haven't we? We can't escape, however much we try.'

She looked thoughtful and turned to look out at the sea.

'I'm sorry. I'm wasting your time. I can't talk, not yet, but I would like to just sit if that's alright with you.'

He nodded, but she wasn't looking. She was lost in some other world he could not penetrate.

'Yes, that's alright,' he said as he opened up the laptop, and tried to turn to Jayne.

CHAPTER FORTY

'Look,' Jayne said, her hand quivering as she held the laptop up so that Jellie could see it. 'What do you think?'

Jellie read the screen. But she was frowning. Not the reaction Jayne expected. 'Yes, I see. Sorry, I was expecting you to go for something, I don't know, more academic I suppose. I'm not sure what you would do with this.'

'But I could make things to sell in the shop, couldn't I?'

'Jayne, that's very sweet of you, but I've got everything sorted here. I mean, I have an oven for cooking up the pastries, and they come in frozen, so I don't have a problem making them, they're just there, waiting. I'm sorry to dampen things down, but, you know, it's one thing helping in the café, but quite another to, well, take it over. At least it feels that way a bit. Sorry.'

Jayne put the laptop down carefully, her eyes full of tears. She looked at Jellie and nodded. Then she stepped forward and hugged her. 'I'm sorry too, I

got carried away, didn't I. I'll have another think.'
She picked up the laptop and walked out with a brief
wave to Jellie as she went. Back upstairs she shed
a tear before going back to look for something else,
but her heart wasn't in it. It wasn't long before she
left the flat. She needed a job. Stuff studying.

Alex sat and watched Lizzie, who was sitting in a dream state, looking straight ahead. There wasn't even a pelican there to see. Lost in another world and, he wondered, what was in that world? What was waiting for her back home? Something frightening? Or just the same old, back to the Crescent and the men Maggie chose for her? But then maybe it was the threat of drugs, the gang moving in, and what would become of her? The gentle life of George Marlin's little club turned upside down. They might force him to stop, and just move **awareness** to another venue, or take over his life. They probably didn't care, as long as the money rolled in.

She turned her head and saw him looking at her, but didn't smile.

'I'm bored. Fancy a walk? We can get a drink as we go.'

He packed up, and they walked along the path together. The sun was high now, and the sand too hot to walk on with bare feet, so he kept to the grass.

'Sorry. I keep saying sorry, don't I, but I feel I'm imposing with no payback for you. I wondered if we could go out somewhere, not today, maybe tomorrow. I'd just like to get away from here. I'm on edge all the time because I don't know what's going to happen next. I have no control over events. Does that sound crazy?'

'No, it's not crazy, and yes, I think it would be a good idea for us both to get out. Shall I book a car? I suspect boats aren't your favourite now.' She smiled at that.

'That's sweet of you,' the familiar hand on his arm. She had become so predictable, 'I think that would be lovely. No need to consult me on where we go. I'll just sit back and be a passenger. Just the movement and a change of location will help.'

They reached the bar, and she surprised him by ordering a beer. She had never struck him as a beer drinker. She noticed his surprise.

'It's hot, this is cold, it's simple.' She grinned at him, and he nodded and ordered the same. They walked the grounds, sipping their drinks.

'I'm just waiting,' she said. 'Waiting for the axe to fall. It's an odd feeling. It has an almost timeless feel to it, as though everything has stopped, and will only restart when we return. I have a bad feeling about that, and whatever happens, I hope you won't feel that I'm a bad person.'

He had to make an effort not to look at her, and wasn't sure why. Was it because he felt she wanted an audience, but didn't want to grant it? Whatever, he just walked, looking at the dry, stony ground. They had left the compound now and about to walk along the grass strip that bordered the road that ran past the hotel. Across the other side, a cow was lying on the tennis court. It had a rope around its neck, with a metal stake attached. A captive on the run.

'Yes!' Torrey exclaimed and threw the phone clattering back onto its rest. The team looked around as one. 'They're in. No damage this time, and the IT guys think they've found a way in as well. Happy days. Deer, come on, let's go and see our treasure trove.'

They had to drive about a mile before they walked into the shed where the technicians had been working. Someone had set it well away from everything else, at the back of a piece of wasteland that, given Bath's expansion, would probably be built on soon. There wasn't much there, just two safes, one open at the back, and looking very black inside, and another, which was on its side, and had its base cut open. On a plastic sheet, some yards away, was a pile of folders and loose papers.

'We thought it best to move them as soon as we could, just in case it decided to go up like the other one. We think it is safe, but, you know, best to be sure. We might have been lucky. If you have a look at the first one, it doesn't look as though there was much in it.'

They walked across and peered into the first safe. It looked as though it had been where she chucked her daily tray of papers and some books. A couple were just badly singed, and Torrey pulled one out, "The handbook of drugs and society". By itself, it said a lot about what they might find in the other safe's offering. He placed it back, and they walked across to the main pile. There were twenty-five A4 lever-arch box files and several bundles of papers, each several inches thick. Torrey picked up a box file and opened it. He read for a few minutes and then turned to Deer.

'We've got them, Deer, we've got them. She penetrated them, right into the heart of them, and was ready to bring them down. Right, I want a secure unmarked wagon down here, with guards and an escort. If they find out we've got this stuff, all hell will break out.'

'Back to the office?' Deer asked.

'Good question. Give me a minute.'

He stepped away and made a call. 'It's all going to London. They're sending an escort, but we have to get it back to ours first, behind locked gates if we can, so I still need the van and escort. This is national now.'

It took nearly two hours for the procession to arrive, familiar faces, so no worries about this being an interception. They loaded the files and papers in, and two officers sat inside with them, a car in front and one behind as they left. Torrey took out his phone again to make just one more call, then nodded to Deer and strode to the car.

'IT has got in and downloaded everything she had. No idea what it is yet, but I want to look before it all goes up the chain.'

As soon as they left the site, he put the lights and siren on and went for it. Not strictly legit, but he wanted to make sure no one else got there before him.

CHAPTER FORTY-ONE

Lizzie and Alex walked along the road, and back through the public picnic area, where people were already set up, or hadn't left from the night before, past Alex's terrace, and back to the bar where they ordered more beer. They had stopped talking altogether. He was just providing company for her thoughts, and they were miles away. As they walked back on the grass towards his terrace, she suddenly stopped and looked up at him.

'I've been terrible, Alex. I'm sorry. I'm not a fit person to be with, really. I want to ask you to help me, but that would be wrong. I can't, mustn't do that, but if you could just be with me until we get back, it would help. Just until we get back. Could you swap the seats around, to make sure you're next to me on the plane? Please. Please.'

He nodded. She was a shadow of the person he had known. There was no spark, no vibrancy to her. It had melted away in a sea of contrition for what he could only guess.

'Of course. As one human being to another, as we swim through... Oh, sod it. Yes, of course, you're getting me at it now. I'd be pleased to do that, Lizzie, whatever you think you've done. Alright?'

She nodded, smiled, took his arm, and seemed to get some of her bounce back with the inevitable result.

'And I'd like a screw before we go. I've got to keep my reputation up, at least with you, after all.'

The woman had no shame. How long ago since Penny had died? Maybe this woman had killed her. Who knew? He shook his head in disbelief. He was wondering what had happened to Penny's body, and if it would accompany them back in an altogether different class of travel. When they returned, he would see if he could find her relatives, parents maybe, and attend the funeral. It seemed right. He had been very fond of her, and if things had turned out differently, well. Then he thought of her other identity. Had she been fond of him or playing a role? He was thinking of the latter, but it didn't matter. He still wanted to be there. For the very end.

'Well, a girl has to ask,' she was saying in response to his silence, but she was smiling now as she clung on to his arm.

They settled back on the terrace, and he fetched his laptop to sit cross-legged with it beside her.

She was fed up with Bath and trudging its streets looking for work. For an unqualified woman, there wasn't much going. At least, until she found the shoe shop and the arrogant woman in charge of it.

Her name was Vicki, and she said yes, she would have a job the following week, which would allow her to sack the useless piece of shit that she had there now. It wasn't a wholehearted endorsement of Vicki's character. But it was all that was going, so she took it. Minimum wage, of course. On the strength of that, and now that she wouldn't be paying out for an expensive course, she shopped around for a new outfit suitable for the job, because Vicki had made it clear she would have to provide her own and expected her to be smartly dressed. It cheered her up anyway, and she returned to the café for lunch in a better frame of mind.

'Can I help?' she asked as she saw Jellie running around with a café overflowing onto the pavement, and for the next hour, she did exactly that, making coffee and tea while Jellie did the rest. When there were only a few people left, Jellie came over to her.

'I'm sorry I was down on you this morning; it came as a bit of a surprise. You see, I've built all this up from scratch, it's my baby, and it felt as though you were trying to take it from me. Want some food?'

They sat and watched the world, and the customers go by, chomping on salad rolls, cups of coffee to hand.

'I'm going to have to tell you this as well. I've been holding back, but It's screwing my head up.'

Jayne looked at her and guessed. 'You and my father? I'd guessed.'

Jellie nodded, and Jayne saw the start of tears at the corners of her eyes, so looked away.

'Yes. It was more than just a casual thing for me. A lot more. It nearly broke up my marriage. I was so into him. There was something else too, something I've told no one else about, especially my husband. My son is your father's, so I suppose he's related to you, isn't he, a half-brother? You can't tell him. Please, I'm relying on you, trusting you, but you know if you happen to visit, as a friend, well, he'll be there.'

Jayne reached over and hugged her close, but Jellie broke away and ran out into the back room, leaving Jayne with a whirl of thoughts.

'Can we settle up, please? That was lovely.' And she was back in the real world, an elderly couple standing at the counter. She sorted them out quickly and went to find Jellie.

'Can I ask what it's about?' Lizzie asked.

'Would you like to proofread it if I can get reception to print it off, or at least some of it?'

'I'd like that. It would make me feel useful, and that's not something I feel very often.'

He went to fetch his keyring and downloaded the file to it, then walked along to reception, who needed to check with the manager. Once that was done, and a rate agreed, they quickly printed the pages for him, and he took them back to Lizzie, via the bar, for another couple of beers. After that, she sat in silence, reading, but Alex, work interrupted, just gazed out at the sea, and drank the beer. After a while, she looked up, smiling.

'How did you know?'

'What do you mean?'

'This is our Jayne, isn't it? The girl Maggie brought in. My understudy, if you like.'

'I don't know. I mean, I met Jayne and went out with her for a short while, but I don't know anything about her, I just used her name.'

'Well, we will see. You're just about to get to the part where she came along to a soiree, as George calls them. Maggie invited her. She saw her when she was out shopping for the clothes you mention at the end.'

'I don't understand. I mean, are you saying that I've written Jayne's story, without knowing it? Without really knowing her?'

'Put it this way, we had some long chats in between sessions as it were, and your story fits everything I remember of what she told me. Maybe **awareness** exists. Spooky, eh?'

'Well, so much for me being an author. I'm just channelling someone's life. Or is there something in this being a **dramatist** thing?'

'Maybe, or is that what authors do when they're in the moment as it were, lost in the words of the story? Maybe they're picking up bits of people's lives and threading them together.'

He shrugged, deflated. How the hell had that happened? **Awareness** didn't exist, he was sure of that now, and yet? He looked down at his laptop and wondered about the words that would come next. Would it be as Lizzie predicted?

'If you've got a pen or something, there are a few things that you might think of changing,' she said, 'but if you'd rather I didn't then, you know, don't worry.'

She looked so pathetic, so apologetic, that his heart went out to her. He looked her in the eyes and came to a decision. Heart over mind.

'Come on, let's have that screw you were talking about,' he said with a smile.

He took her arm, and she rose to meet him. Arm in arm they went into his room, where, gently, they kissed, and step by step put her back together. Back to the Lizzie he had known. Before Dave. Maybe just… before.

Torrey stood in front of the Circus house, Deer at his side.

'I'm not letting this go, Deer, there's something we're missing. I know there is.'

'Shall we go in then, sir? It's a bit wet out here.'

It was true. The rain was sheeting down, but Torrey in his big belted mac didn't seem to notice. Deer just had an umbrella. They walked over to the now-familiar door, and Deer opened up. The place smelt stale, unoccupied, unloved. They started in the kitchen diner, and worked their way around room by room, and then into the garden. Back inside, Torrey looked at the door to the cellar, and after a hesitation, they went down. The bottles of wine probably had an extra layer of dust on them, but nothing else had changed. They turned to leave when Torrey turned.

'I've been stupid. Have you got a tape measure?'

'Sorry, no.'

'Right, let's pace it out. Number of steps each way.'

It took Deer seven paces across and twenty, front to back. They went back upstairs and carried out the same exercise. Twenty, front to back, but seventeen across. Torrey, looking jubilant, ran back to the cellar steps. As soon as he was down, he examined the wine rack closely. It was metal, and far more solidly built than necessary. But he couldn't see what he wanted.

'Let's take the bottles out, there must be something here.'

They went from left to right, carefully placing the bottles along the opposite wall, until they were left with just the bare rack.

'Look,' Torrey said, pointing at the outline of a door on the other side of the rack, 'there must be a way of moving this thing. Look, in the middle of it, casters, the damn thing wheels out, it's just finding out how.'

It took them more than an hour, and it was Deer who found it. A little switch that was hidden in the racking, the wiring in the metal tubes that made the racking up. He got Torrey to stand back and touched it. With the lightest of touches, the rack swung open into two halves, which allowed access to the door. Which was locked. Two mortice locks, one at the top, the other at the bottom, and no handle to the door either. Frustrated, Torrey called for a locksmith. The man who came was the one who had fitted it years before, so knew exactly what to do. Bath might be a city, but in many ways, it was a small place.

CHAPTER FORTY-TWO

Alex and Lizzie had just a few hours of peace before lunch, and strolled along the grass towards the bar, feeling relaxed and happier with the world. They saw several fishing boats making for the building. Maybe it was their lunchtime too. Three of them peeled off and made directly for the beach in front of the hotel, coming in fast. While two peeled off to wait, one kept going. Its outboard lifted just before it hit the shore so that it came right onto the sand before it stopped. Three men leapt out. One pointed at them, and Lizzie screamed. 'Dave! No!'

There was one white man and two locals. The white man was holding a gun. Alex was no authority on guns, but it looked real enough, especially when Dave stopped, held it at arm's length and fired. There was a crack of glass behind them as a patio door took the shot. Alex threw himself on Lizzie as another shot rang out, and he heard a thud in the grass beside them and something grazing his upper arm. There was nothing else he could do except brace himself for the next shot, and surely that wouldn't miss. They could only lay there, Lizzie still and panting, him on top, barely daring to breathe.

There were shouts from the hotel and shots rang out, but not from where Dave had been standing. The feet of men running past them from the hotel, then more shots. The sound of outboards starting up, followed by more shots and one outboard coughing in its death throes. Then a voice, right next to them.

'Well, Mr Torrey said to me, he said, "make sure you deliver those two safe and sound to the aeroplane," and that is what we shall do.' Alex rolled off Lizzie, knelt, then stood to see the figure of Superintendent Henry smiling at him. He offered a hand to Lizzie, which she ignored, scrambling up on her own. They looked across towards the beach. Dave lay face down, two policemen next to him, while other policemen escorted three men away. The boat that had beached was still there, as was one other. The last boat was a speck in the distance. Henry followed his gaze.

'They won't get far, look over there.'

On the horizon and coming in fast was another larger ship.

'Trinidad and Tobago navy. They'll have them in a minute. Now,' he turned to them, 'how are you both? Hopefully unscathed, or I will have to apologise to DI Torrey. Ah, Mr Ash, I'm sorry, but a plaster from the hotel will deal with that.'

'We're both alright, I think. What's the expression? Shaken not stirred.' He looked at his left arm, where a red line of blood was flowing down. It didn't hurt yet. One of the hotel staff ran over with tissues, ointment and a large plaster and sorted it out. He thanked them and turned to Henry.

'Very good, Mr Ash, very good. All is well now. If you'll excuse me, I have some paperwork to do and some people to talk to before I ring the police in the UK. I don't think you'll be bothered again during your stay, but I must ask you not to leave the hotel grounds, for your protection. I still have some men here to ensure that we keep you safe.'

'Thank you, Superintendent, that's very kind. Please thank your men too, they saved us.'

'It's no trouble, it's helped me too. I believe I now have at least two members of a local drugs gang in custody, so I'm happy too. Enjoy the rest of your holiday, and my regards to DI Torrey when you see him.'

The police left, and they looked out to see the patrol boat rendezvous with the fleeing fishing boat. No doubt someone would tidy up the other boats in due course. Lizzie put her arm around Alex, kissed his plaster, and they made their way to the bar to be greeted with more questions than they felt up to answering, so they apologised and continued into lunch.

'No trip out then. I'm sorry,' Alex said as they tucked into swordfish. 'Just a few days of sun, sea and…'

'Sex,' Lizzie finished for him with a grin. She was much more herself now, although he wondered what

325

awaited her back at home. No doubt the anxieties would recur nearer the time, but for now, maybe they could just enjoy themselves. 'I'm sorry you got hurt, are you alright?'

'It's going to be sore tomorrow, but for now, it's fine. I must get some more plasters, I don't think this one is going to hold, and I don't want to walk the beach dripping blood.'

'We'll get some on the way back. I think that one's a bit small. You could do with two that size. Anything you want to do after lunch, apart from me?'

'Lizzie; down, girl. It's lovely to be wanted but there are limits.'

'Oh. Tell me what they are.'

He shook his head. He never knew when she was joking. They finished their meal, collected a couple of beers, and then picked up some plasters from reception before returning to the room. There, as tiredness overcame him, he lay on the bed. She nestled in beside him, and they had an unplanned siesta.

It was nearly five in the evening when Lizzie awoke, but Alex was still sleeping. She hesitated, and then went to her room, collected some money, and went outside to where a small cabin housed the taxi owners, or at least someone who could call one. She was in luck, and a large woman took her over to her massive American sedan. No air-con, but the experience was fun. They pulled over just out of Black Rock, where she could see a phone box. She went in, made her call, and returned with the woman to the hotel.

Alex was still sleeping as she crept into the room, so she changed into her sarong, opened the patio door, and sat on the terrace. Bored after a few minutes, she set off for the bar. Several guests were standing around, pre-dinner drink in hand, so she joined them, and they immediately asked her about the shooting.

When Alex woke, and walked over to the bar, thinking that she might have retired with another male companion, but she was unsteadily recounting the story of the shooting again for those who had just arrived. She smiled and put an arm around him, more for stability than affection he felt. It was probably going to be like this until they went home, but better that than being shot at.

After a quiet dinner, they retired to their room, and he opened up the laptop.

Jayne stood in the café, alone. No customers, and no Jellie. But her mind was full of the revelation that her father had a son, Jellie's son. How strange the world was that you could stumble through it not knowing something like that. Something so important, something that blew your mind. Shaking her head, she wiped the counter down, and then started on the coffee machine. Displacement activity. Yet she felt displaced already.

Everything cleaned, she went into the back of the café to find Jellie. She was standing, looking at the wall, lost in her thoughts. Jayne went over and hugged her.

'That's an awfully big secret to keep to yourself all these years, love,' she whispered.

Jellie turned around, and they hugged. Jayne could feel Jellie's sobs until they subsided, and Jellie looked up, her face a mess, mascara running. Jayne went to wipe it, but Jellie shook her head.

'Don't worry, I'll sort it. Thanks for that. Yes, it's been a long road, and it's odd. Sharing is a relief and yet it feels kind of odd as well. I have to trust someone else now not to tell, and not to blow my world apart. I hope you understand?'

'Of course. I'd love to meet him, but only when you're ready, and on your terms. There's no way I want to cause a problem for you. It must have taken courage to tell me, so thank you.'

'I had to. I couldn't live with myself otherwise. Imagine him growing up, never seeing his half-sister, and you never seeing him. No, whatever the risks, I couldn't do that.'

'Would you like me to keep going? You could stay here, or even go home if you like, I'll be alright.'

'No, love, that's really kind, but I have to face up to life. I can't just run away. As for going home, well, to be honest, I'm here because I run away from that. I'll have nowhere left soon.'

'I'm not sure if it's the right time to tell you, but I've got a job. In a shoe shop. They want me to start next Monday.'

Jellie went quiet for a moment. 'Well, yes, you'd best have your freedom. I hope it works out for you.'

'I know, it's difficult, but I think it's best if I try to be independent. It might be rubbish, who knows?'

He stopped. He was nearing the end, he could sense it. He looked across at Lizzie. She was fast asleep. So he joined her.

CHAPTER FORTY-THREE

The last few days of their time in Tobago passed quickly, but Alex, a little guiltily, was pleased when it came to an end. Lizzie had become both edgier and needier, and while she could be said to be lovely in small doses, it felt claustrophobic when she was there all the time. She was constantly fiddling with her hair, her hands, anything handy, always on the move, constantly touching him, and using drink and physically exhausting sex to mitigate her worries. Maybe this was the real Lizzie? He changed the plane seats back, so that they were together again and was surprised when they told him he had a refund due from Penny's seat. But that brought back thoughts of her, and Lizzie became even more stressed as he went into himself for a while, just remembering Penny. Soon, though, it was time to pack and hand the cases over to the airline, who did a hotel check-in. That was it, just a few hours to while away before the journey home.

They touched down on time at Gatwick, and Alex soon gathered his belongings together and was ready to go. He looked across. Lizzie was still in her seat, looking down at the floor.

'Want a hand?'

She shook her head and looked up with a weak smile. 'No, sorry, just thinking.' She stood up. He helped her get her bag down, and she started packing the bits and pieces she had out for the flight. He had to duck into his seat because passengers were disembarking, but a few minutes later and she was ready.

'Let the rush die down, and then we go, OK?' she said. He saw that she had been crying.

'Hey, you alright?' He dodged across the aisle and hugged her.

'Yes, I'm alright, I'm just afraid of the future.' She looked into his eyes and kissed him deeply. He felt her shaking as he held her close. 'Don't think badly of me, Alex, please don't.'

'You can do what you want to now, though, can't you? Now that Dave's gone.'

'No, Alex, you don't understand. Dave is a tiny cog in a bloody great machine, and that machine has not gone away. I doubt it ever will. There's always someone who wants to shove you back on the treadmill, because to them, the treadmill is more money and more power. Sorry, but that's the way it is. Come on, there's a gap here.'

She pulled away, and they left the aircraft, trudging through the corridors and into passport control. Lizzie joined a queue that wasn't for the automatic scanning, so they had a while to wait. It was as they shuffled slowly forwards that he noticed several people making their way to the same queue, except that they were on the other side of the barrier. Just a few more to go and they'd be through. Lizzie was silent, looking down, so he put his arm around her. She didn't look up, and she was still shaking.

They were next at the barrier, and Lizzie pushed him to go first. The Immigration Officer handed his passport back, and he walked through, turning to wait for Lizzie. She looked to be in a dream as she handed her passport over, which was checked, handed back, and she walked through. They continued towards the stairs and baggage collection.

'You alright?' he said, but she didn't answer, just kept looking down. They collected their baggage and made their way into customs. As they walked through, several people walked towards them. A woman stood right in front of Lizzie.

'Please come this way, both of you, thank you.'

They followed the woman towards a door, which she opened, and they filed through in the centre of the group, the others behind them. They took their luggage trollies from them, but they were pushed to one side, so this wasn't a customs' check then. The woman looked at Lizzie and spoke.

'Mrs Emily Edwin, I wish to question you regarding the murder of Miss Elizabeth Westbrook...' she went on, but Alex could only stand and stare at the silent Lizzie, or whoever she was. Yet again, he'd been duped. Who the hell was Emily Edwin? There was no expression on Lizzie's face, except maybe sadness as she looked at the floor. They went to lead her away, but she turned sharply, looked him in the eyes, and kissed him on the lips. 'Sorry, Alex. You're a good man, too good for me,' she said, and was gone.

'Mr Ash.' Alex swung around, and there stood a rain-coated man with a serious expression looking at him. It was odd how there was sadness in his eyes, just like Lizzie.

'We'd be very grateful for your time answering some questions if you'd be so kind. We advised your taxi firm they wouldn't be needed, but I can offer a ride to your house if you need it when we've finished.'

They took him back to Bridewell police station in Bristol and gave him a coffee in a claustrophobic room. After a while, two men walked in. Both had been at the airport.

'I'm sorry to have kept you. As you will have gathered, we have detained the lady you were with, and I'd like to cover a few points concerning her. Are you prepared to answer these?'

'Yes, of course, anything I can do to help.'

'Excellent, then we can proceed,' he nodded to his colleague. 'we'll be recording this. It saves mistakes and misunderstandings later. Now, how did you come to know Mrs Emily Edwin?'

They asked many questions but didn't answer his, and he felt exhausted by the time they had finished.

'Thank you, Mr Ash, I'll take you home myself if you don't mind,' the older, shorter of the two said. 'You've been very helpful. Just a word of advice. I don't think it would be wise to visit Mr Marlin's house at the moment. From what you've said, I'm sure you can understand why. Otherwise, I think that is all.'

He sat in the front of an ordinary saloon car for the forty-five minute journey home, his mind running over everything that had happened. His companion didn't say a word until he left him and his luggage at the curbside. He looked up at his house. How pleasant and ordinary it looked. It was good to be home.

'We'll be in touch, Mr Ash. Just let us know if you're thinking of going abroad again. Thank you for your cooperation.'

And that was it. He went into his house, which felt the same and yet, and yet the recent weeks had left their scars. Images of Jayne, of Lizzie, of Penny, flashed through his mind. No, life wasn't the same. He dumped his case and bag in the front room and went to check the fridge, sighed, and set off for the Bear Flat Co-op to buy some food. Some things never changed.

CHAPTER FORTY-FOUR

He sat at his desk, looking out over Roundhill, and at the rows of houses surrounding the grassy protrusion. He was lost in thought, although if asked he wouldn't know what about. Then the call came.

'Mr Ash? DI Torrey. I would like to update you and ask you a question. Are you free today? I'm happy to come to your house.'

'Yes, of course. When are you free?'

'I can be with you in about half an hour if that's convenient.'

It was less than that when Alex saw the car draw up into the only free space on the other side of the road, and Torrey walked over. After Alex had made coffee, they settled into the two armchairs in the front room.

'Thank you for seeing me. This is a lovely room the view is enviable. Now, this is unofficial, I just thought it right and proper if I updated you. As I believe you know, we arrested the woman, you knew as Lizzie Westbrook. She was, as we had worked out, her sister, Mrs Emily Edwin. Mrs Edwin has admitted to all this. I think she was desperate to do so. There comes a time when someone who has committed a capital crime finds that the guilt weighs on them. It becomes a relief to admit what they have done, even if it means that they then have to face the punishment because they understand they deserve it. I don't say every criminal is like that, but certainly, in her case, it is true. As a result of our investigations, I can clarify some things that happened, comfortable that she will be pleading guilty. I would be grateful if you keep this to yourself. It should not be public knowledge until after the trial. Is that agreed?'

Alex nodded. 'Yes, of course, thank you.'

'Mrs Emily Edwin and her sister were opposites, in that Miss Lizzie Westbrook was studious and quiet, and was quite content to concentrate on her studies and take little notice of the outside world. She rarely went out, had everything delivered, and kept her head down working on the learned publication she was preparing. Her sister, though, is best described as having always been a wild child. She married Mr Edwin, an accountant, though I wasn't sure about her explanation, given everything else she did. This was that she needed the security of a steady income, and to know she had a place of safety, a place of last resort. Whatever happened, whatever the reasons. As soon as she had married, she began to sleep around. But I don't think she had ever been anything different. She says otherwise, it's just my opinion. She has always been athletic, and was at one time a serious athlete, a gymnast, and used this

to captivate numerous men friends.' He looked quiz-
zically at Alex, who nodded. That was something he
had definitely experienced.

'When she married, her extramarital activities
were all done under the cover of her Pilates and yoga
teaching, but that business did not exist. I suspect,
but she would not admit, that she sometimes, maybe
frequently, took money for her services, which she
then presented to her husband as the results of her
work.'

'Then her father died. Which might have been
fine, had he not left everything to Lizzie. I don't
know why, so I can only speculate that he knew of
Emily's lifestyle, and didn't approve. Who knows?
It threw Emily into a fugue, and then a rage, and she
determined to have what she considered being hers.'

'She contacted her sister and arranged to visit her.
That visit was to be never ending. At first, I understand, although this is Mrs Edwin's version, she was
welcomed, and they went out together and got on
well. In fact, according to Mrs Edwin, she introduced
her sister to the theatre and restaurants, a life that her
sister had eschewed. Whatever happened, at some
point Emily met Maggie North. Being both attractive and shall we say, game, it was suggested that
she attend the **aware** soirees. Now, this is where it
doesn't necessarily make sense. You see, she says she
introduced herself to Maggie as Lizzie Westbrook.
Now, I must make clear that the sisters were twins,
not quite identical, but close enough for most people

not to realise it was one or the other. From this point, the real Lizzie's fate was sealed. Emily, while roaming Lizzie's house on the Circus, had found a cellar, and a large room there that could be locked. One day she enticed Lizzie down there and imprisoned her. No doubt her athleticism enabled her to do that with some ease. Later she had the wine rack built to hide it. Gradually she equipped it for Emily so that when we walked in, it was a bedsit with a desk and all the research materials that Emily could want. I think we are right with our timings, but if I can ask you one question?'

Alex nodded.

'You said, and Mrs Edwin confirms, that you went down into the cellar to fetch some wine.'

'Yes, that's right.'

'When you were there, did you hear or see anything that was, let us say, out of place?'

'I think there was a rustling, behind the wine rack, and Lizzie, or Emily I suppose, said it was mice I didn't think anything of it.'

'Yes, that accords. Of interest, Mrs Edwin says she liked to take visitors down there for the thrill of having them so close to her secret. In the meantime, as I understand she told you, she was being sucked into the world of the **aware**, and Maggie North. She was a very willing participant, even the instigator of some of the activities. Sex had always been at the forefront of her world, and to have a range of different men, and women, provided for her, was something she revelled in. Maggie was careful. First, her new recruit was introduced to a man as a friend and given the option of an upstairs room for an hour or two. Then two, then sometimes an orgy. At this time, she didn't know that Maggie was charging the participants, and had people lined up to view as well. That changed when one woman complained that she hadn't been paid enough for some act she was being asked to perform. Emily was shocked and completely lost it then. She went to George Marlin in a rage and demanded to know what was going on. She says he pretended not to know, but she'd seen him in the upstairs rooms, although he'd never been with her, so she doesn't believe that. He sent her back to Maggie. Now Maggie had a problem of her own making. If she'd been upfront with Emily, or Lizzie as she knew her, then I suspect all would have been well, and Emily would have gone along with the plan. I mean, as well as the steady supply of men, she would have been paid, and she had no other income. After some shouting, Emily says they came to an arrangement and a back payment for all that had occurred to that day. So, life resumed. Then you arrived. Emily says that she was instructed to reel you in slowly, using the **awareness** thing. Maggie viewed you as a lamb to the slaughter as it were, a naïve potential regular source of money. Unfortunately, it would seem, Mrs Edwin fell for you. I know, unbelievable, isn't it?'

'To add to her problems, as she was, err, busy loving you, her sister managed to escape from the room. Emily doesn't know how, and I couldn't work it out at first, but there are clues in a number of bent paper clips in the cellar room. I wasn't convinced, but I've reconstructed the scene, and, because it's an original old unsophisticated lock, yes, after many attempts, I can confirm that it is possible. Using multiple paper clips and a larger, thicker clip she had. Emily came back one evening to find her sister on the loose. She couldn't escape the building because Emily had the keys, and there were mortice locks on the doors so they couldn't be opened from the inside. It would have been possible to smash a window, but either she hadn't thought of that, or hadn't had the time. Out of interest, we had noticed that there wasn't any internet connection to the house or a landline, so Lizzie was unable to contact the outside world either.'

'Emily says they argued, and she lost her temper. Her sister wanted to call the police, but that wasn't going to happen. They were upstairs in the bathroom at the time, so Emily walked downstairs, opened a cupboard she'd been using for tools, took out a mallet. Then she ran back upstairs and hit Lizzie with it. Completely premeditated. She completely lost it, she says, but it appears to be far more cold-blooded than that. I think she wanted to make sure that any distinguishing marks were erased.'

'She pulped her sister's head, and when we first saw her there was no way of recognising her from her facial features. Which of course left her with a problem. It was then that she suggested a holiday to you and staged a scene for us to find to mask her crime. It was a bit odd, but I suppose I can see her logic. She left the front door open, but in such a way that it didn't swing open immediately. It was probably the wind that opened it. She intended to make us think that someone had been allowed in at the front, and left that way, leaving the door open. But she didn't count on the numerous CCTV cameras that are around these days. They showed her leaving and carefully putting a piece of cardboard under the door.'

'Later David Makepeace entered by the back window, which she had left open for him. Again, CCTV from neighbours covered the back alleyway and gate that allowed access to the rear of the property. We think he was supposed to remove the body, but, for one reason or another, decided not to. Maybe he thought the risk too great, and Mrs Edwin dispensable. Maybe he thought her story plausible enough to fool us. But of course, he couldn't lock the rear window. He seems to have been reluctant to use the front door, but then there are often people around out there. Mrs Edwin isn't saying, I don't know why, so we'll never know. Maybe she doesn't know.'

'There was something else happening up at George Marlin's at the time. Maggie had contacts with a drug supplier. I don't know who approached whom, but it happened, and she started to offer supplies to her clients. She was very careful, and never did so openly, but after the number of interviews we've now carried out, we've established that she was, without doubt, a dealer. The drugs world isn't an easy one, and one thing led to another. The supplier up the chain wanted more. He saw it as a profitable route into Bath society, and he wanted to take it over. The whole thing.'

'By this time Maggie was providing numerous sex partners to their clients. In all, I believe she had over twenty girls working there, mostly part time, with Emily as the main attraction. Her athleticism made her the port of call as it were, for many a man.' He looked steadily at Alex, who nodded his understanding. He understood only too well, as visions of Lizzie expecting sex in incredible positions flashed through his mind. He still couldn't understand why they were necessary.

'So, there we are. Oh, David Makepeace, and there is a misnomer if ever there was one, was tasked with enforcing the wishes of the gang who wanted to take over the Marlin operation. He covered the loose end that Emily had left behind, namely her husband. He would have recognised her from her sister, and he was becoming discontented with Emily's absences, which of course had become more frequent. In fact, she was almost permanently in Bath by then. Makepeace decided to remove him, and went over to their house, took a rod from the garden and hit him. But when he found out that Emily or Lizzie had gone to Tobago with you, he panicked. He got the first flight he could and the rest, I think you know, until he was shot and killed. I think that just about covers it. Charges are being brought against Emily, Maggie, George, and several other participants. That, as they say, is that. Do you have any questions?'

'No, I don't think so. Can I ask if you're charging Jayne Sutherland?'

'Ah yes, she said you knew her, but not in her professional role. If you had moved to the upstairs rooms though, well, you might have met her there. No, we weren't able to get enough evidence to do so. The clients weren't keen on talking, so there wasn't much we could do. Any particular reason?'

'Just interest, I went out with her for a short while, that's all. She seemed a nice enough girl.'

'I see. Well, if that's all you want to know, I'll get going. If you think of anything else, just give me a ring at the station. Thank you for listening, and for your cooperation. I'll let myself out.'

Alex stayed sitting. He was having trouble taking it all in and wondered if he should see if he could visit Emily, but then dismissed the idea as daft. It was strange to be in an intense relationship with someone one day, and the next to hear that they were a murderer and a prostitute. Oddly, he wasn't too bothered about the latter but had difficulty coming to terms with the fact that he had been so close to the real Lizzie, without knowing she was imprisoned there. There was nothing he could have done, nothing he could do, but that didn't make it any easier.

Then there was Jayne. Jayne. Her story. He ought to find her and give it to her. But what was the point? A fiction that just had her name attached to it. Yet Emily or Lizzie thought there was more to it. That he had written things that only Jayne would have known about. It was this sort of weirdness that made him wonder about life, and about the idea of **awareness**. He knew he was going to have to find her, show her the story, and see her reaction. It was the only way to set his mind at rest.

CHAPTER FORTY-FIVE

The sun was shining on Bath as Alex walked from his house and down the Beechen Cliff escarpment into the city. He had one aim, to find Jayne, and show her his story, but he didn't know where she worked or lived now. There was one logical starting point, the shoe shop, so that was where he was heading. He stopped outside and peered in. He couldn't see Jayne, but another woman he'd seen with her was serving a customer. He waited until she had finished, and the customer had left and then walked in.

'Can I help you?'

'I hope so. I was in here a while ago and met someone called Jayne, Jayne Sutherland. I need to talk to her, but I don't know where she is. I wondered if you might know?'

'I remember you. Alex, isn't it? I haven't spoken to her, but I saw her in a café a few days ago. Look, I'll show you where it is.' She took out her phone, brought up a map of the city, and showed him a road near to the theatre. 'If you see her, tell her I miss her. I'm Amy. We didn't always get on after she became a manager, but it's not the same without her. I didn't feel that I could just go in and talk to her.'

He thanked her, promised he'd tell Jayne, and walked on. It wasn't far. The café was slightly out of the way. But there were plenty of people inside, and he could see Jayne going from table to table. He hesitated, but with sudden determination, walked across the street, and in the door. There was one table free. So he sat down, and after a few minutes, Jayne walked over.

'Hi,' he said. She did a double-take, she'd been concentrating on her job, and hadn't recognised him.

'Oh, hi. Can I get you something?'

He ordered a cappuccino and a couple of pastries.

'I have something to show you. Would you be free later?'

She hesitated.

'I suppose so. I work through lunch, it's our busiest time, but if you came back around two,' she shrugged, 'I should be free for a while then.'

'OK, I'll come back then.'

He settled down to eat and looked around the café. It was a comfortable place to be, unlike the chains that were made for slick service and a fast turnover. This was a place to linger, enjoy, and probably keep ordering while you were there. Which was exactly what he did, taking a newspaper out of a rack by the door to pass the time. Jayne was a little edgy around him, but as the customers thinned, she came over.

'So, what is it you wanted to show me?'

'I've been writing a story. I started it when I first

met you, so I put your name in as the principal character. I just wanted to show it to you.' It sounded a bit odd when he said it, and he wasn't so sure what her reaction would be. When he'd started from home, he'd be convinced that she'd like it, be flattered even. But now? He looked up anxiously.

'Alright then. I've never been in a story. Leave it with me and I'll read it. What's your number? I didn't keep it. I'll give you a ring.'

He passed it to her, and she walked away, so he finished his coffee and left. Maybe that was it. Maybe he'd never see her again. He remembered Amy and said to her as he left. 'I meant to say, Amy, in the shoe shop would like to see you again. I don't know what happened between you, but she said she missed you.' She looked surprised but didn't speak, just nodded and went on with her work.

He wandered the city, took in a bookshop, bought a couple of books, hesitated over new clothes, and found a café for lunch, where he began to read one of the books. He was just finishing his food when his phone rang.

'How did you fucking know? This is mental. I want to talk to you now.'

He settled up and walked back to the café where Jayne worked. There were butterflies in his stomach. He must have done something wrong. Maybe he shouldn't have included her in the story. Maybe she felt it was nothing like her. Shit.

She was waiting for him and showed him up to

her flat. It was more expensively equipped than he expected, but then… the story.

She sat down and motioned him to do the same. She didn't offer him a drink.

'How did you know? You've written about stuff I've told no one about. So how did you know? I just don't understand. Have you been bugging me? No, that doesn't work, there are things in here that even a bug wouldn't pick up. I don't understand.'

She was close to tears, he could see, but he couldn't do anything about it. It wasn't as though he could cuddle her.

'It was on my mind. That's all I can say. I wrote what was in my mind. Are you saying it's true?'

'Every single fucking word. Everything. I don't know what to say. I have no words. It's as though you were living my life. Inside my head. And that's scary. Really scary. You've got to promise me you'll stop. Please. Now. I don't like it.'

'I'm sorry, I really am. I didn't mean to scare you.'

'I don't understand, though. How did you do it?'

'I can't explain it. I promise you I would if I could. If I still believed in it, I'd say it was **awareness**, but that's all gone now.'

'I know. I read about George Marlin in the paper; the ordinary phones with a special App that generated phoney past lives and with a Bluetooth connection that buzzed if another App was near. All that. I suppose a lot of it was in our heads. I mean, if you think you're special, then events that are just coincidences appear to be something else.

The police even interviewed me about my role with Maggie. You know, I'd been wondering what was going on, I'd even started to make notes on it. I'm sorry, but I thought you might be involved. Anyway, I thought they were going to charge me, but they didn't. Just warned me off. I don't know, Alex, I'm going to have to think this through. In some ways, it's strange, yet comforting to have a record of what happened, but it is scary. I hope you can see that.'

'Yes. Sorry. Are you settled here now?'

'Yes, I think so. I've decided to go to college and get some qualifications, but I haven't decided what yet.' She smiled. 'Not bakery, that scared Jellie. Something else. Maybe I should try something more academic, but I'd be shit at exams, so something without them. Have you been doing much?'

He hesitated. So much he didn't want to talk about. 'I've been around, you know, writing.'

'Your story's a bit behind. Johnnie left to do a masters up in Durham, so we called it a day. I'm free tonight if you fancy a drink.'

He walked away, wondering if he'd done the right thing.

The next morning, he sat at his laptop. He'd typed up the rest of Jayne's story. The conversation with her enabled him to bring her story up to date. Now he sat, the cursor poised for the next chapter. But he couldn't write. He knew he should write the words his subconscious was telling him should be written. But he couldn't. He just couldn't. He could see her future all too clearly, and it was not a future she or he would want. Not a future anyone would want. Maybe there was something in **awareness**, maybe a writer could affect the future, and he had to face it, he'd seen her past. So, if he wrote all that was in his mind, would that make it true? What if someone was writing his future at this very moment? His death?

He stood up and moved away from the keyboard. There were other stories, other lives to write, but he wasn't ready to do that. Not yet.

Acknowledgements

Having finished my masters at Christchurch Canterbury, I dithered over publishing the semi science fiction I'd been writing there, or make a complete change and write about a place I love. So, Alex Ash came into being. I hope he brings with him a curiosity about the city of Bath in the UK and if you haven't visited already, a desire to do so. The two science fiction books remain on the cloud, and may see publication, one day.

My thanks for their love help and assistance with this series goes firstly to my wife, Briony, for her support. To the late lamented Evie Cat for providing a role model for the unnamed neighbour's cat, and my tutor Peggy Riley, for her help and encouragement, clearly there are no comma splices in this work, whatsoever. Tessa Tilley for beta reading it first, Helen Baggott for proofreading, and Andrew & Rebecca at Ardel Media for their skill and patience with the series cover designs.

To the Royal Crescent for the second World of Alex Ash

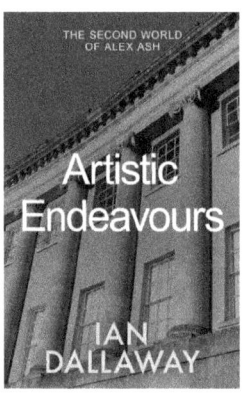

Alex has already encountered George Marlin, who runs various questionable enterprises from his house on the Royal Crescent in Bath. Now George is selling artworks, but being George, there seems to be something more to his scheme. Then there is Maggie, his live-in lover, who has her own enterprise in the rooms above.

Alex becomes involved in an investigation into the production of the artworks, as the story he is writing takes a similar route. He romps his way around, at one time finding himself unexpectedly in bed with two women in the Second World of Alex Ash.

Alex goes to London for the Third World of Alex Ash

When Ginny, a friend from the last book, asks him to go to see her in London Alex becomes enmeshed in her world. A murder at the jazz club she introduces him to launches a series of dramatic twists and turns that sees questions posed over the whole basis of her family life.

In Bath, however, another death, and yet joy and celebration at the culmination of a project.

This is the third story in the Alex Ash series, as Alex steers his way through life, death and love writing as he goes